Jaxyl
Warrior Princess

Ruth C. Mitchell

Ruth C. Mitchell

ISBN: 979-8-218-47870-4

Cover Art by Teressa Pelliccio DeVito
Graphics by Ashley Stouten of Wild 4 Life Design
Formatting by Sarah Jennings of TechScribes, Inc.

Printed in the United States of America

Reviews for
Jaxyl Warrior Princess

"From the moment you dive into the pages, Jaxyl's vibrant personality and fearless spirit leap out, capturing your attention and never letting you go. She's a character full of contradictions—naughty yet noble, brash yet brave—and her choices, while sometimes questionable, always drive the story forward in exciting ways." – *The Review Universe*

"a book that not only entertains but also inspires. Don't miss out on this captivating and engrossing novel." – *Kindle Library*

"Mitchell's storytelling is both engaging and thought-provoking, ensuring readers are fully invested in Jaxyl's journey. *Jaxyl Warrior Princess* is a must-read for fans of thrilling adventures and strong female leads who defy convention and save the day." – David Wilson, *Goodreads*

"The novel's fast-paced narrative is enriched with feminist themes, captivating love scenes, and epic battles. Mitchell's world-building is immersive, and the unique languages add a layer of intrigue… it is a standout in the genre. – Nikhil Soni, *Goodreads*

"Mitchell has truly crafted a gem with *Jaxyl Warrior Princess.*" – Alex Ben, *Goodreads*

"A rollercoaster of emotions…Ruth C Mitchell skillfully weaves a narrative that blends action, romance, and adventure. Jaxyl's character is multifaceted and relatable, making her journey both thrilling and heartwarming. This book is a fantastic addition to the genre." – Shivani, *Goodreads*

"An engrossing tale and fantastic choice to those seeking a thrilling and empowering read with a strong female lead." – Erik Heg, *Goodreads*

"The narrative explores the impact of personal and communal loss, and how these experiences shape and strengthen individuals and societies. Jaxyl's journey is a testament to the burdens and challenges of leadership. Jaxyl Warrior Princess is a captivating addition to the science fiction/fantasy genre, offering a blend of personal growth, political intrigue, and interstellar adventure. Ruth Mitchell has crafted a compelling tale that resonates with themes of leadership, resilience, and the relentless pursuit of peace and justice. Fans of epic sagas and strong, multifaceted protagonists will find much to admire in Jaxyl's story." – Charles Templeton author of *Boot: A Sorta Novel of Vietnam*

Dedication

Jaxyl Warrior Princess is dedicated to anyone who needs a hero, a role model, a SFP, or a light to guide them. Jaxyl is bold, entitled and brave, but most of all she just rocks. Is she perfect? Absolutely not. Her oversized ego and libido get her into adventures that cause timid creatures to cringe and blush. If the universe needs a savior, here she is, no apologies needed, because it turns out the Warrior Princess was born to save the cosmos and that's no small challenge.

So dear readers I invite you to partake in this exciting journey and to escape into the marvelous world of Merth and beyond through the adventures of a mystical and divine creature whose destiny is not to be ignored.

Like any book this length, there are many advance readers who guide the way with their reactions and valuable opinions. I have many to thank including the cover authors: Wendy Taylor Carlisle, Webb Hubbell, and Siobhan Curham, all wonderful writers in their own right. To my ARC readers, thank you, I am so grateful to you all. To Ashley Stouten and Sarah Jennings, thank you for your skilled services, and to the amazing Teressa Pelliccio Devito for her wonderful cover art.

My dachshunds are often by my side, or in my lap preventing me from typing when I'm trying to write so they too should be commended for their service to this fantasy world of Merth. My family as always lends me their encouragement that makes all the endless hours of work meaningful.

But it is you dear readers that bring the wonderful characters of Merth to life when you spend hours with them escaping into their rich fantasy world. Bless you, for your reviews and shares.

Book I

Queen Ali and
the Cup of Light

Before

There is a place where beauty flourishes in the fickle wind dancing between tall and robust trees, sometimes swooping down to ruffle the waters of crystal blue lakes and tickle the golden fronds of cultivated fields. The oracular planet of Merth is where two moons hang in the night sky on the farthest elliptic cycle of *Gluta Marin* within sight of the great Immense. It is a place of innocence and strife, where the people are ruled by the benevolent Karda family who are guided by the powerful and omniscient Matong, a divine orb which they bond with for instruction to guide their people.

Merth is now ruled by a young Queen, Aella Anemone, who has been devastated by the loss of her would-be mate Fontar, the 'cup of light' chosen for her by the prophetic Matong. Most recently, she and her family and the country, have been shattered by the tragic sudden death of her father, King Poma. 'Ali,' as her family calls her, is the first ruling queen born to the role and while she has been groomed for this position since childhood, the young queen struggles to find herself as the supreme leader of Merth.

Ali's mother Queen Aadya, who began her life as a lowly peasant, is responsible for changing the fabric of Merth's society–once an unenlightened people. Aadya struggled to become a warrior, unheard of in her time. When she became the chosen wife of Prince Poma, she was able to elevate the status of women, who were referred to as 'breeders' and her lifelong pursuit was to educate all Merthians.

1-The Ring

The dreams continue to haunt Queen Ali throughout the first dozen or so rotations after her coronation. *It is as Father described; the ring is overwhelming.* "Those early days, of wearing the ring after the coronation, were exhausting." He once told her. "The ring bombarded me with information. I couldn't focus and my sleep was filled with bizarre dreams. If it weren't for your mother holding me steady, I would have imploded."

The youthful Queen Ali looks at her left hand. *Married to Merth uh huh, and I have no one to lean on like my father had my mother.* The ring had molded its shape to her petite finger and in doing so created a new distinctive pattern, it was breathtakingly stunning on her hand, but it was there forever now, always present to remind her of her duty to her people.

Ali's dog Robic, a wedding gift from her beloved Fontar who died tragically a few days before they were to be wed, straddles Ali and licks her face, telling her it is time to rise and begin their busy day. He has grown into a massive dog with white, silken curly fur. His dark blue eyes mimic the deep pool just inside the *Lystyl* Cave on the far side of Compana. A sharp blade of light from the morning star slices into the room. Waking alone, Ali's thoughts turn to Martyl again, and the one night he came to her bed before her father had the tragic hunting accident plummeting her into her premature reign as queen.

Ali's sister, Galen the healer, had helped her devise a plan whereby the widower Martyl, who was known by Galen to be infertile, became Ali's discrete lover. For her protection, Galen gave the young and lonely Queen Ali an elixir to keep her from falling in love. In this way, she would be ready to receive her 'cup of light' when the Matong finally delivered on its choice for her royal consort.

With the coronation uproar behind her, Ali's mind wanders often to the mysterious night when she was one with a man for the first time. *I should invite him to dine with me.* She had taken to dining with her rapidly declining Grandmother Queen Mother Mesa, with whom she shared occupancy of Katara's opulent and rambling residence, and her newly widowed mother, who didn't always come using her standard excuse, "It is not the best time of day for me to venture far from Compana."

I am like an old spinster! I don't care if the servants gossip. I will invite him. I am queen now! If I were a man no one would give my trysts a second thought.

When Martyl arrives, it is as if her great thirst has been quenched. They embrace like old friends more than lovers although she is awakened by his masculine embrace. "I need to increase my circle of influence," she tells Martyl, whose icy silver-gray eyes unsettle her. "Not tonight, of course, there's only the two of us." She looks at him and realizes he can see through her like water. *He does not judge me but dutifully comes to serve the queen.*

He bows his head slightly, his silky brown hair falling forward, and with a wholesome smile says, "The pleasure is mine." Her heart pounds in her ribcage like pummeling rapids in a swollen stream and she bites her lip, feeling not much like a queen and more like a petulant adolescent who wants her way. She resolves to start entertaining a revolving body of friends and family and to quit acting like a *scared little child and more like a person of rightful power.*

Ali holds to her plan and her circle of influence grows steadily but Martyl is almost always present at these frequent and jovial soirees. He dutifully says his goodnights publicly but returns to her chambers late in the evening on most nights, even dining privately with her the morning after his nocturnal visits. Ali occasionally seeks his counsel when she wants a man's point of view, but also her meetings with Princes Bonder and Parsa and the others in the high council, including her mother, Aadya, are what determine the true course of Merth.

The ring too, with its historic perspective leads her and gives her confidence in her decisions. The very act of wearing it diminishes her need to seek bonding with the Matong as much as she did in the very early days of her reign.

Her older sister Galen is her most valued confidant, however, especially in her relationship with Martyl. "The potion you gave me once before I became one with Martyl...it still works. I do not have love for him in the way I loved Fontar. I do love him, but it is not the same," Ali tells her sister one day while visiting her at her home, the artistically designed *Glaufstanhall.*

Galen bathing her little one, Olza with the brilliant red hair, smiles at her baby first and lets her gaze stretch to her sister which fades to a look of quiet regret. "The potion I gave you is permanent. Under no circumstances will you have Martyl as a mate. I chose him for you because he is infertile. I told you; he is not your 'cup of light.'"

"Oh Galen, I know, but it is depressing. When will the Matong let me find a mate?"

Galen squeezes the soft cloth in her hand letting the tepid bathwater drip down the baby's back, which causes the little one to giggle. The radiance in her baby's eyes melts her mother's heart. Galen turns to Ali, Queen of Merth, and leveling her tone reminds her sister, "You must focus on your people now, it is what the Matong has planned for you. To dwell on something, you don't have is a waste of your time."

Ali lets out a deep breath and her shoulders drop slightly. "Yes, of course, you are right. I am going to create a task force to solidify the loyalty of the Omi, who are still unsettled in their peace with us. I will draw Mother into the talks although her thoughts can sometimes be overbearing. She is the one who began this enlightened society of ours, educating everyone and bringing the contributions of women to the forefront."

It is at the very next council meeting when Ali's first real challenge raises its draconian head. "My Queen," Oofar, the harried diplomat tells her with a shaking voice and trembling hands. "The Omi are building a structure across the Sonnatong River!"

"What?" she feels her breath tighten like she has inhaled smoke. "What kind of structure?"

"They call it a bridge and it is going to span the river. Some say it will make trade more bountiful, others are suspicious of the Omi's intentions."

Her brother, Roark, breaks in to ask the diplomat, who is built like a lumpy sack tossed over two thin stalks of *weedlum*. "Where is this taking place?"

"Actually, close to our old border where the river is narrow and deep, above Howker Falls."

"This will not stand! We must arrange for a meeting at once," the young queen roars. Aadya stays silent, observing where this obstacle will take her daughter.

"I will send an envoy," her uncle Parsa breaks in. "We will escort them here at once. We leave no wiggle room for their impertinence."

"I want King Brechnole, his sons, and most of all, Tildyn in attendance. This is unacceptable and they must not breach our trust. We will act accordingly," Queen Ali says decisively, surprising even herself. Heads nod in agreement with her directive and a pulsing energy fizzes through the room as the group wrestles with ideas for dealing with the Omi's defiance.

"May I say something, Queen Ali?" Alatoi, who is often included in such gatherings because of her strategic importance, speaks up though she is not high-ranking enough to be a part of decision-making.

"Of course, what is it?" Ali's ring is humming with information, but she doesn't have the focus to pay attention. "I want to remind you, as I am an Omi myself, we are like wild boars, you must deal with us decisively."

The crowd rumbles with humor and a smile surfaces on Queen Aadya's lips, Ali's mother, as she recalls how many years ago, led by the Matong sight, she had killed an attacking boar in the dark of night, only to nearly be gored to death by another feral hog who her beloved Poma slew.

As the group breaks up, Ali retreats to the Matong chamber where her mother Aadya is also approaching. "Good, Mother you are here, please stay while I bond with the Matong. I need your counsel."

The message they receive from the omniscient orb surprises both women. Ali turns to her mother, "I must be mistaken, I was told to allow the Omi to build their bridge." Aadya has the same troubled expression on her face as her daughter. "How can this be?"

Aadya shrugs and feels an emptiness in her heart for her beloved husband, King Poma, who would surely struggle, but ultimately overcome this startling news decidedly after conferring with his advisors, including herself whose judgment he trusted the most. Aadya knew her counsel was not so revered by her daughter who was eager to prove herself.

"Yes, but there certainly must be conditions and parameters for such an action," Aadya finally says, not willing to withhold her opinion despite its possible rejection.

"The worst part about this," Ali says, "is they are still acting independently from us. No one asked for permission or explained why they are doing this."

2-Heads Will Roll

It takes several rotations to convene a meeting of Omi leaders, which gives Ali time to assemble her thoughts as to how she is going to deal with their gross misconduct. This is the first significant challenge she has had since her father, King Poma, died and the first time a queen has been the ruling monarch during such a major infraction of a treaty.

"They will expect me to be weak and indecisive," she tells her mother.

Aadya laughs, "Of course they will, that's why you must not stray from your command, or lose faith in your power. Treat them like their heads will roll if they do not respect your authority. You are a great warrior on the battlefield. Do not let our hard-earned peace soften you." Aadya gives her powerful daughter a compassionate smile. "We will respect and support you. You wear the ring now my dove." Aadya strokes her daughter's hand and the ring on her finger. "Much has changed in my lifetime. They used to refer to us as 'breeders.'"

"I know, and you are responsible for most of the change, Mother."

In preparation for the summit, Ali spends more time with the Matong than she has since her coronation. As usual, the holy oracle does not tell her directly what to do as if to challenge her faith, which at times it does, but she is still bolstered by the energy and strength it feeds her.

Occasionally, with the royal ring, she even hears her father's and grandfather's voices in the ring's demonstrative parlaying of Merth's history directly into her consciousness.

Ali also spends time riding with Martyl and sometimes her brother Roark, oftentimes visiting Galen at her home, and her mother Aadya at Compana. She lunches with her uncles Bonder and Parsa and even confers with Alatoi. Dinners include others, such as Galen's husband Kandar, a mighty warrior himself, Oofar the Omi ambassador, and others suggested by her close circle of advisors, who might be helpful in strategic planning.

"I don't understand what the purpose of the bridge would be. No one has even attempted such a project although our scientists have speculated how it might be built for crossing our rivers," Ali says to Roark, who has been dedicating himself to the novel study of science. He is the one she respects most for knowing the why and how of so many things now.

"We will have to wait and see what they are up to. We need to utilize Alatoi and her special skills at spying." Roark's words make her uneasy. Spying has associations with her of the vile war with the Omi in recent times.

On the morning of the first day of the summit. Ali, who has slept alone for the past few nights to focus, readies herself with quiet detail as to each item she will wear and refers to the mirror to practice her facial expressions, reminding herself not to smile or frown too much, but to stay neutral. The heavy metal crown she will wear is the official signature of her importance and she practices walking around her spacious quarters while wearing it, looking to appear confident. Once her handmaidens place it on her head, the royal ring on her hand buzzes with information she doesn't find particularly helpful until she distinctly hears her father's voice. BE FIRM BUT OPEN TO THE PROMISES OF THE FUTURE. *Oh, Father, I want to be prepared for this, but I am woefully inadequate to deal with those pistoids!*

3-I Must Change This

When Ali enters the great hall of Katara, everyone else is already seated, as the advance committee had planned. She glances over toward the enigmatic Tildyn, once her close friend who made her twinge with a peculiar and confusing desire. She sees him seated beside his father King Brechnole and his other vulgar half-brothers; they on the other hand *make my skin crawl.*

There is someone else seated with them, a man with the deep rich skin color of the Hoffa nut. She has never seen anyone like him, and it is hard to not stare, she takes in his green eyes fluid like water, another rarity, and wonders who he is and why he has been brought to the summit.

"We meant no harm Queen Ali," King Brechnole stands and does his best to grovel, a concept more foreign to him than dancing with women.

"If this were true you would have consulted us with this project before beginning." The strength of her voice surprises even Ali. "So, what is this about? Do you not understand the terms of our treaty? You are no longer an independent nation. We have delivered our end of the bargain far beyond all expectations." Using her focused eyes as weapons, Ali stares down the rugged Brechnole with fierce intensity she did not know was within her.

King Brechnole is visibly unnerved by her tone. He looks around the room to muster support from his cronies. "Your Highness we only..."

"Please be seated, King Brechnole. Look around you, we are all seated. There is no need to stand when you address me." A murmur spreads across the room as heads bob toward each other.

"Yes, Your Highness," he mutters.

"Now, tell me who oversees this project? They should tell me what is going on and why."

Tildyn stands, breathes in sharply, and finally speaks. His slight build and fashionable clothing are in sharp contrast to his brutish father. "My Queen Ali," a subtle smile crosses the queen's lips as she notices he has used the familiar to address her. The 'my' is window dressing, but she allows him to continue. Without speaking, Ali raises her arm, lets it pivot at her elbow, and drops her hand down, signaling Tildyn to be seated. He looks around the room awkwardly as his knees buckle, lowering himself back down into his seat.

Deflated, Tildyn takes another breath and begins again. "We have brought with us a gentleman from parts unknown, who has delivered to us a...rather unbelievable tale. We found his story unusual and didn't believe in him at first. So, we began work in earnest to test his theory. We wanted to bring you the gift of the bridge and show you the advantages of bringing trade to all regions at a faster and safer pace than we have ever known."

"Thank you Tildyn, who is this man? I would like to hear him speak."

"His name is Ahshen Owanu, he may address you now."

Ali's heart races like a wild bird unleashed in her chest. *I'm doing this. I am perceived even by Tildyn, who used to try and diminish my status as a leader. Thank you, One True God who has transformed me, into a queen.* Ali looks around the room at the impressive assembly of Merth's most distinguished persons and notes not nearly enough are women. *I must work to change this.*

4-Ahshen Owanu

"Queen Ali, may I address you as such? I am not familiar with the proper ways of your planet." The stranger does not attempt to stand but heads bob again, and the murmur of the assembly grows when he speaks.

"Please continue…"

"My story is particularly peculiar I hesitate to tell it in this large assembly for concern it may be misconstrued."

"You need to proceed and let the leaves fall where the wind blows them," Queen Ali urges him on.

"I am not from here. I was dreaming in my bed on my home planet Fantu when I woke up here on Merth. As you can see, I look very distinct from everyone else." He looks to her for acceptance and turns to gauge the audience. Some people are shaking their heads in disbelief. Others, driven by curiosity, hold their breath as if doing so will encourage the stranger to continue with his bizarre tale. "Perhaps I should have handled my surprise at being here differently. If so, this controversy might not have been created. But I did not know. It was as much a surprise to me to find myself on the bank of the Sonnatong River, literally where the bridge should be constructed, as it was for those who found me and have assisted with my well-being during such an unexpected journey. You see in my home planet; I am what is known as an engineer. I design and build bridges and dams and aeroports, etc."

The beautiful dark man uses a few peculiar words Ali, and the others are unfamiliar with. To compensate he uses his hands demonstratively.

"My Queen!" Tildyn jumps up and tries to intercede. Addressing her in this manner makes it difficult for Ali not to smile in triumph, but she resists. Instead, she holds her hand up, and the massive hall becomes drenched in silence.

"This is what we are going to do. We will adjourn for today and reconvene tomorrow. We will meet with this," she wants to say *strange man*, but instead says, "visitor now, in a more manageable setting. I need Roark, Princes Bonder and Parsa, Queen Aadya, Princes Tildyn and Olafar, King Brechnole, and Alatoi now in the Offen hall to address these issues in a more contained environment where we can better grasp this unique situation."

Chairs being pulled back make a resounding screeching noise across the stone floor as dozens of officials depart the great hall.

The nearby Offen hall is named after the skilled craftsman who designed and constructed the tall arched, crystalline windows, which sparkle uncannily, filling the room with dancing light. It is a perfect size for the group.

"Mr. Owanu, your story was quickly going toward the fantastic and I didn't want too many people in the know if you can understand?" Queen Ali says to him.

"I do understand Your Highness," his eyes light up when he speaks, and he makes a slight bow in her direction. "Forgive me if I am unfamiliar with your ways. And you may call me by my first name, Ahshen if you so desire. I am aware my story sounds unbelievable, but as I said, I was truly dreaming when I awoke to your planet. My home is called Fantu, and you can see it in your night sky as a bright light near the Tuumus constellation. The light comes from the reflection of the Nebris belt of stars, well that's what we call them."

Those in the room of the Royal Karda family who had experienced bonding with the Matong, do not see his story as totally outrageous, others have more disbelief to untangle.

"We believe he traveled through the Immense somehow, although there were no signs of a carrier. All we have ever found is Owanu himself," Tildyn has clearly designated himself as the Omi spokesperson, relying on his previously friendly status with the queen.

Owanu breaks in, undeterred by Tildyn's desire to interpret for him. "I have brought a scale model of the bridge I plan to build. I was only responding to my hosts, who have graciously taken me in and cared for my needs."

"I understand, but you have to understand they contravened our treaty in taking on this project without our permission."

Owanu's expression craters softly into an undefined contortion. "Forgive me Queen Ali, the loss of my home and family sometimes overtakes me unexpectedly."

Compassion for this stranger engulfs her like a sweltering mid-day heat, but Ali knows she must push forward. "May we see this model you speak of?"

Owanu, looking relieved to move forward, motions for the bridge structure to be unveiled. Tildyn and his brother Prince Olafar lift it onto the broad wooden table and pull off a dense red cloth.

Miraculously the room seems to radiate with even more light, and everyone in the room is struck by the details of the tiny wooden bridge, with its geometric angles, arches, and elongated span.

Prince Roark, Ali's brother, who has made it his life's work to become a scholar, is the first to speak. "This is a marvelous structure." He looks at Owanu with admiration. "I have never seen anything like it."

"These are commonplace on my home planet."

"Where did you say you are from?"

"Fantu, although I cannot tell you how far away it is," Owanu lets his gaze fall to the floor hanging his head slightly. "I presume I have no hope of ever returning."

Perceiving the silent agony of the handsome stranger, with a dimple in his chin like a provocative talisman, Ali experiences, a sharp physical pang in her ribcage. It is as if an idea is trying to surface but she dismisses it, remaining focused on the conversation.

"But here, let me explain how the bridge works. Here you see these arches?" He points out the two negative spaces beneath the bridge. "These are what support the span, and these struts are designed mathematically to brace the whole construction of the bridge."

5-Our Time is Limited

It is an exhausting afternoon of questions and puzzled expressions, but Ahshen Owanu wins everyone over. It is decided the bridge will be built with the supervision of Roark and each end of the bridge will be guarded by a select team. Oddly more time is spent on these negotiations than anything else. "The sentries must include Omi, it is after all our bridge, er" King Brechnole seems to regret his bold statement as soon as it comes spilling out of his mouth.

Queen Ali glares at him. "I don't think you need to brandish such treasonous statements, sir!" To which King Brechnole pushes his chair back impulsively, but he has nowhere to go. He calms himself and delivers a more diplomatic response.

"Of course, not my Queen, I meant to make the point we are the ones constructing it."

My Queen! Did I hear right? My oh my! The old pistoid called me his Queen! The young Queen Ali struggles to stifle the smile straining to rip across her face.

She nods her head to her protocol officer nearby and whispers into his ear when he draws near to her side. "Be sure to seat Owanu beside me tonight at dinner and keep Brechnole and his sons at a distance."

"Yes, my Queen." The steward nods.

It is during dinner conversation with Ahshen Owanu, Queen Ali becomes absorbed with his melodious voice and impeccable manners. Her secret consort, Martyl, seated at the other end of the table even mentions the obvious focus of her attention later that evening in her chambers.

"You like him," he teases her.

"Don't be silly, I have much to learn from this man, this strange visitor to our world."

Martyl touches her neck pulling her silken hair behind her neck, and grasping her shoulder he pushes her gently back onto the pillows of her bed. "Our time together is limited. One day your 'cup of light' will appear, and I will be history."

"Don't be so dramatic. You and I are never to fall in love."

"Aye, it may be true for you, your sister the healer, gave you an elixir, but she did no such thing for me, and I have been in love with you from the moment we first became one."

A sadness washes over Queen Ali, as her imagination travels back to her courtship with Fontar, the man the Matong had delivered as her 'cup of light' only to allow him to die in an ambush, she survived.

"I am hesitant to love anyone, my love only brings death to those who love me. My purpose was to sleep with you discretely, but half the kingdom is talking about our relationship. I think even my mother knows, although she will not approach me with the topic. She understands how devastated I was to lose Fontar."

The two lovers stop talking and slip into a silent but sensuous coupling with a sadness folding over the two of them like a shared dream. Martyl is gone before she wakes, aware she has an early morning appointment with Ahshen Owanu.

6-Less Than I Would Like

"Please tell me more about the other world you come from," Ali had asked Ahshen at the dinner banquet the night before.

"It is much different there, we are much more developed technologically on my planet, there are many things I could tell you about, but you wouldn't have the context to understand."

"You view us as a primitive society?"

She could see him scrambling for the words. She had put him on the defensive. It was a newfound quality developing in her conversational skills—putting people on edge thus giving herself a tactical advantage.

"For instance, we do have the ability to travel here, if we could find you. But that simply is not how I got here."

"Perhaps your people secretly brought you here and left you," she teases him. Owanu laughs releasing a soft breath, which paradoxically makes him more masculine in her eyes. "I have given it much consideration but dismissed it. I think it has more to do with interplanetary schisms. You know one slide over here, results in a crack over there. I think I literally fell through a crack so to speak."

She laughs, "Now you have lost me."

"I understand you have kinetic sight and there is a divine orb here. Is it true?"

"You must be speaking of our Matong." Ali looks at her hand which is jolted with a vibration from her royal ring. She turns in her chair to face him better. "Where did you hear this? The Omi's understand little about our Matong."

"King Brechnole told me early on he feared you because of it. His whole premise was we needed to rush to get the bridge built before you discovered us at our work. He felt you were less likely to nix the structure once you could see how it benefits trade."

Ah, the old pistoid fears us now. "I see," she says distractedly. "The ink is barely dry on our peace accord." Queen Ali takes a sip of her wine. It has a slightly minty taste to it, making it unusually piquant.

"Can you read my thoughts?" Ahshen Owanu asks with a quizzical expression trying not to expose his growing concern. It is the first time he has said something ordinary since she met him, and it makes him approachable and more desirable all at once.

"More than you would want, but less than I would like."

She clears her throat and wipes her lips with her napkin, the conversation taking a turn she is not ready to approach. "You need to always have my brother Roark by your side. What he doesn't know, you will teach him. Is this understood?"

"Yes" Your Highness," he salutes her with a peculiar hand gesture she assumes is respectful, as he gives her no indication he is anything but dutiful to her.

Giving pause like a *wickleworp* before it leaps, with its black eyes bulging in calculation of how far it must travel, Queen Ali looks straight into Owanu's distilled green eyes and says," I have a crazy idea. We could ride out early in the morning, the three of us, and examine this bridge."

"It will take us at least two rotations to travel, wouldn't you have to prepare for such a trip and bring along your entourage?" He questions her with the modesty of someone who has been unexpectedly caught snacking off the serving plate.

Ali laughs, "But we have Matong horses at our disposal."

"Come again?"

"I don't know of any incident where a nonroyal has ridden a Matong horse, they may not even be able to perform under such conditions, but the Royal Karda family has horses we have bonded with the Matong. They can leap into the air and make the journey in half the time a regular horse can."

Ahshen Owanu takes a deep breath and relinquishes his misgivings. "You are strong and skilled at riding are you not?"

He chuckles having only ridden a *dupospol* once on his native planet Fantu, a similar but different animal with four legs. "I suppose so."

"You will do just fine." She gives him a reassuring look.

7-The Draw of the Bridge

It is barely light when the three of them race out of the stable, their Matong steeds have been readied with provisions and no time is lost as they quickly greet each other. After a few tense moments, where Ahshen imagines plummeting to the turf below, he catches on to riding a horse that leaps more than runs, traveling four times as far as a normal horse in one stride. The ride is so exhilarating they arrive ahead of schedule, about midday.

As they round the last low bluff the bridge comes into full view. It is somewhat of a shock for Ali as she has never seen such a large manmade structure. It takes her breath away. She pulls up on her mare, the daughter of her mother's horse Fowtyl, who nickers unsteadily, spooked by the sight of the bridge. The other horses stop abruptly, and Ahshen, still in motion makes a clumsy grab for his horse's mane, a butterscotch-colored gelding named Myxa.

"It is huge!" Queen Ali stammers. It feels uncomfortable to see such an object, already spanning the river. "It feels invasive of the landscape." She says, trying not to sound judgmental or negative. "Will it be safe?"

She turns to Ahshen who has pulled up beside her, his pride visible in his posture.

"Oh, yes, my Queen, it will be more than strong enough. A whole army could cross it and it would hold."

"An interesting hyperbole, it is exactly what we fear from its construction, the Omi will use it to overtake us when we least expect it."

"Worry no more, there are safeguards built into it."

"What do you mean?"

"There are gates beneath it which can be opened. I built those in for when the time comes you will have large boats traveling the river. But they can also be engaged to block traffic from coming across. Perhaps this is why the Omi, also wanted sentries to protect both sides."

"I can see this structure, will be the impetus for villages springing up nearby."

"It sure will," Roark, who up until now, has been rather quiet. "I see great potential."

Suddenly they spot several horsemen advancing toward them. Roark raises his shield with the royal insignia on it and they slow down approaching more cautiously.

"Stand down, the Queen of Merth is in our party." He tells the approaching horsemen.

"Oh, pardon us, we had no idea, no one told us. You travel without the royal guard." A youthful Omi soldier observes. Suddenly a spark of panic ignites Ali's insecurities. Memories of the attack on her and Fontar, which led to his death, grip her heart. *I have been too impulsive I know better than to travel without a guard detail.*

Reading the concern in Queen Ali's face, Owanu says to the young men, "Fellows you look familiar, I am Ahshen Owanu, designer of the bridge. This is your Queen Ali and her brother Prince Roark. We have been engaged at a diplomatic summit at the Capitol city of Valtar, concerning the bridge. I request Captain Viscoht be summoned immediately."

"Certainly sir," the leader of the group spins on his spirited horse and takes off with the others close behind. The three Matong steeds stand firm and still as stone pillars.

Once Captain Viscoht gets word the Queen is present there is a lot of scrambling to attend to her presence. "My apologies, ma'am, we had no idea…" His words trail off like the call of a faraway bird.

"We wanted an impromptu visit," Ali looks at Ahshen who is maintaining a stern look despite the distraction of his pride as he gazes upon his work.

Roark, who is armed with one of the superior swords and shields made from metals deposited from the Immense in the Great Targa storms, is suddenly feeling limited by the protection he offers. "We are surrounded by Omis he reminds his sister quietly. I am going to engage troops to escort us home, but it may take some time to assemble them. I suggest we put off the tour until they arrive."

Owanu shakes his head slightly. "I don't think there is much cause for concern. I've worked side by side with these men, most of them are young and anxious to learn a new trade."

"Good to know. We can make use of this and put them to work on other projects we have," Roark says. "We need to integrate our people as one." But feeling surrounded by

Omis, Roark is insistent they don't begin their tour of the construction until reinforcements arrive, and he does not let them dismount.

8-To Look Up is to Invite Dizziness

As the inspection party approaches the bridge, it looms above them. Its massive beams and stone pillars are at immense proportions compared to any structure they have ever seen before. To look up is to invite dizziness, but the group continues. "The arches are what give the span its strength." Owanu points out.

"What do you mean?" Roark quizzes him.

"On my planet, we have utilized arches for eons. They are self-supporting through compression. This makes them stable and efficient. They can support greater loads than horizontal beams. And this why we typically use them in bridge design."

Queen Ali and Prince Roark study the incomplete but impressive span arcing across the river. A light breeze blows, and Queen Ali's horse nickers softly. "My science team needs to see this," Roark says softly to his sister.

"Can we ride our horses on it?" Ali asks Owanu.

"Yes, we'll ride out to the middle." He turns his horse to the path which winds up the hill. As they ride to the entrance, the sounds of hammering and men shouting increase.

"Aaw *shwiza*, I hit my *fluming* thumb again!" Ali, Roark, and Owanu smile at each other. And their guide, Captain Viscoht, looks chagrined. He murmurs to one of his men to ride ahead and cease production momentarily.

The horses' hooves echo on the bridge as they slowly begin to proceed to the middle of the span. "The most difficult part is getting the two sides of the drawbridge to meet perfectly. We don't have any advanced tools, but the workers have proven to be resourceful," Owanu explains.

"It is truly incredible; you have built this amazing structure and we have not provided any funds so far. I guess the joke is on the Omi's," Roark grins.

"Oh, we'll pay," Queen Ali tells him. "This is a Merthian structure. It will never belong to just one cadre. It belongs to all." She looks over at Owanu, who studies the bridge as he has done every day for many revolutions of the moons. "This is much more impressive than I was led to believe. I'm glad we came, but I must get back."

"Before you go, you must see the draw bridge operate. The one on this side is fully functional." Owanu beckons to a nearby worker and signals him to begin the process of raising the span. A bevy of workers scuffle as shouts more joyous than serious call out with orders from the top.

"Aye, there, get '*yer flops to grit*,' and focus on the capstan afore your *arse* is mush."

"They like to lift the span…still a little disorganized, but it's their favorite thing to do." Ahshen tells Ali leaning toward her.

"I can tell," Ali smiles as she watches the fervor of the men.

There is a great creaking sound and the bridge beneath their feet trembles. The Matong horses typically stand like statues, but the vibration causes them to prance and rise above the ground by several feet. Owanu, still a novice at riding a Matong steed, hardly notices he is so absorbed in watching the bridge slowly rise into the sky.

"I love it!" The excitement in Queen Ali's voice is sensed by all present, those bending their strength into the motion and the observers. While the movement is slow, there is much drama created by the groaning of both men and timbers as the massive draw bridge gradually rises. Ali cranes her neck and shields her eyes from the afternoon star. A *cutole* bird, with its enormous wingspan, glides past, its size dwarfed by the immense bridge span now raised high above them.

9-It is Important to Understand My People

"It looks like our escort detail has finally arrived," Roark nods to the distance where a group of horsemen comes thundering toward them with a pulsing halo of dust shadowing them like an angry *bouton* ray.

"I wish I could stay here with you Ahshen," the queen hesitates. "I require you to send a daily report of your progress, and we should meet soon."

Turning to Roark she asks him if he will ride back with her. "The escort will not be able to keep up with my Matong steed. I need you to return with me. We should get back by nightfall."

"Yes, of course, Faynyl will be expecting me."

"Perhaps I should return with you?" Owanu asks her.

"Aren't you needed here?"

"Of course, but my Omi escort doesn't even know I have left Valtar. I think I came with you; I should return with you and help secure your safety."

Ali doesn't argue, besides the Matong horse needs to be returned home. *It would be negligent to have the horse not secured at the royal stables.*

"All right," she smiles at the thought of more time spent with this intriguing stranger. Roark rides ahead to converse with their escort which leaves Ali alone with Ahshen momentarily.

"Tell me," she gestures with her hand nervously. "You said you had a family back at home?" She couldn't remember the name of his planet.

"Yes, I have a wife, had…although…" Ali wants him to continue but his face flushes with conflict. "My wife and I had been happily married for a few years, but just before I came here actually, she told me she was taking a new job far from our home. We had not had a chance to work out the details, but she was not clear about me coming with her." He tips his chin down slightly as if embarrassed to go on. "I was very busy building a huge aeroport at a great distance from our city. I hadn't been home much for the last year, and she may have decided to replace me." He says with a self-deprecating laugh. "We were going to meet for dinner the next evening and discuss our future when I disappeared and woke up here. So, as you can see, I left some loose ends back on Fantu. I'm afraid Ellania will never know what happened to me."

Ali can feel the depth of his emotion but doesn't want to frighten him by letting him know. Owanu's normally gentle smile fades as he tries to control his feelings. "Forgive me, I have been too familiar with you."

"No, not at all. I can't even fathom what you have been through. I need to understand my people, and now, whether you want to or not you have become part of us."

Roark comes stampeding up to them. "They will escort us but want us to take another route that keeps us in the open more, so even if they fall behind, which they will, they will be able to keep an eye out on us."

10-Put Him in Prison Until He Rots

As they begin their mad dash back to Valtar, Ali's mind is filled with visions of the amazing bridge and its designer who now keeps up the frantic pace beside her. Roark guards the rear, and ironically now, as opposed to the early morning ride without the escort, the riders are acutely aware of their vulnerability. *I don't know what I was thinking to travel without an escort. Yes, I do. I wanted to be free of entanglement. Such folly. So here we are now in the bright light of day Where anyone can see us. I was too impulsive.*

The royal ring on her finger buzzes with activity, but the queen cannot pause now to focus on the information it provides, but suddenly she gets a clear message as if she is bonding with the Matong. BE ALERT THERE IS DANGER AHEAD. Ali reacts by pushing her steed to greater speeds. It is nearly impossible to stay astride, and yet Ahshen and Roark keep up with her. *At this pace, we will arrive before dark.*

Suddenly an arrow crosses their path with a whistling noise. Where it comes from is impossible to tell without slowing down. The Matong's warning, the arrow, everything comes at once. Queen Ali lowers her head and grips her horse tightly with her legs when the squeal of another arrow passes close past her ear. Roark and Ahshen are both slightly behind her. Looking for cover she spots a few rocks ahead which might afford some shelter. *Out in the open my faoltol! This was planned.*

The three of them manage to swirl around the stones like frenzied water in a storm.

"Surely this is not our own men firing on us!" Roark shouts.

"No, look over there, riders are coming at us from our flank," Ahshen says.

"I only have my knife with me!" Queen Ali shrieks. *By the One True God, what was I thinking to take off spontaneously like we did?*

"Is it the one I had made for you from the Targa metals?"

"Yes, thank the One True God. It will hit the mark no matter how badly I throw."

Roark laughs nervously, "Our escort isn't too far behind. We need only hold them off briefly." They are all breathing heavily but feel more protected behind the stones. Ahshen gives Ali a worried look.

"I can cause a diversion, lead them another way," Ahshen says.

"Don't you dare leave my side. We need you here." She spits her words out like barbs to hold him.

"I have no weapon," he says softly, remorsefully, more to himself than his comrades.

In the distance, they can see the cloud of dust marking their security detail, but closer still is a lesser cloud now within shouting distance. Another arrow barrels toward them and they duck, but it falls short.

"I'm going to speak to them if they would stop firing arrows at us," Owanu says.

Ali pulls at his arm. "No, let Roark do it he has his shield, and the security team is not far off." Memories of her holding Fontar in her arms as he lay dying flood Ali's mind and she curses herself for being naïve. *Never again will I pull this stunt. I have my people to lead. I care more about them than my own life. But if I'm dead I will be useless to them.*

Roark guards himself with his shield and stands slowly as the riders, three of them, approach. "How dare you fire upon us. You commit treason, do you not see the royal colors our horses bear? You shall spend the rest of your life in prison for your insolence."

"I think not." A burly man dismounts and approaches. One of the horses behind him rears and the rider pulls a sword. "Surrender the breeder now and we will be off." He turns to his partners who brandish various crude axes and hammers. "You are no match for us," he boasts.

"You speak rubbish. Who are you anyway?" Roark demands.

The stubby man now on foot, grins, and spits on the ground. "Just a couple of Omi, refusing to be harnessed by living under the rule of a breeder."

Ali gasps and stands, but recognizing the voice, Owanu rises and speaks before Ali can say a word.

"I know you; you are working on the bridge."

Suddenly a rope comes swinging toward Queen Ali. Astonished she grabs at it, but it lands around her arms making her struggle to reach her knife. Owanu moves in and grabs the rope which is tightening around her. Roark leaps forward and slashes at the rope when Ali's horse thunders toward the other horses and breaks them apart from each other. The attackers quickly get the sense they have bitten off more than they can chew, and they scatter. One of them draws his bow, at too close of range, and pulls it. Roark deflects it with his shield. By this time the queen has her knife in her hands and throws it at the marksman. Roark lunges toward the man standing on the ground, and armed with nothing more than his anger, Owanu rushes toward the third rider pulling him off his horse. Grabbing him by his collar and punching him in the face, Owanu pummels the culprit until his face is bloody.

"Nice work guys," Ali pulls her shiny knife out of the body of her assailant, now lying on the ground. She wipes it in the grass and surveys the situation. They tie up the one fellow who is left alive and when the royal guard shows up, hand him over. "Put him in prison until he rots," Roark tells them.

11-You Could Never Be a Rump

"It's comical those three thought they were a match for us," Roark grins at Ali.

"They are ignorant," Ahshen Owanu says. "At home, we have a word for such unfortunates. We call them rumps, as they don't know their heads from their rears. It's sad really, some people see no value in bettering themselves and they cling to foolish beliefs."

"I feel a little foolish I masterminded this fiasco," Ali brushes off her sleeves. "I don't regret seeing our remarkable bridge, Ahshen. I am in awe of its size and intricate design. But I of all people, should know better because I was once captured by the Omi, I should never have pulled a stunt like this. I guess I was acting a little bit like a rump myself today."

Ahshen laughs, "Oh no never. You could never be a rump." She gives him an impish grin and turns toward Roark.

"We will travel back at the pace of our escort and send word of our revised return. Faynyl will be worried sick for you, Roark."

"Nay she knew how far we had to travel."

Flanked now by forty or more warriors, this gives the travelers a much greater sense of security, but Ali is not prepared to let them stop and rest for the night. So, they press on not pausing for meals but instead, snacking on provisions brought from home, while they keep up their frenetic pace.

As the afternoon star settles against the sloping horizon, tendrils of phosphorescent color splash across the canvas of the darkening sky while the two moons rise in the luminescent indigo expanse just above the horizon and the stars high above begin to shimmer as if they are in a fierce competition to be the brightest.

"You have grown quiet," Queen Ali says to Ahshen who rides by her side. Roark has drifted off to converse with some of the other horsemen.

"Ah, I was taking the countryside in." He scans the skies wistfully. "Merth is unlike anything I have seen before. It is quite distinct from my home."

"In what way?"

"We have many more people than you, this brings with it more chaos. More people means more ideas to process. There is a constant barrage of information, and at some point, it just becomes noise. Merth is such a peaceful place."

Ali laughs, "And you say this after this afternoon's encounter with those crazies?"

He looks at her as the rhythm of their horses' hooves glide beneath them in unison. "The Omi are so much cruder than your kind. And violent."

"Yes, they are, and they are sneaky too. We are called Kardians, but we rule the Omi now. We are trying to cultivate a place for them in our culture," she pauses. "But truth be told, it is a tremendous burden on my mind."

As the sky continues to darken, soldiers in the guard detail light lanterns to illuminate the way through the subdued glow.

"I have been thinking how we must revise our language, so it is not the Omi's or the Kardians, or the Dupes. We are one people now and we are all Merthians."

"It is wise to think in those terms," Ahshen agrees. "Unite the people as one."

"What did you mean when you said there are more people on your planet and thus more ideas?"

He looks at her, perhaps considering how to phrase his answer but decides to go with what comes to mind. "A couple of centuries ago our people made the observation certain ideas, for say, advancements in technology or music, or art were being discovered simultaneously in other parts of the world. Some scientists chose to explore this hypothesis with scientific data, and they determined ideas have energy and they multiply with greater numbers of people, so…one person might be writing a play in a remote part of the planet, and someone else comes up with the exact same premise in another faraway place. It's hard to imagine ideas can float through the air, but some hypotheses include the possibility ideas can be transmitted from one being to another through the air like a virus. A carrier of an idea might not even be aware of the idea themselves. If their knowledge is restricted, then their consciousness of an idea is restricted. People can't articulate what they don't know."

"Fascinating," she says turning toward him. "I wonder if the same is true here?"

Ahshen shrugs. "Perhaps. I'm no expert in this field, but we might investigate it."

"My mother, Queen Aadya, whom you have not met yet, was responsible for encompassing all our people into the circle of learning. That was pretty recent in our history. She was born a simple peasant, so when she became queen through marriage to my father, she was adamant about educating all, especially women who were considered to be nothing more than 'breeders.'"

Ahshen turns to her as they ride and studies her expression. "Am I to understand the royal Karda family gets messages from a divine orb, and you can converse silently with each other?"

"Yes, it is a natural power we alone possess. I can share my thoughts with Roark for instance, but I rarely do. He is just my brother."

"This is something I would like to know more about."

"As you wish," she says as she urges her horse to speed up.

12-Where Nasty Things Thrive

When the weary travelers arrive home it is near the time when the morning star rises. The two moons hang low, close to the horizon and Queen Ali wants nothing more than to steal off to bed and get at least a few hours of sleep, but first, she must bathe. "I am too filthy to go to bed like this," she tells her domestic staff. They swiftly draw a bath for her, adding mintus leaves and *calezl* drops into the steaming sunken tub, to help her sleep. She sinks into the luxurious bath and enjoys her back being scrubbed by one of her attendants. Occasionally if she bathes before bed, a small ensemble will play stringed instruments for her, but the night is short, and the peaceful quiet is like a blanket, warm and soft. She nods off, but someone gently taps her awake and carries her off to bed.

When the queen stirs from her sleep it is because the bright light is peeking through the drawn curtains, and she squints at the intrusion. She is starving but has invited Ahshen Owanu to dine with her for breakfast. "Just bring me some tea and a couple of those buttery," she motions absently with her hands, "you know, those cookies I love."

"Yes, Mum," her trusted Sauza smiles, returning shortly with a plate of dainty, bite-size cookies, fruit, and her favorite sugar-encrusted flowers.

"Thank you, Sauza, but I don't have time for all this. Have the kitchen prepare a breakfast feast for Owanu and me."

"He has been waiting for you in the Maultu dining room. We tried to serve him, but he's waiting for you."

"Aw *shwiza*, I didn't mean to oversleep."

"It's all right Your Highness, Prince Roark showed up and they've been conversing."

As Ali enters the room Roark and Ahshen both grin and stop talking. "About time you got up your Royal Highness," her brother teases her.

"Aye, I was exhausted."

"Please join us, Owanu, here has been filling me in on some amazing ideas. He says it's possible to fly through the air, and he was sketching a machine; it has wings like a bird."

"Oh my, it's too early for such tales," Queen Ali admonishes her brother.

Owanu stands, "Please sit and let them serve you."

"Tea first," she beckons to the attendant, then sits down and pulls the paper toward her. "So, what is this contraption? It looks like an arrow with wings on it."

Owanu points to the drawing. "We call this a mini-cortar after the aeronautical engineer who first designed it. There are aeronautical ships much larger than this, but I believe I can propel this one using some of Roark's... ah what did you call them?"

"Targa metals. They fell from the sky during the great Targa Storm."

"Yes, as he describes them, I think I can polarize them to build a small engine, for propelling the mini-cortar."

"Slow down guys, what in the heavens is an engine?"

Ahshen Owanu takes his charcoal and begins to sketch rapidly drawing two circles with lots of arrows making the orbs look as if they are spinning. "Using the polarity of the metals, I should be able to create a small engine. I won't know for sure until I get my hands on them, but from Roark's description, I think we are talking about *aludadyones*. I'm going to take these materials and work on them in my spare time while I supervise the bridge."

"Speaking of that, Roark I want you to accompany Ahshen back to the bridge and get some more suitable lodging for him, and the other workmen. Sounds like they are crowded into a few primitive residences. And you need to sort out the bad seeds from the good. We don't want any workers there like the ones who accosted us."

"That would be most welcome, Queen Ali," Ahshen looks intently into her eyes with gratitude.

"Yeah, we need to build a village overnight before the Omi's *fondraduff* seeps into everything."

Ahshen looks confused. Ali laughs. "It's the stench of where nasty things thrive."

"Ah, yes, the Omi do have their own disgusting smell," he agrees.

"And Roark, I will also need a lodge I can come visit and keep an eye on things."

Roark rolls his eyes at his sister. "Of course, my Queen. Of course, for you anything."

Ali bites into a delicious cheese and *fotu* leaf omelet served to her on a crystal plate and Ahshen joins her.

"Mmm, delicious."

13-A Once Cherished Friendship

"In the short time we have known each other, I have grown to, ah," Ali is careful to choose her words. "I have, well, I've gotten used to having you around." Ahshen Owanu squeezes the hands she has offered, understanding no one is to embrace the queen unless she offers physical contact first. Her hands are cold to the touch, and he struggles with what to say to her. "I must finish the bridge of course."

"Now Roark is in charge, the project will go much more smoothly."

"I'm certain of that, the Omis are no picnic."

Ali looks confused, "What does this expression mean?"

He leans toward her almost inappropriately close and speaks softly. "It means there is no joy in working with them."

Queen Ali laughs. "We know this too well. But perhaps this is the opportunity to become more united."

Owanu mounts his horse and smiles down at her. As she looks up at him, the shadow of his face is silhouetted by the morning star above him, creating a tiny halo effect, causing Ali to shudder.

In the background, Faynyl and Borzok are saying goodbye to Roark. Ali pauses to see what the commotion is about. Borzok is inconsolable as his father mounts to leave. Ali makes her way over to him. "Get the royal lodge built quickly. I will visit before the moonlight dims in the next Asunder."

"Bring Faynyl with you," he grins.

"Queen Ali, may I have a word?" It is Tildyn, he has shown up in the group that is leaving. "We never had a chance to talk, just you and I," he jerks his horse back and pulls out of the line of horsemen.

"What is it Tildyn?"

"I wanted to offer some suggestions for the bridge."

She looks puzzled, "the time is past, it has been settled." A visible irritation floats up into his face, but he tries to suppress his annoyance. "That may be, but if your brother is in charge now, I am concerned…" He leaps off his horse to meet her face to face. "I am concerned he will have a disciplinary problem with the men."

"And why do you think this?"

"You are asking them to take orders from someone who is not their kin."

"Thank you for your concern, but my brother is an excellent, well-educated, leader and he will organize an efficient chain of command. I have every confidence in him."

"You have not taken into consideration the bridge is an Omi project."

It is difficult for the queen to hold back her scowl, especially with the daylight shining into her eyes. "My dear Tildyn, you seem to have lost sight of the fact, your family enacted war upon us in recent history, a war in which I fought. We won the war. Then your family authorized a bridge to be built without our permission, and despite this, we are accepting of the construction. This is a public-use roadway governed by our agreed-upon laws. I suggest you get used to the idea Prince Roark is in charge. There is no changing my command." Her voice hardens and she must use restraint to not shout.

"But you will be sorry!"

Disgusted the queen turns away to dismiss Tildyn. *What arrogance, and to think I once cherished his friendship.* She pauses again and turns to him just as he is again about to mount his horse. "Tildyn, if there are any problems among the ranks of the Omi, I will hold you personally responsible. And do not tell me again I will be sorry, or you will find yourself behind bars! Do you hear me?"

All the color in Tildyn's face drains, leaving him pale and even more repulsive to her. He fumbles to give her a shallow and awkward bow. "It would be prudent for me to apologize for my impertinence, my Queen."

"Don't just talk about it, do it!" The words come thick from her mouth, and she wants to have him hauled away but thinks better of it. "You need to resist your urges, Tildyn. There could be a place of honor for you in my court, but you must prove yourself loyal first."

14-A Resonating Clamor

Once the envoy has left Katara, it gets a lot quieter, but within the calm is a resonating clamor for action by the queen and her advisors. The distance between the bridge and Valtar is enough challenge for concern because a lack of communication could be destabilizing, but there are many more issues to resolve.

"We must be made aware of what is going on at all times. We shall need to have a relay of dedicated riders. They will traverse a day's journey to pass information back and forth." Queen Ali's uncle Prince Bonder proclaims at the very next council meeting.

"Yes, an excellent idea. And we need to build lodging for the workers and for us when we journey to check up on our investment." Queen Ali tilts her head and daintily brushes back her hair with her left hand that bears the royal ring. She hardly notices its mild vibrations and the messages it delivers to her cognitively, "I think we need to recognize and accept there is an enormous need for expansion of goods and services to this area, we must build a village at breakneck speed. The Omi's in their ignorance, did not provide enough forethought for such a large undertaking." She notices her voice has become more commanding without her having to consciously deliver it that way.

"Food is already problematic, the Omis don't take such good care of their workers." Prince Parsa, who is less outspoken than his brother Bonder, comments. Queen Ali notices his hair is starting to turn silver and his hairline has receded slightly. He no longer wears a stylishly groomed beard but is now clean-shaven.

"This will be a good committee for you to head up. Prince Parsa, you will take care of communications. This relay idea of yours can also work for food and other sorts of supplies."

Queen Ali pulls at her leather sleeve, like her mother in her youth, she is always dressed in practical, but comfortable garb so she can leap onto her Matong steed in an instant and be ready for battle. "Alatoi, I want you to accompany the next group going out. You shall serve as a close advisor to Roark. I want you to use keen eyes to watch for trouble, and you will serve as the Master Captain of our guards to ensure a lawful community." Queen Ali gives a hard look at the woman who still wears her long, black silken hair in a ponytail which falls halfway down her back swishing past the sword scabbard she proudly bears. Alatoi carries the sword Queen Aadya gifted her many moons ago. The one her father, Zolan Vannatu had used in battle. It was the queen's way of honoring Alatoi who had been mostly responsible for rescuing her long-lost father those countless revolutions ago. It was an extraordinary personal gift, which Alatoi did not take lightly.

"I will write up your orders to take to Prince Roark." Alatoi bows, her history with the queen and the growing trust Queen Ali has for her, ever since Alatoi rescued the queen from her Omi captor, has transformed Alatoi from the days when she came from Omi land as the merchant,

Petra Kilva's lover. She was a sullen and gifted artist then, now she serves as a valued emissary because of her Omi heritage and her skills as a spy.

"Chard," Queen Ali motions to her aide, "bring Kysal Toltor to me. I need to speak with him immediately in my antechamber. Everyone else," she looks at the crowd of council members. "Please keep meeting and make these plans work."

"Kysal, thank you for your quick response. From here on out you shall be part of the council. Your skills as a gifted scientist are invaluable at this juncture in our development. I am sending you to Roark's side for the time being at the bridge. He is working closely with a man named Ahshen Owanu. Ahshen, as I presume you know, is our visitor from another planet. His science skills are way beyond ours. I need you to mirror him and soak up as much knowledge from him as you can. He mentioned a device to me, using the Targa metals, whereby he could fly through the air." Kysal sucks in his breath, "I had always speculated flight would someday be possible, that we could mimic the birds. It will be a great honor to fulfill this task."

"I want you to take a handful of your best students to assist you in your mission. They must be smart and hardworking. Madam Alatoi will be moving out with the next *possel,* and you and your aides will accompany her and her staff."

Kysal backs up, bows to his queen, and heads out the door.

15-Building Bridgenstyl

The hammering and grunting by the work crew is like the rhythm of a thunderstorm, only incessant. The melodic sounds of nature in the area, the large flocks of the *cacophono* birds, the hoots of the bulky *owlicans*, the frenzied flow of the river, and the howls of the wild *fontons,* can only be heard at night when the noise, like the prickly *gozan* shrub, is lifted and the heavens glow, not dimmed by the dust of construction. Alatoi finds the noise invigorating and wears the badge of authority the queen has bestowed upon her, on her chest with pride; occasionally polishing it with the back of her sleeve in private. She is among her countrymen the Omi but has never been prouder to be a Merthian. She, Roark, and Ahshen have been given quarters in a nearby house recently purchased from a farmer. It is modest but large by surrounding area standards. They have a cook, a grizzly Omi, whose skills aren't up to the standards they are used to, but no one is losing weight.

On a typical day, Alatoi traverses the project on her horse, a saucy bay that nickers loudly when a disturbance erupts among the men. The horse enjoys breaking up their little conflicts as much as Alatoi and only occasionally does Alatoi have to hold her ground, flashing her heirloom sword and cursing a would-be opponent. The unruly workers fearing Alatoi, subvert their anger by telling ugly stories behind her back. Because she is in a position to police their actions, she avoids sleeping with any of them and instead has taken up with a serving girl at the newly established pub inside of what was once a barn, but there is a new woman, a construction worker who has caught Alatoi's eye. She will save this dalliance for later, because of her conflict of interest.

Because Alatoi is open about her diversity of sexual interests she is completely startled by Roark's advances. "You *flowkin* pistoid!" she spews at him one night in the bar. They both were drunk. He whispers into her ear several lewd suggestions and even lets his tongue touch her ear lobe sending a spasm down her spine. Despite the fire that leaps inside of her, Alatoi summons her restraint, hard baked by her loyalty to the queen. "You are drunk Prince. Go home and think about your beautiful wife and pleasure yourself. For the love of the One True God don't ever try something like that again, or you will lose an arm."

To the point of stumbling, Prince Roark backs off, clearly surprised by her rebuff. "Oh, that's how it is, you are the ideal citizen now because of the badge you wear?"

As always, armed with Prince Roark's grandfather's sword on her back, Alatoi peers around trepidatiously. "Sir you are out of line," she hisses, "and you need to recuse yourself. Do I need to get one of my aides to take you to bed?"

Quickly Roark becomes self-aware of his conduct and sucks in a deep breath. "No," he tells her. "Forgive my transgressions." He brushes off his chest as if his behavior were instead breadcrumbs flaked upon his tunic.

Upon awakening, Roark's guilt pounds within his head like a clapper in a warped bell. It is late when he goes down for breakfast and thinks this is an advantage to avoiding Alatoi, although it won't be possible forever. He decides lack of memory is the best path to take. When Alatoi is still at the breakfast table finishing off her plate, he feigns ignorance when she snickers at him for his indiscretion.

"Don't worry handsome prince, your secret is safe with me and only a handful of other drunks at the bar."

This is bad. I must not drink so much. He silently glares at her, hating himself for his illogical attraction to her.

"You have simply misunderstood my actions. I have a beautiful wife at home."

"Whatever you want to tell yourself, but your wet tongue upon my ear was nothing to be mistaken."

Roark stops in his tracks and looks down at her staring at the sultry woman, her eyes, like black *obsidiantia* meet his with equal challenge. "You are a valuable member of this team, but do not forget you are replaceable," he snarls.

She stands abruptly and as she does, she spits on the ground barely missing Roark's feet. "You would be advised never to threaten me again. Especially…especially if you have any hopes of indulging yourself in your fantasies with me!"

Roark turns and walks away from her, his head still pounding, his brain tissue like a dehydrated fruit flopping around inside his skull. He does not miss Alatoi has left a door open to him. He shrugs off the vitriol of his worst self and waves off a servant who tries to bring him something to eat. "No, thanks, I must catch up with Ahshen. It's getting late."

16-Embracing Change

Back at Katara, Queen Ali has begun an exploration of the grand library hall where she has begun soaking up the knowledge once contained in a few safely guarded books limited to the royal family's use only. She has gotten to know the quirky, thin-limbed librarian, Belhana, who has taken on the mission to anticipate the queen's curiosity, and in her enthusiasm is sometimes seen hanging by one arm off the rolling ladder to procure a rare title for the queen.

Feeling a need to embrace the changes in the kingdom, Queen Ali has also disciplined herself to meditate and pay more attention to the royal ring on her finger as it conveys its messages to her. Matong visits, too have become more frequent. "You'd be proud of me Mother; your influence has steered me toward a greater appreciation of knowledge. I can be more confident in my leadership abilities when I understand every topic presented before me. Our world is quickly becoming more complicated." She tells Queen Aadya who has joined her in the reading nook for tea and conversation.

Queen Aadya glows with pride. To have her daughter express such validation of her life's work is rewarding beyond words, but she does not let the honor land on herself, instead giving her son, Roark, credit for the freshly expanded library.

"Roark is the one who has done this," She sweeps her arms wide to encompass the huge room created by opening up eleven smaller rooms in Katara. "He is responsible for pursuing scientific knowledge."

"It is absolutely surprising how he has turned out." A delicate smile comes to Queen Ali's full lips as she thinks of her brother in his teens, a spoiled, arrogant prince with no larger goals than wanting to impress girls.

"Look at him now, he has a beautiful wife and child." Queen Aadya beams although her words invoke in Aadya the intensity of her daughter's emotional loss of Fontar. YOU WILL FIND LOVE, A PARTNER TO SHARE YOUR LIFE WITH. Aadya lets her thoughts be transferred to her daughter.

I WISH I HAD THE SAME CONFIDENCE YOU DO. Ali turns from her mother and pets Robic whose massive furry body is curled up on the cozy couch with her. She sips on her tea and peers out the tall leaded windows to the courtyard below. YOU CAN ALWAYS SEE STRAIGHT THROUGH ME, IT ISN'T FAIR.

Aadya laughs, I used to feel that way about your father.

"There is someone I am interested in," Queen Ali speaks softly, cautiously.

"You needn't say more, I know about your consort."

Blood rushes to Queen Ali's face, "No, I'm not talking about Martyl."

A smile guiltily creeps into her mother's still captivating face. "Oh?"

Queen Ali fidgets, clutching Robic's fluffy white fur. Blushing she turns toward her mother. "It doesn't matter I am supposed to wait for the 'Cup of Light.'"

Aadya's face falls as she sees the disappointment in her daughter's expression. "Honey," she reaches out to stroke her daughter's hand.

They look into each other's eyes and Queen Ali, shrugs. "I have no time for love anyway. My people need my full attention."

"Oh, but you do, and you will meet your 'Cup of Light.'"

17-Distractions

"You seem distracted tonight my Queen," Ali smiles wickedly at Martyl. She likes it when he calls her 'my Queen.'

"You are beginning to know me too well." She purses her lips as she considers his intentions.

"Perhaps you don't want my advances tonight." She sits up in her bed, clutching the silken cream-colored sheets to her waist. Her full breasts, like the shimmering sheets are illuminated by the moonlight which filters through the trees outside.

"No, I do want your company and I do want your advances, but at this moment I would like you to pour me more wine and touch me softly. You know how you do, barely touching me, so It's hard to define where I stop, and you begin."

He looks at her curiously, but knowing what she wants, reaches for a translucent scarf nearby and lets it fall lightly, randomly on her breasts and thighs. She shivers and he stops to reach over to grab the cut-glass crystal decanter filled with a cherry-colored *fontiel* sparkling wine. The trickling sound of the wine pouring into her long-stemmed glass floods her senses and she lifts the lily-shaped stemware to her lips.

"Don't stop," she pleads. He continues to tease her body with the scarf, until he takes her glass away from her and begins to use the scarf selectively, tying and untying it to tantalize her and surprise her. "Would you be this creative with me if I weren't 'your Queen?'"

Martyl laughs, "Most likely not. I would throw you across the bed and ravish you and demand your loyalty to my body."

"Right now, it's looking as if your body is pretty loyal to me," she grins. She touches him lightly in a way she knows drives him crazy and succumbs to his embrace. As the night swallows them in sleep like warm bath water, Queen Ali reaches her hand over to him and lets it flop casually onto his stomach. "I'm leaving tomorrow for Bridgenstyl. I'm not sure when I will be back." Her words sound rehearsed like an oft-delivered line in a dramatic play.

He takes her hand in his and ventures to ask, "May I go with you?"

"No, you will stay here." She can sense his disappointment in the heaviness of his touch.

When there are many people gathered for traveling, the noise of the horses, the wagons, and the people shouting over those noises, creates a storm of confusion. Remembering her first slightly catastrophic visit to the bridge, Queen Ali is comforted by today's uproar. With a steady flow of trade now between Valtar and Bridgenstyl, the journey will be much more comfortable she reminds herself.

She has not notified Ahshen she is coming, but certainly, he has learned of her upcoming arrival through

the servant's gossip. She mounts her glossy mare and
like the prancing of hooves beneath her Ali's spirits soar
knowing she will soon be in Bridgenstyl.

18-A Startling Visage

"**L**ook! Up there it is a giant bird!" The warning ripples through the horde of travelers like still waters disrupted by a hurled rock. Queen Ali pulls Elita to a halt, and using her hand to shield her vision, peers up into the clear afternoon sky. It is unlike anything she has ever seen. The startling visage soars and dips like a massive bird but is too large to be one. Paranoia of ominous trickery swells through the wary crowd.

"It's coming toward us we must take cover!"

"Halt!" The queen raises her gloved hand, and her escort detail hovers around her like pollen on water. "If it is what I think it is we shouldn't be frightened." She looks again up into the sky as the giant bird soars and loops. *This must be what Ahshen, spoke of the last time we talked. Hopefully, that is all it is.* "Scatter through the crowd and calm them," she tells her guards.

As they approach the burgeoning village, Roark rides out to meet them. He arrives astride his Matong steed who is foaming slightly at the bit. "Make way, make way," he shouts and the confused crowd parts to let him through.

His grin rips across his face. "Is it not amazing?" He pulls his horse up abruptly before his sister. "That's Ahshen up there!" He says pointing at the broad wings now looping precariously close. Roark embodies the joy of a mischievous adolescent in his face. "Isn't it absolutely *fw-nataal*?"

While the sight is astonishing, Queen Ali does not like the disruption. She had envisioned a much different reunion with Ahshen Owanu. "Surely, he has seen you from above and will land soon. He took me up yesterday and it was bizarre! We must waste no time clearing the landing strip."

Roark spins his honey-colored steed on his heels. "Attention guards get these people and lead them over there." Roark points to the road they came in on but have now scattered with the unruliness of pack animals searching for food. "Get the people off the landing strip," he waves his arms wildly and it becomes more apparent what he is talking about, a wide and level path parallel to the road with two worn trails, makes the landing strip look like an extra wide road.

"Where's Faynyl?" Roark asks his sister. Queen Ali shrugs.

"She wanted to come but the stewards said there was not enough available lodging yet."

"That's ridiculous, she could stay in my quarters."

"They didn't think that was sufficient. She'll come next time, I'm sure."

"They have a recently constructed lodge for you, but it is more basic than you are used to. Laborers have been working their *astos* off for you, my Queen." The 'my Queen' part in Roark's voice is tinged with the slightest sarcasm, only her brother would dare breathe.

"Tell my guards where it is, I'm not going to sit here and wait for him to come down."

"You don't want to miss it. That's the most exciting thing about it; the launch and the landing."

"How in Merth does it launch?"

"The engine is lightweight and enough to sustain flight, but he has been catapulting the aero wings by a sophisticated loaded spring system, off the bridge."

"The bridge? Doesn't that get in the way of construction?"

As if harboring a fair portion of guilt, Roark explains, "He only launches once a day, and the workers merely clear the deck of the bridge. Beneath them, work continues on the piers and struts."

"Obviously, once the bridge is completed, there will have to be another launch pad. Ahshen is already exploring options when he takes flight and can see from the air, what might be suitable for this."

Ali feels a headache coming on and only wants to get to her lodge and wash off the dust of the road. "I'll see it another time. Please, Roark, escort me to my lodging."

19-This is not Katara

"They'll be adding more rooms on the far end over there," Roark waves his arm as they enter the spacious lodge. "Perhaps my bride will be allowed to come when they have added more square footage," he says with a noticeable twinge of bitterness. "Servants should not be encouraged to make decisions for my family."

Queen Ali hardly notices his discontent as she is shown to her quarters and the steaming bath prepared for her. She sinks into the luxurious tub only to be startled by pulsing waters whispering to pummel her body. "What is this?" she asks Sauza, who has traveled with her to oversee the local staff.

"I understand Sir Owanu created this delight for you," she answers.

"It's amazing, I'll have to ask him how it works." Ali sinks further into the crystal tub, thinking it is more luxurious than the one at home. *I would like to bring Mother here so she can experience for herself these innovations.*

It isn't until much later in the day when Queen Ali first sees Ahshen. Roark has taken her out to the bridge to view construction and Ahshen is embroiled in a loud discussion with one of the workers. When he sees she has arrived on the site, he gives an insulting gesture with his arm to the subordinate and walks off disgustedly in her direction.

"Working with these Omi is so frustrating, Ali." He says with a scowl. "They have no idea what they are doing and don't want to learn. This bridge could have been finished many moons ago."

This is not the romantic reunion I had hoped for. "It must be safe," she says.

"Oh, it is. I personally check every crucial structural component as it is constructed."

"We need to pull in more of our men," she turns to Roark. "They are more educated and willing to work."

"That could be problematic too, it will cause a stir among the Omi, who like the steady pay," Roark tells her.

"I want to meet with Brechnole and Tildyn tonight at dinner."

"But they are not here. They have left Olafar in charge."

A sour taste rises in her mouth. "Of course, they did. He is the least competent person, but he's not as arrogant. We will use this to our advantage."

At dinner, Queen Ali still has not had a moment alone with Owanu, much to her disappointment, because talks with Prince Olafar take precedence. *No one will ever be able to say I put my interests first before my people.* As she listens to Prince Olafar drone on, she swallows and takes a deep breath. "Stop, where you are! I have put Ahshen Owanu in charge, with my brother Prince Roark as his commander. We are bringing in more workers from Valtar and you will do as I say."

Olafar grinds his teeth and looks down. "My king will not go for this!"

"Your father has already agreed to my sanctions. Prince Roark is my eyes and ears. You have no choice."

Observing the seething going on inside of him, Ali lowers her voice. "Look, we are here to support your worthy efforts. I understand you are used to having your way, but we are embarking on a fresh path together. You must trust me, and we will all profit."

"But…"

"Olafar, you must obey me or find yourself behind bars." She folds her hands in her lap, "Or, let me assure you of the wealth you will acquire should I reward you for your valuable service. Wealth independent of your Omi royalty status."

For a brief moment, she feels him acknowledge her words, until a shadow crosses his face, leaving her with doubt as to his sincerity. She looks over to the aide standing by the door and signals him to draw close. "As part of my pledge to you for your loyalty, I am assigning Traxfor to assist you. This will lighten your load and give you the presence of mind to evaluate your loyalty to me."

His expression reads both hot and cold, but there is resignation in Prince Olafar's voice. "As you wish Queen Ali."

20-Nothing Could be More Complicated

As the plates are cleared and the candles extinguished, Queen Ali invites Owanu to join her for dessert in her outer chamber. A fire is laid for them and tiny glasses of sipping *chaltarn* are brought for them to enjoy. Her favorite *clontons* and sweet, crystallized blossoms are also served. The effervescent drink and the sweet and tart delicacies create a lightness of mood. Queen Ali finds herself giddy as she gazes upon Owanu, his broad shoulders and now, shoulder-length hair tantalize her, but it is his smile, only for her which makes everything he murmurs seem enchanting. She wants him but acknowledges she must not rush. She is curious how he might pursue her.

"The bathtub, thank you, it is amazing."

"I thought it would be something you would enjoy." He lets his thumb slide up and down the crystal stem of his glass. "I have many other inventions you will benefit from."

A slight chill runs down her spine causing her to shiver. She looks at him intently unable to contain herself and no longer believing the 'cup of light' will someday be delivered to her. She leans over and lets her lips touch his lightly. Her brain tingles with delight and her body vibrates with desire.

She pulls away as softly as she had reached out. He stumbles for words. "Ali, Queen Ali." He corrects himself, "I don't know what to say or do. To allow myself this supreme indulgence—is this your invitation?"

Laughter, nervous and impulsive plummets from her lips still tingling with the sensation of his kiss. "Forgive me. I couldn't resist. I am attracted to you, everything about you. The physical and the *phsyzk* spark of your mysterious appearance here on Merth."

Ahshen reaches over to her, touches her neck lightly, and pulls toward her, his body drawn to her like the gravity of water plummeting down a steep incline. Before either of them acknowledges mentally what is happening, they are tearing at each other's clothing. His hands at first respectful, in the placing become entangled with her desire. The two miscreant lovers grope fitfully for mutual satisfaction which only comes after several rounds of passionate parlay.

Awakening, Ali feels a warm hand grasping her breast. Her smile is interrupted by her panic. *What have I done? This is not what is supposed to happen. The Matong is to provide the 'cup of light'. I have allowed my passions to get the best of me.*

She feels a slight squeeze of her bosom eliciting a *shiverous* response deep inside of her and Ahshen raises his head like the morning star rising. Grinning like a little boy with a new pup, his charm is irresistible. *By the One True God, he is handsome. I am totsle!*

She leaps from his grasp, but he doesn't let go. Empowered by their nightlong dance of passion he uses the advantage of his strength and size to subdue her. *I am queen I should put a stop to this!* But Queen Ali does not enforce her sovereign reign and lets her lover take one more opportunity to elevate their mutual passion. Allowing herself to become powerless in this way is so frightening she rebuffs him afterward, becoming cold and distant.

"You must go now, my maids will see you out through the back door. No one must know of this." Owanu dresses silently, frustrated but respectful of her mood. As he sobers to the dawn of day, he wonders what to do. He has slept with the queen, and nothing could be more complicated.

21-Away from the Matong

"We must talk," Queen Ali looks down at the drawings before her rather than Ahshen.

"Yes," is all he says.

"I have allowed myself to succumb to my desires for you." He remains still with the intensity of a hunter watching a stray *voxen* in the wild. She turns to him with less courage than she'd like. "I am away from the Matong which I would consult in such matters. This is a vulnerability I have by being here rather than being in Valtar at Katara."

At first, Ahshen says nothing, letting out a careful breath he still does not meet her gaze. Finally, he answers. "I believe I have a solution."

"And what would that be?"

"My flying machine could take you there in short order. My only conundrum is where we would land once we get there. Where I have been landing is a bit dangerous. I have a good idea where there is a better place, but I have not scoped it out thoroughly."

Queen Ali's smile spreads unpredictably across her face. "Me, the queen, a passenger in your flying machine. I think not."

"Why not? It's perfectly safe."

Queen Ali briefly lets her imagination soar to such a ridiculous place, letting go an uneasy laugh.

"Can you guarantee my safety?"

"Sure, what I propose is, I will take Roark first, he is adventurous and familiar with the terrain. We'll land and make sure it is safe. I'll return and come get you." He meets her gaze. "It's a very short ride via the aeroplane."

"It would certainly simplify my life if I could be transported quickly between the two locations. I want to stay close to this project." *And you.* But she doesn't share her thoughts with him.

"I'm on this." He reaches for his soft leather jacket and races away.

"Ha! This is amazing." Roark says as he peers down at the ground below. The wind in his ears echoes as he turns his head back and forth for a maximum view.

"I knew you would love, it. You will probably have me building you one soon."

"*Dauffle* straight!"

Elation swells through Ahshen Owanu as he takes the plane higher, then dips to spin and rotate. The force of the turn pins them both to their seats.

"By the Almighty One True God. What are you doing man?" Roark punches him lightly from the back seat. Laughter peals from Owanu whose spirit and body are soaring together in one tightly pulled knot. His face takes on a more youthful demeanor as he runs the flying machine through some aerobatic moves.

"Holy *frap*! Are you trying to kill us?"

"No, I thought you might enjoy a thrilling ride."

"I think I've had enough." Roark beginning to feel a little queasy in the stomach, wonders how much further they must journey. As if reading his thoughts, Owanu points to the horizon.

"Over there is the city of Valtar. Can you see the towers of Katara now?"

Squinting against the light of the morning star, Roark is thrilled by the sight of the city from above. "We'll be there in a few minutes. I'm going to do some surveillance from up here, to find the best landing site. Any suggestions?"

"There's a field close to Compana on very even ground. The *wavu* grain was harvested recently, so it may be ideal. It's over in that direction." Roark leans forward to point where Owanu can see his motion.

"I'll head that way."

Owanu guides the plane in the direction of Roark's hand and soon begins a descent. "I hope we don't scare anyone."

Owanu chuckles, "It is why I brought you. I hope to land quickly before a crowd gathers and gets in our way." Taking a sharp turn, the flying machine sinks rapidly. Roark holds his breath with the sensation his breakfast will come spewing out his mouth.

"You will have to be much gentler with my sister." A warmth bursts into Owanu's chest fueled by both shame and a bit of unexpected joy. *Surely Roark couldn't possibly know I slept with his sister. Or does he?*

22-A Joy Ride

Roark, now without a way to return to Bridgenstyl, plans to stay home with his family for a few days. When he surprises Faynyl with his presence, she is delighted. She hugs him and quickly hands him Borzok. "Here, you two need to reacquaint yourselves. I haven't had a moment to myself since you left." Roark is a little taken aback she doesn't greet him with the passionate embrace he had been anticipating since Owanu first invited him to take the test flight with him.

Still bubbling with enthusiasm despite the less-than-amorous greeting, he tells her. "You won't believe how I got here."

"Don't tell me you arrived in the mechanical bird; everyone is talking about."

"Yes, it was quite amazing. I want Owanu to take you up so you can experience it."

Borzok, giddy with his father's return giggles and pulls at Roark's hair.

"I only have a short time before I must return. Let's get a servant to keep Borzok for a while and later I will surprise him with a special gift, I've been considering."

"He is too young." She gives him a stern look.

"What?" He shrugs his shoulders.

"I won't even say it in front of him, but you know he's too young. He'll get hurt."

Setting the boy down Roark reaches for his wife and kisses her with pent-up passion grasping her hungrily. "Ah Faynyl, it's been forever why didn't you come to see me?"

"They told me the nice quarters only had room enough for the queen."

"Then you shall come and stay when she is not there. I can't live my life without my wife and child. I won't do it. I shall have a house built just for you."

Faynyl snorts, "I'm sure your needs will be put before the queen's."

When Queen Ali is escorted by Owanu to the slick-looking compact flying machine he has built, she admires the black matte finish with silver signature swirls along the edge of the cockpit and runs her hand across the smooth, mysterious Targa metal as if getting acquainted with a horse she is about to mount. And while she knows they will be jettisoned off the bridge to reach airlift, the acceleration she feels as they boomerang across the length of the bridge deck is bizarre, frightening, and amazing all at once. She clutches the smooth, wooden handrails tightly not allowing herself to look down at first. Once she does, she is mesmerized by the sight of the light dancing across the brilliant blue river like twinkling gemstones beaded randomly upon a ribbon sash. Below the trees and fields are a living patchwork quilt dotted with farm animals. It is the sight of the horizon, which surprises her the most as it glows with a mysterious haze she never realized was there. *This is extraordinary, much like riding a Matong steed, only faster, higher, and much riskier.* The rushing of the wind drowns out any hope of conversation, but Ahshen turns and smiles to check her demeanor, "I can make it more exciting if you'd like," he shouts.

She laughs, "I'm sure you can, but I think we should just get there alive this time." He nods affirmatively. She can only see his thick, dark hair pulled back by a leather thong and the side of his face now shadowed by whiskers not shaved in several days. *He makes me feel safe and on edge at the same time. I must always find a reason to keep him by my side.*

And as her thoughts manifest, temporarily reassuring her, he tells her to hold on tight. "What? No! Please don't do anything foolish!" She shouts with futility. The aeroplane, which feels more like they have strapped on wings rather than riding in an airship, dips steeply toward the ground. The strap holding her inside the open seat directly behind him suddenly seems insanely inadequate. She hears a squeal coming from deep within her, which peals involuntarily out of her lungs like a caged *drazon*, the barbaric species Fythls keep to feed their enemies to.

Ali, a veteran of the battlefield who was once captured by her enemies, is laughing and crying at once. She is ready to slash her sword straight through the gut of the man in the front seat, the one with the helm who went from being her supreme protector and adoring lover to the designer of her instant death.

"You must not treat your queen this way!" She shouts falling back on protocol this man has clearly chosen not to follow.

"What?" he says cupping his palm to his ear in an exaggerated expression of false concern.

"I will have you quartered and fed to the dogs," she screams.

"What? I still can't hear you."

When she has her two feet firmly planted on solid ground, the landing, in and of itself frightening, she is so angry she cannot speak. He observes her, trying not to show his pleasure.

"I had to show you what the little flying machine can do so the landing would not scare you."

She has no words to confront his impertinence, a masculine grunt issues from her body, a tone she doesn't recognize and vows not to look him in the eyes until he apologizes, which he never does.

She swipes at her leggings and pulls her tangled long hair to one side. Humiliation like fog creeps into her and she tries to rationalize why she entrusted this maniac or even worse why she has allowed him into her bed. "Well, it certainly didn't take us much time to get here," she says trying not to overreact.

Then a strange transformation takes place as Ahshen takes his arm and wraps it around her squeezing tightly. All the terror and rage she felt melts, and she is once again grateful for his protection. *It's so odd what this man does to me.*

23-Melting Like an Icicle in the Bright Light

Surely this is not right, Queen Ali plants her feet and focuses on comprehending the message from the Matong. BELIEVE IN THE ONE WHO HAS COME. HE HAS MUCH TO OFFER MERTH. YOU WILL HONOR HIS WISDOM AND SOON I SHALL REVEAL THE 'CUP OF LIGHT.' YOU SHALL BE WED AND BEAR A CHILD.

On my life, the Matong has finally reassured me I will have a mate. Shuddering slightly, she grasps at her collar to pull it away from her throat.

"I will stay here at Katara for a few more days she tells Ahshen later. You may come back and get me, but only if you assure me, you will not take unnecessary risks with my life. You don't understand I have to be careful. I am the leader of the land." Even as she says this, she is reminded how insistently she had joined the battle in their most recent war with the Omis. *I was only a princess though; my father was alive and ruling king.*

"By the way how do you launch without a bridge to boomerang from?"

Elated he has not completely alienated Ali, Ahshen Owanu explains how a group of people rolled his aircraft to a nearby cliff and pushed him off. He hadn't been certain aerodynamics would take over with the moderate boost from the craft's small engine, but it did, and he hadn't been dashed on the rocks below. To make the aerocraft dependable he was going to have to design a more powerful engine.

"You're going to love that part," he tells her not sure if the added weight of a passenger will change the lift dramatically. "How much do you weigh?"

"What? Why is it any of your business?"

"I need to run some calculations."

Taller than her mother, Queen Adyaa, but still petite with an athletic build, Queen Ali was not accustomed to sharing such intimate details with anyone. "I'm not actually sure."

"Then we will have to weigh you," he says letting his boyish grin spread wider.

Too late to depart with darkness coming on, Ahshen joins Queen Ali for supper. They eat on a cozy veranda in the fresh night air. The tall candelabras sputter in a light breeze as the staff bring them dish after scintillating dish. "I especially love this wild boar," Ahshen smiles broadly, "and the fruit glaze is superb. That's one thing about Merth which excels over my planet, is the food."

"May I remind you; you are eating dishes prepared for the queen."

"Even at Bridgenstyl, the food is excellent, much better than on Fantu where technology is the focus, even in our more exotic lands."

"You don't talk much about your home."

"This is my home now; I have accepted it. And to be here with you is all I need."

Still furious with him for his dangerous flight, Queen Ali softens a little. *He thinks I will allow him back in my bed. By the One True God, I think not!* Her wave of anger does not build as familiarly as it often does but lands softly like a gentle wave caressing a moonlit beach. *Perhaps I am being too arrogant. Why deny myself the pleasure of this man? The Matong gave me no stipulations for my relationship with him.* And as if she has no control of her body, she reaches her hand across the dining table where glistening crystal and ornate dinnerware are set to enhance the experience of the fine cuisine before them.

He meets her gaze; his dark eyes haunt her, and his grasp is warm and comforting. "There are issues at play."

He sighs and lets his eyes fall to the table. "I'm sure."

"Being with you at Bridgenstyl. We had privacy. It's complicated. I am a female at risk of pregnancy, and…"

"That is something easily dealt with."

"I'm sorry. What did you say?"

"You have plenty of Mauvil flowers here, and that's all you need to ensure your safety in this matter. Or we can, you know, just fool around."

Blood rushes to Queen Ali's cheeks in a way she is unaccustomed to. "What? I don't believe even my sister, Galen the healer knows of this protection."

"This isn't the romantic conversation I had hoped for after such a thrilling day."

"No, it's not." Queen Ali wipes her lips with her soft linen napkin delicately embroidered by talented *craftousai,* and wonders if she should mention Martyl to him.

No, but he deserves to know at some point, and it should come from her not Katara gossip.

She pushes her chair back, noticing the elegant cutlery twinkling in the soft light, she wishes life could be more simple for her. "I'm sorry, I seem to have lost my appetite."

She doesn't stand immediately, but he does. *This is a direct insinuation of disrespect he probably has no clue about.*

"Let me escort you to your chambers," he says dropping his napkin on the table.

A dullness invades her brain with the firmness of a palm clasped over her mouth and she finally stands, mostly so he is not in direct violation of protocol. *Why does the Matong not intercede with this relationship if there is truly to be a 'cup of light' for me?*

Her first inclination is to deny his assistance and then a wave of indignation unfurls. *Flum this! I am the queen.* She grabs her very tall and delicately crafted wineglass still full of rich *verdeu* and takes a deep swallow of its delicate nectar. She snaps her fingers. "Get me some *jocelyn*" she commands uncharacteristically of the staff. "Chilled *joceyln* and crystal blooms. The ones I prefer. Bring them on a tray and leave please."

They are about to depart the veranda when a servant comes out with a tray. A few of her favorite *chozos* have also been added to the gilt serving dish as artistically decorated with food as a painting worthy of hanging on the walls of the palace. "Shall I follow you, my Queen?" The loyal servant asks.

"No, let Owanu carry it for me on his way out."

Ahshen sheepishly grabs the heavy silver tray and with downcast eyes takes it from the girl and walks with Queen Ali to her private chambers.

"You can set it over there," she points at a table near the roaring fire. There are two crystal shot glasses on the tray for the chilled *jocelyn*, but Owanu is confused is he is to stay or if he needs to go.

"Shall I join you or are you ready for me to leave?" It feels as if a large clammy hand has covered his beating heart, but he is careful not to let his emotions seep into his voice.

"Stay please, forgive me. We should talk, but first, let's have a little of that incredible Omi distilled liqueur. I don't even like to admit I drink it, but we have to have it available for when they visit."

The sound of the clear gurgling alcohol filling the crystal shot glasses bolsters Ali's resolve. They toast to each other and down another after clinking their glasses together. The fumes are so aromatic the room fills with the vapors of the drink. "It smells like winter and *shaunton* berries, doesn't it?" She says as she pours a third round. Ahshen is quiet but friendly, unsure of how to handle the situation. Sensing his reluctance, she set down her glass. "I'm going to make this easier for you," she says pulling off her silken dress the pale-yellow color of the Merth sky when the first moon, Ava, sets. Her graceful neck still bears an assortment of gemstones from a sparkly *sotor* to a pale *ona* stone. One is generously large, the other encrusted with shimmering *gylas* as clear as the liquid *jocelyn* they now drink.

The glow of the fire silhouetting Ali's curves makes Ahshen unsteady. He sets his crystal glass down and approaches her. "Not yet, you first have to tell me how much I weigh," she laughs. "Because I don't know. It's not something we keep track of."

"Really? I guess you Merthians don't need to as most of you are fit." He touches her lightly on the arm and grins. He comes closer, but she pushes slightly on his chest with her outstretched palm.

"No, sit down, not yet." It is getting harder for him to resist her. He goes over to the fireplace and adds another log to the fire. She sits down in her chair like a wilted flower, her mind swirling with the strong drink.

Ahshen sits down as she has requested not able to take his eyes off her, he subdues his rising energy. "If you want me to weigh you, you must sit on my lap," he jokes.

Queen Ali, now wearing only the gems around her neck and some delicate ankle boots carefully swings herself into his lap, with a shrewd smile. He grasps her around the waist, but his hands quickly wander. They both giggle and their resolve melts like an icicle in the bright light of the morning star.

24-A Missed Message

Queen Ali wakes with a frenzied gasp of air. *What the flum have I done? My foolishness is going to get me pregnant. I will look like a total faoltol when my bulging belly gives me away. I have thrown out reason and the hard-won power my mother fought so laboriously to achieve for women. She handed me the throne in unheard of precedence and I am throwing my dignity away for a fling with some handsome stranger. It is different for men who may cast their seed without consequence.*

"Wake up Ahshen! You must get out of here."

Startled awake he asks, "What is wrong Ali?" It is the first time he has called her by name without her title. It is both shocking and pleasant.

"I can't do this! It appears I can't resist you, and yet I must." She hears the gurgling flow of the bath being filled in the adjacent room. "You need to leave but now you can't," she says through gritted teeth. "The maids will discover you here. You must hide." Ahshen is absolutely stunned by the queen's remorseful attitude.

"Aren't you their supreme ruler? Can't you do what you want?"

"You don't understand, I have no privacy. No, I can't do what I want. A ruler must put her people first." In her panic, she thinks only of going to the Matong. "You must hide, pull the covers up over you, and try not to give yourself away. I will handle this." She is still arranging the covers to bury him with when a servant girl knocks.

"My Queen your bath is ready."

"Oh, thank you, Lilith, please let me be. I am a little queasy this morning."

"Shall I call your sister to attend you?"

"No, I was up late entertaining our guest." Owanu playfully punches her leg and they both restrain a giggle. "Leave me be I'll be fine." Once the maid is gone, they both slip into the bath, amply large enough for the two of them.

"We'd call this a party tub on Fontu." Owanu playfully squirts her, but Queen Ali's mind is racing again with concerns.

"I've got to get to the Matong as soon as possible," she says slipping out of the tub. "Please excuse me, we must talk this afternoon. You need to get out of here without anyone seeing you."

As she enters the sacred chamber of the Matong, she senses something is wrong. The orb is alternately dimming and brightening in a way she has rarely seen. Placing her hand high on the globe it feels colder than usual.

As she waits for a message, it is slow to materialize. MY PRECIOUS ONE, YOU ARE CONFUSED. I SENT YOU A SIGN LAST NIGHT BUT YOU DID NOT RECOGNIZE MY MESSAGE BECAUSE YOU LET YOUR GUARD DOWN AND CONSUMED TOO MUCH OF

THE OMI POISON. The tone of the Matong is reproachful, almost angry.

Fear seizes her making it difficult to swallow. Yes, she had allowed herself to drink too much. While she enjoyed much privilege, she was always queen, and responsible to her people. BY THE ONE TRUE GOD, WHAT MESSAGE DID I MISS?

I HAVE BROUGHT YOU A TRAVELER FROM FARAWAY GALAXIES TO ADVANCE YOUR PEOPLE. YOU ARE TO WED THE CUP OF LIGHT.

Trembling, Queen Ali tries to control the frustration in her voice. I AM QUEEN ALI, ROYAL DAUGHTER OF KING POMA AND QUEEN AADYA. WHY DO YOU TAUNT ME? I AM READY FOR THE CUP OF LIGHT. PLEASE MAKE YOUR WILL KNOWN!

YOU WILL SOON BE WITH CHILD. Stunned, Ali slaps the almighty Matong reflexively which causes her royal ring to spark. She is instantly appalled by her involuntary action but does not stop there. I DON'T THINK THIS IS AN ADVISABLE WAY TO TREAT YOUR BELOVED, LEADER. WHY DON'T YOU TELL ME WHO I AM TO WED? IS IT AHSHEN OR SOMEONE ELSE?

PAY ATTENTION: SINCE YOU DID NOT VISUALIZE THE HALO AROUND HIM AS HE STOOD BEFORE THE FIRE LAST NIGHT. GO NOW AND ASK AHSHEN OWANU TO HOLD ANYTHING. IT WILL GLOW WITH FIERY LIGHT. HE IS THE CUP OF LIGHT. Ashamed, Ali feels like her body has been thrust into ice water, and she is still shivering when she sends for Ahshen.

25-It Gets Worse

"I don't understand," Ahshen utters as the silver goblet he is holding lights up with the intensity of an arc from an artificial *saltar* flame.

"It's as I have told you before the Matong proclaimed over two revolutions ago I was to wed 'The Cup of Light.' I went on the quest as instructed yet when I was united with my dearly beloved Fontar. He was struck down… murdered. I was so bereaved, the only thing that brought me back was my dog Robic, Fontar's wedding gift to me; and of course, there was my father who shamed me with his expectations of my succession to the throne.

"It gets worse," she tells Ahshen. He is still holding the silver cup she handed him, and it continues to glow with a piercing light. "After our wedding ceremony, you will be received by the Matong, and you will be privy to many kinds of mysterious privileges. My parents, when my father was alive, often communicated without words." On the battlefield, Queen Ali has proven herself dauntless, and yet she is terrified to tell Ahshen the rest of it. "I can see by the look on your face you are overwhelmed."

"I presumed I was on the receiving end of the affections of the sexiest woman I've ever met," he grins. She impulsively decides to let the rest of her news rip from her lips. There is no one but her who can convey what she has to tell him.

"I am to have a child."

Ahshen's handsome face curdles with bittersweet joy. "Wow," is all he says still clutching the glowing silver goblet. Noticeably shaken, he steps to set it down on a nearby table. "I'm going to be a father. You've got to understand this is way over the top. Even for a guy who woke up on another planet."

She spins on her heels impulsively. "But you have not asked for this and perhaps it is not your desire."

Ahshen's smile filled with obvious desire lights his face. "I am overwhelmed, but I am most willing." He grows still and takes her hands in his. "On Fantu there is no hierarchy, every person is considered an equal. So, to be a royal leader, this is what will be most difficult for me to adjust to."

"But who takes care of the least of you?"

Ahshen shrugs, "Each individual is given the same opportunity and education. Everyone takes care of themselves."

Ali cannot imagine what he is talking about. It is like he is speaking another language, which essentially, he is. Oddly, ever since waking up on Merth, Ahshen has understood the language of Merth and can speak it. This is as curious to him as his inexplicable arrival.

Ali considers this enigma of a man before her suddenly realizing how unique his situation is, and how challenging it must be for him, although he has gracefully adapted. *And look at him, he is now to be my husband and rule with me over all Merthians.*

"I should suppose your life with me will be a lot like the aerocraft plane ride I had with you. Sometimes you'll have to hold on for dear life."

"My sweet Ali," he picks up her hand and kisses it. "I ask you to trust me and become my wife." His words spoken with profound sincerity center her attention and Ali responds with the confidence the Matong has delivered to her.

"So be it," she declares.

26-This is it?

"We must arrange a royal wedding quickly," Ali tells her sister Galen.

"Oh? What is the urgency?" Ali shakes her head knowing her sister, the great healer, probably has a viable idea.

"Because my 'Cup of Light' has been found for me. I am anxious to get on with it."

Galen grins knowingly.

"Ah, *ditzo*. We have only been together twice. I am not with child yet, but I'm not waiting around. There is no going back. This is the Matong's plan. We just need to pull this together quickly."

"Yes, I will not intercede. And Ahshen? He is prepared for this?"

"Certainly not, but he's willing and over the moon to have a child with me."

Ali bites her lip. "There is something I need your help with."

"Yes? What is it? It seems as if there are many things you need my help with."

"Martyl." Ali's dry lips stick together as she says his name. "Surely, he knows something is up. But I haven't had the time to see him and certainly not to explain."

Galen sighs, feeling the burden of having been the one who put them together. "You must see him in person and tell him."

"I will write him a letter and you give it to him. I don't even want Ahshen to know about him."

Galen doesn't try to hide her disappointment. "No, that's not right. You must speak with him personally."

"*Ditzo!* I can't."

"Oh, but you will."

"Have I ever told you what a demanding *faoltal* you are?"

"I'll do this much," Galen offers. "I'll have him come to our house this afternoon. You can ride over and talk to him yourself."

Ali looks around cautiously as if someone might be listening and nods. "Yes, I can do it."

But when the time comes, Ali has never been so ashamed. "This is it?" The first words out of Martyl's mouth fall on her like broken shards of *chozel*.

She approaches him slowly. "I wanted you to hear it from me."

"The walls have ears; I am not stupid. I knew for certain when Galen sent for me."

"Please don't be bitter," she reaches for his face as if to comfort him. It is more than he can bear, and his eyes soften with disappointment. "You needn't trouble yourself with me, Ali, I knew it wasn't ever going anywhere."

"I disagree Martyl, we are steadfast friends. I shall always seek out your counsel."

An uncomfortable laugh rattles out of him "I have nothing to say to you right now."

Ali came to do what she could and now didn't see any benefit in prolonging Martyl's discomfort. Still, she lingers wondering if she should tell him more. "It's Ahshen Owanu, who the Matong has chosen for me."

Lifting his head slightly he nods "I know."

"Thank you for coming." She turns away to leave but he extends his arm to touch her and kisses her on the lips, respectful but still laced with optimism from their time together. "Goodbye Martyl."

As Queen Ali races back to Katara on her horse her sadness evaporates and is replaced with joy as she nears the royal residence. With Martyl behind her, she could focus on the future. *Much to do in such a short time.*

"I'm sure you are anxious to get back to 'your bridge,'" Ali asks Ahshen as she begins the process of organizing their plans.

"It has crossed my mind."

Stopping in her tracks she looks him straight in the eyes. "If you don't mind, I don't take much interest in this sort of thing, wedding plans, I'd like to let the others handle it. There's no reason you can't get back to work, but I should stay here for now. I'm not sure you even need to be here for the announcement. It's not like we must have our marriage approved by anyone."

"Okay," he says.

This is unlike what I have experienced with Fontar. I was such a child then.

"And you should understand, until you make this flying machine safer, I won't be riding in it."

"Of course," he says. "Where were you?"

"I had an errand. I had to see my sister Galen to wrap up some loose ends to begin planning our wedding ritual."

"And she's the great healer everyone talks about?"

"Yes, I believe you have met her."

"Does she have special kinetic sight like you and the others, Roark, and your mother I presume?"

"Oh, she is the most gifted of us all. She can heal people. That's why she abdicated, and I became queen, so she could pursue her art of healing. She saved thousands in the wake of the Great Targa storm. I should have her and Kandar over tonight for dinner before you leave so you can get to know them better. They are going to be your family going forward."

"I would like that very much."

"The whole family should come, and we will get this wedding announced and begin the preparations. I haven't even told my mother!"

27-What's the Rush?

"Hello darling," Aadya hugs her daughter gingerly, and Ali inhales her mother's soft fresh scent as if she had recently been walking in the garden at Compana. Aadya's eyes sparkle with anticipation as she draws back from her daughter and grabs her hands. "I understand from the Matong you have news for us."

Ali sucks in a breath, *so much for privacy.* "It is joyous news!" Aadya squeezes her daughter's hands, holding them longer than usual. Her penetrating smile is a bit unnerving. "I told you there would be a mate for you."

I WAS WAITING FOR THE RIGHT MOMENT TO TELL YOU MOTHER.

Aadya turns to Ahshen to greet him and gives him a slight bow of her head; it is an unusual show of respect for the man who will soon be the father of her grandchild. It is only the third time Ahshen Owanu has crossed her path.

Once everyone is greeted and seated, Ali stands and begins her well-practiced speech. "I thank everyone for coming on such short notice, Ahshen and I have some news and we ask for your assistance." She meets his gaze and places her graceful hand with the royal ring upon his shoulder. "This has happened rather quickly, but the Matong has finally revealed who the 'Cup of Light' is. Ahshen is here on Merth, as you know under unusual circumstances." Each word she utters has been carefully reviewed in her mind for impeccable value. "We have much going on in our kingdom, with the bridge and the growth of Bridgenstyl. I see no value in wasting time. We will be married in twenty rotations of the moons."

"Forgive me Queen Ali, but what is the rush?" It is Faynyl, Roark's wife who asks. "A royal wedding is rare. We should delight and honor your union with great fanfare. We can hardly prepare a feast in such a short time let alone a fitting festival and ceremony needed for such an event."

While Faynyl, as a princess, has access to the Matong, it is clear she has not been awarded the knowledge of the upcoming wedding. An awkward silence descends upon the room like the soft downdraft of a *sorton* cloud. Aadya masks a smile behind her napkin. Someone lifts their silver goblet, and the landing of the heavy object is heard with a soft thud.

Ali takes another calculated breath. "This is what the Matong has decreed. Our job is not to question our deity, but we must have faith. We must follow as directed."

It is Galen who backs her sister up. "Faynyl, the staff will move as directed. We can do this; it is for the best."

Faynyl looks down into her lap and back up toward her husband Roark. Sometimes like now, she feels awkward in the presence of her royal family. Once a brilliant scientist, she has abandoned her official position to focus on her child. Her level of discomfort flares up at gatherings like these.

28-More than Two

"She is amazing!" Ahshen tells Ali as they return to her sleeping quarters.

Ali's face lights up. "Galen? She must have touched you."

Ahshen's expression goes inward. "Why yes she did, and I have felt euphoric ever since."

"That's why Galen doesn't hug or touch much. Every time she does, it drains her. With us…family it's a bit different, but you are not family yet." Ali takes his hand and begins to explain what to expect. "Immediately after our wedding, you and I will bond with the Matong. I think you are going to like having kinetic sight. If you think we are close now, you will be amazed to feel what it is like when we can share our thoughts without speaking."

Ahshen studies Ali, feeling regret about leaving her side. "I leave very early, at first light. I have already arranged for a crew to help me get the plane launched. And…" as the future begins to sink in, he mutters. "Don't we get some kind of time after the wedding, to be alone together just you and me?"

A strange feeling overtakes Queen Ali. *This is real.* "That would be ideal. Can we make it happen on such short notice?"

"I have an idea." Ahshen snaps back. As he sits on the bed and pulls off his shirt. The sight of his muscular chest distracts Ali temporarily.

"And what is that?"

"There is a ledge I know of on the other side of the river from Bridgenstyl. I can get my men to build us a small lodge quickly. It will be very secure there. There would be only one way in. Your guard detail should have no trouble protecting you there."

"But we only have twenty rotations, how can they possibly build something that fast?"

"My love, my men and I can do it. You just leave that up to me."

Ali sinks into the bed and rests her head on his lap. "I am going to instruct the wedding planners to keep our ceremony small and the festivities at a minimum." She turns her head up to him and wraps her arm around his waist. "I do have one request. Can you have them build one of those bubbling tubs like at the Bridgenstyl house? I love the luxury of it." Ahshen's grin is one of pride and anticipation. "Of course, I will have one built big enough for the two of us."

"Tell Roark our plans and he shall arrange for all the materials and labor you need."

29-Time on the Ledge

The newlyweds, hardly make it out of bed for their time on the 'ledge', as Ahshen likes to call it. I HAD NO IDEA LOVEMAKING COULD BE THIS IN-CREDIBLE. Ali shares with him. The ability to communicate their thoughts telepathically since Ahshen bonded with the Matong is new to both of them.

YOU ARE SUCH AN INSPIRATION! BUT I DO FEEL I AM MORE NOW...I HAVE BEEN TRANS-FORMED BY THE MATONG.

REALLY? I WAS A SMALL CHILD WHEN I FIRST BONDED AND I CAN NOT REMEMBER A DIFFER-ENCE. BUT I DO SEE A CHANGE IN YOU.

I AM SMARTER SOMEHOW. IDEAS ARE BOM-BARDING ME. THERE IS MUCH FOR ME TO DO HERE ON MERTH. YOU CAN'T BEGIN TO IMAG-INE THE PROGRESS WE CAN MAKE.

Having been apart until just before the wedding has made their reunion even sweeter. The wedding as prom-ised, was an elegant but small affair held on the beautiful grounds of Compana, beneath the tall, profusely bloom-ing *clossal* trees, whose flowers shed their delicate white petals upon them as they said their vows.

"It's still very rustic," Ahshen apologized when he first brought her to their romantic hideaway construct-ed from the massive logs in the forest nearby. The abun-dance of natural light and the tall ceilings make the space seem more expansive than it is, but there is definitely an unfinished feel to it constructed, as it was, in such a brief space of time.

"No, it's amazing. You even made the special bathtub I requested. And that carving of me in the column in the living room, I had no idea you had such talents."

Ahshen grins proudly, "That's how I spent my lonely evenings away from you. Carving your likeness from my memory."

"You seemed to have captured my breasts precisely." She gives him a shameful grin.

Now as they lay on their bridal bed, Ahshen lets his fingers dance across Ali's hip in a way that makes her shiver. She is overtaken by his seductive touch, and they spiral into each other once again.

Breathless after their entanglement Ali flops over on her back and looks up into the night sky through the window he has built into the roof. "I love to see the stars! It is such a delight." He rolls over and grins. "I like it too. This is very common on Fantu, but I've never seen sky windows built here."

TO BE WITH YOU HERE IS LIKE DRINKING WATER AND I HAVE AN INSATIABLE THIRST. But they both know their time together in this dream state is temporary. In just a few short rotations, Ali will have to return to her duties at Katara, and Ahshen will have to stay here and finish his bridge.

MY BRAIN IS MUSH. IT IS PROBABLY BEST I WILL BE GOING BACK TO KATARA IN A FEW ROTATIONS AND YOU WILL REMAIN HERE IN BRIDGENSTYL TO FINISH THE BRIDGE.

YOU ARE ANXIOUS TO BE RID OF ME?

YOU KNOW THE RESPONSIBILITIES I HAVE, THE BURDEN OF LEADERSHIP, AND ACCORDING TO THE MATONG I WILL SOON BECOME A MOTHER.

I WILL FINISH THE BRIDGE AND GET BACK TO MY PLACE BESIDE YOU.

YES, THAT IS MY GREATEST DESIRE. She allows her emotions to well up into her eyes but shakes off her weakness for it serves no purpose.

Ahshen reaches over and grasps her hand, rubbing her slender fingers in his rough fingertips. YOU ARE PERFECT JUST THE WAY YOU ARE. A smile surfaces through the murk of Queen Ali's self-doubt. *I am in the right place. I finally have the 'Cup of Light' promised to me.*

30-I Couldn't do this Without You

"I must be pregnant," Ali reports to Galen soon after returning to Valtar. The *helitons* are rampaging through my body. One minute I'm laughing the next I'm crying. I can't be this way I have to be level-headed to rule. You must give me something."

Galen subdues her laughter, but her mirth is not easy to contain. "My dear sister, forgive me, but there is no 'cure' for pregnancy, not everything can be served to you upon a silver platter. Giving birth is not so simple as to take a potion."

Queen Ali's frustration gives rise to a sour expression. "I'm sure you have a tea or powder that will alleviate my symptoms. You don't understand I am the supreme leader of Merth. I snapped at my aide this morning and she did nothing wrong."

Galen's humor subsides and she touches Ali's arm tenderly. "Yes, of course, I have calming teas that won't affect the baby, but you will also have to learn to curb your emotions during pregnancy if you want to be trusted by your people."

Ali spins around. Her thoughts propelling her. "Part of the problem is Ahshen is not here with me, but we have to finish that *flowkin* bridge!"

"It would be best for him to stay there for now. When it gets closer to your time you will really need him."

"I guess I must announce the pregnancy soon. It would be better if he were here by my side."

"Nonsense, he doesn't need accolades. Send the word out by messenger and the impact will be more subdued. As the first ruling queen of genetic ascent, you don't want to emphasize your reproductive role."

"Perhaps you are right." Ali's face brightens. "I couldn't do this without you, dear Galen."

"I am always here for you little sister." Ali closes her eyes and lets Galen's healing touch soothe her.

Despite Queen Ali's early anxiety, the pregnancy passes without a hitch. Ahshen overjoyed to become a father remains by their side for nearly a half revolution of Merth doting on his 'little cherub' as he loves to call her. The name Jaxyl Alexis is given to her by the Matong. It means Great Defender of the People.

31-I Have the Advantage Now

Queen Ali opens the letter she has received from Ahshen. *My dearest love, I miss you and baby Jaxyl greatly. We have completed the aero hangar and are beginning the setup for the factory to build a fleet of aero ships. Prince Roark and Faynyl saved the day by learning to replicate the Targa metals. The Omis have become surprisingly motivated as hard workers. Who would have ever known respect combined with monetary reward would be the magic solution? I am coming home in three rotations for a respite. I can't wait to wrap the two of you in my arms and squeeze until you beg for mercy!*

Ali lets her hand holding the letter drop. *At last, he returns to me. When I allow him to make the decisions on his whereabouts, he is happier and better company. When I insist, he comes home, he is moody and miserable. His mind requires challenging work. I want more time with him, but it's hard for both of us to get away from our duties.*

Ali leaves the chamber and joins her mother and Jaxyl, who is beginning to crawl. Queen Ali keeps the precious child nearby unless royal protocol is involved. Aptala, Jaxyl's nanny, is adept at handling the baby's moods and needs. Ali has allowed Jaxyl's golden curls to flourish atop her head without ever having trimmed them. Sometimes she pulls her daughter's curls up into a ponytail in the way Ahshen often wears his hair when he lets it grow beyond his shoulders, which is most of the time now, only Ahshen's hair, the color of rich chocolate is silky straight, and her child's golden curls are as thick and tangled as *paltar* sprigs.

"He's coming home, Mother!"

"Excellent. It wears on you when he is gone for an extended time." Aadya picks up her granddaughter and makes a sour face because the baby's dirty diapers are rank.

"He is advancing our society by leaps and bounds. It is foolish to stifle his industriousness."

Her daughter's bravado does not fool Queen Adyaa, who raised her three children with her husband, King Poma, mostly by her side. "This girl needs a change."

"Let Aptala handle it. It is what she is here for."

"No, she is my granddaughter, I will take care of it."

Queen Ali rolls her eyes. Changing diapers is not on her list of things she likes to do. "Mother don't be a martyr."

"*Pish pottle*, leave me alone. I'm happy to do it." As her mother carries Jaxyl out, Ali's *exant* aide comes in. "Your majesty, excuse me but Prince Tildyn has requested an audience with you." Luce, the studious slender man charged with keeping up with her schedule, tells her. She now has a prime *custadore* who hires her aides. It has simplified her life. *Even so, this chain of command does not get rid of Omi Prince Tildyn. Ah, what a curmudgeon!*

Queen Ali looks at Luce and tells him to schedule the prince for some time tomorrow.

"But he says it is urgent. He must meet with you today."

"It is always urgent with him. Don't let him get to you." Her aide looks slightly chagrined for his insistence, apparently unwarranted, and backs away from the queen with a slight bow. She returns his smile as she broods over what superfluous demand Tildyn is going to make now.

"Have him meet me in the council room just before dinner time." *He will be hungry and tired I will use this to my advantage.*

When Tildyn arrives for their consultation, he does indeed look drawn and pale. "Thank you for this audience, my Queen." He grasps her hand and kisses it which feels completely hypocritical when she knows he is there to subtly harass her. He has never forgiven her for not taking him as her mate. She pulls away hastily. *He shouldn't even be touching me, he knows this.* "I have come with tidings you don't want to hear. I am aware of this." His voice falls lower and grows silky. "There is trouble brewing at the aero factory in Bridgenstyl."

"Oh, and how is that? No one else has come to me with problems, they are just getting started."

"There is dissension over the grueling hours and paltry pay."

"No, I don't believe you." Ahshen says the workers are happy."

"It's mostly about the extended hours and so little time off." He adds to bolster his claim.

Studying Tildyn she can sense the clutter of his dark heart, like a fallow field of stubble, useless and brittle.

He is still obsessed with the idea he should be the king. He thinks I should have chosen him. He thinks he should be ruling Merth. He doesn't understand our mighty Matong. He is such a despicable creature.

Everything about this man whom she once called 'friend', is annoying to her now, his uncommon white hair which stands like floppy stalks of wheat atop his head, his thin physique, now more bent over than should be for a man his age. His lips once cherry bright, are now stiff and gray like a roadmap to his dreary ego. Her affection for him has leached out like an open wound and she wants him out of her realm. Queen Ali instinctively straightens her spine as an antidote to this anathema before her.

"Tildyn, we use Omi workers only regarding our allegiance for peace with the Omi, to build a better world, but there are limitations to what I am willing to do. Your men can easily be replaced. Now, I'm asking you to leave, don't push me to make more of this incident than it has to be. This is a warning, please heed it."

"But"

The queen raises her palm into the air. "No, I don't want to hear another word. Ahshen and Roark are in charge. Now, I suggest we consider your reassignment to a post that will suit you better." Tildyn's eyes grow large as he considers this recent development which could be turned to his advantage if he is clever.

"Queen Ali, what did you have in mind?"

"I'm not sure yet, I will have to give it some thought, but as it stands now, I am no longer willing to continue to have these little quarrels with you. Ahshen will be home very soon, and I will consult with him as to the best role for you going forward."

She sees Prince Tildyn's thoughts churning in his expression as he considers how to manipulate the situation. She stifles the smile rising to her lips. *I have the advantage now.*

32-A Startling Revelation

"**Y**our Highness, would you like to receive the little one?" Aptala holds the baby out to Queen Ali. Jaxyl has been groomed and dressed in preparation to greet her father. Her eyes, the color of the Sonnatong River sparkle and dance with expectation when she is lifted into her mother's arms.

"Ah my little darling, you look beautiful!" Ali embraces the plump toddler as the baby's nanny hands her off and rubs her face up against the rosy cheeks of her child which feel cold to the touch like soft river stones. "This is new?" She surveys the pale gossamer gown, its hand-stitched collar adorned with tiny pearls. "It's beautiful, but can she get those pearls loose and swallow them?"

Aptala shakes her head, "No, Mum, they are stitched by Mistress Dorial."

"Oh, then no, of course not." This is the first time Queen Ali has held the child the entire rotation, and she regrets it now with Jaxyl hugging her tightly, her little body conforming to the Queen's as if filling in her empty spaces. *I should make more time for my family, but the demands of duty thwart my good intentions.* "Any word yet, has Master Owanu landed?"

Aptala shakes her head, "No, but I can go ask again."

Energized by the baby's warmth and touch, Queen Ali rocks her anxiously as she begins to push against her mother's chest to get down and discover what she can on her own. When this doesn't work Queen Ali bounces her up and down awkwardly feeling rejected by the brief encounter. *This child is my most precious gift. I forsake everything to keep her safe.*

Jaxyl wins the power struggle and Queen Ali sets her down only to be surprised at how fast the child can make her way across the room away from her.

"Yes, Your Highness Sir Owanu has landed and will be here shortly," Aptala beams with the tidings she knows will make her mistress happy.

"Oh, thanks much. I want you nearby in case we need you, but we will want privacy too." Can you make that happen? Queen Ali says with her expression and slightly tilted head.

"Yes, of course, I will be nearby but not too close, just ring the bell. Shall I take the child?"

"No, no, Ahshen will want to see her. Leave her here with me, I will entertain her until he comes. Where is her box of toys?"

"I'll bring it," Aptala says as she spreads her palms across the waistline of her skirt.

"There you two are! I thought I'd never make it home." Ahshen drops his bags on the floor and rushes to embrace Ali and Jaxyl. Ali feels his warm breath against her cheek and her body softens. Jaxyl squeals as her father squeezes her and nuzzles her with his wiry beard.

"Ah, my sweet, sweet girls, I am so happy to be here with you." Jaxyl pulls at her mother's hair and giggles.

Queen Ali hardly notices she is busy taking in the sweet fragrance of reunion. Ahshen reaches over to kiss his wife. It is a prolonged and thirsty kiss.

"We have time before dinner to 'retire,'" she says demurely.

"Ah yes, we should retire for sure. What about the baby?"

"I will have Aptala entertain her until dinner." Queen Ali pulls away and hands Jaxyl to her father. "Here at least hold her for a minute while I call Aptala." Jaxyl is bubbling with joy as her father bounces her in his arms and sings her a nursery ditty from his home planet of Fantu.

"What is this?" he asks Ali sharply. "Aren't her eyes blue?"

"Yes, why?"

"Look! As I spun her around, her eyes have changed, they are a light violet."

"What?" Ali sets down the bell she has rung to call the nanny and hurries to his side. She pulls Jaxyl out of his arms and lifts Jaxyl before her, scrutinizing her daughter's face. "By the One True God, what is this?" By the time Aptala has shown up to take the baby, they watch as Jaxyl's eye color changes from a light violet to a milky blue.

Stunned, Queen Ali takes another hard look at her child. "We must take her to the Matong to understand this." The two parents bolt from the room. Aptala looks at them helplessly as they leave.

"Your Highness, may I help?"

"No!" she mutters as she races past cradling the child's head into her breast.

THIS BELOVED CHILD HAS POWERS BEYOND YOUR GREATEST IMAGINATION. DO NOT BE FEARFUL. YOU WILL BE GIVEN FURTHER IN-STRUCTIONS AS NEEDED. DO NOT BE FRIGHT-ENED BY HER ABILITIES AS THEY ARE REVEALED.

Queen Ali looks at her husband. His face speaks of a thousand questions. Her throat constricts, making it difficult to speak. *There is no longer any room for me to be a willful child. I must surrender my frustration with the Matong and practice my faith.*

I DON'T UNDERSTAND? Ahshen propels his thoughts to her and reaches for his child. Queen Ali lets go reluctantly but understands his need to hold onto her, so she embraces them both.

She wants to share her thoughts with him but honest-ly doesn't want the Matong to hear her. *As if I could ever hide from the Matong!* "Let's get out of here."

33-Busy as Two Bittles

The hours pass until the moons begin to rise. Their child's eye color has changed four times since they first noticed the phenomenon. "It seems to be rooted in her moods," Ahshen declares as his drowsy child falls asleep in his arms. They have been absorbed in surveying her for hours. As they put her in a sleeping gown for the night, Ali realizes they have never stopped to eat dinner.

"I can hardly drag myself away from her right now," Ali says as she and Ahshen look down into the crib of their sleeping angel. "I think I'll have dinner brought to our bed chambers. You must be starving."

"Ah, dinner in bed. It suits me," he says gently placing his curved finger under her chin and lifting it subtly. "We never got to 'retire.'"

"Well, sir let's get on with it," she says pulling at his vest and deftly unclasping his shirt until she reaches his bare chest. "I think I've spent more time with Jaxyl this afternoon than I have her entire lifetime. I'm ready for a suitable distraction."

His pleasurable smile digs into her like a sharp blade. "I must have you, and then I must have you again," she declares.

"Such a task it is to satisfy my Queen," he tells her pushing into her with a deep-throated kiss, his strong palm bracing her back as he places his other hand on her alert breast sending shock waves across the landscape of her body. Eventually, they realize they are in their daughter's nursery and should relocate to their sprawling bed chamber.

Vigilant servants have anticipated their needs. A heavy silver tray, laden with a variety of savory and sweet noshes including bite-sized succulent meats glazed with sticky sauces, pungent cheeses, and crunchy fruit-encrusted bites, awaits them on the table near the roaring fire. But first, they must finish their passionate entanglement they've longed for these many rotations while Ahshen has been away.

The pull of their two bodies is as fierce as a *magnetar* unleashed. —Ali, Ahshen, Ali, Ahshen— they are one until they are not. It is bittersweet to separate, but another type of hunger comes upon them like a *snootle in a snap*. Queen Ali giggles uncharacteristically. "I'm glad to have you back." Without dressing, she picks up a tiny drumstick from a *froltol* bird and begins to nibble, then licks her fingers. "I had no idea I was so hungry."

"You are hungry," her beautiful husband grins.

"Yes, and after I finish this snack, I would like to satisfy that hunger some more."

"Ah, *flum*, we need to figure out how to be together more. It's your turn to come stay with me, we need to open up the lodge on the ledge again."

"It's not adequate if I bring Jaxyl."

"Then the first order of business, when I return, is to expand it."

Ali looks at him as if it is the first time she has seen him tonight. "That's an excellent idea, what took us so long to figure it out?"

"We have been a little busy. Busy as two *bittles*." Ali looks at him strangely. THAT MUST BE ONE OF YOUR FANTU SAYINGS. I AM UNFAMILIAR WITH IT.

He loves it when she speaks to him telepathically. It gives him a slight sexual buzz, but he is still finding it takes a lot of energy to respond to her without words. "It's something I picked up from the Omi," he tells her.

34-The Problem of Tildyn

"What is it, Luce? We are eating our break-fast and do not want to be disturbed." Luce bows slightly. "Pardon me, Your Highness, this is when we normally go over your schedule."

The queen shakes her head absently, "Of course, I am in Ahshen land now." She squeezes her husband's hand who is juggling Jaxyl on his knee as he eats. "You are spoiling her. I never hold her while I'm eating."

"I'm sure," he says trying to subdue the judgment in his voice. She shoots back a look of disfavor he has become too familiar with.

"When shall I come back?" The aide asks.

"We're nearly done, let's meet in the more comfort-able anteroom. Give us a few minutes please."

She looks over at Ahshen again. "I've been meaning to ask you. I want to get Tildyn out of Katara, is there something you could find for him to do?"

"That *flowkin* rogue. He is already underfoot too much."

"Your language, please in front of the child." Her hus-band clamps his lips together sternly.

"Yes, of course, she is clever, and will be repeating ev-erything we say soon."

"Galen tells me there is no history in our family with the changing eye color. She has researched it. She thinks it is because of the mixture of your cell contribution to mine."

"You don't think it is the Matong's doing?" he asks as he pours steaming tea from the intricately adorned teapot.

"It is the Matong that brought us together in the first place."

"Yes, of course, that's what I meant."

"So back to Tildyn…"

"I have an idea. It's a bit farfetched." He pauses to let Jaxyl, who is squirming down onto the floor, free of his grasp. "But I think it might work." He leans over to hand Jaxyl a stuffed *pytal* toy.

"What? Please continue."

"A man like Tildyn, is devoid of any excitement in his life. He holds the title but has nothing to claim for his own except to harass us. We need to divert his attention, and I think I have the perfect ploy."

"Tell me please!"

"Recently he asked me if I would take him up in one of the aerocrafts, so I did. And he loved it."

"Puzzling. Who would have thought?"

As they talk, Jaxyl wanders toward a nearby table and has pulled herself up to a standing position.

"Look it's the first time she has ever done that!"

"She's our child, isn't she?" Ahshen beams. They both watch as she wobbles and sits down with a plop.

"Oh, my little girl!" Ali goes over to pick her up and Jaxyl, looking very pleased with herself, giggles. Queen Ali nestles her child close and blows in her ear playfully.

In response, Jaxyl takes her two chubby hands and holds them over her ears.

"What is it you have in mind for Tildyn?"

"Why don't we have him called in and the both of us can tell him of his new role in our burgeoning society."

"And what is that exactly?"

"We shall train him to be a pilot."

"A pilot? You mean you will teach him to fly the aero machines?"

"Yes, and he can teach others. We'll get him so distracted having fun he will leave us both alone."

Queen Ali spins Jaxyl around in her arms, pretending to let her fly. Profuse joy bubbles from the child as her irises begin to glow with a golden spark of color. "It is brilliant, I hope it works."

35-We Have Won Him Over

Tildyn's face lights up for the briefest moment until his skepticism eclipses his mood. "And why do you want to do this? Make me a pilot." Ahshen and Queen Ali have called him in to announce their plans for him.

"I saw how much you enjoyed the ride recently. I think you will make an excellent pilot among a chosen few. If everything goes as planned, you may be promoted. Who knows you may become a commander of the air overseeing aeronautic operations."

Tildyn valiantly tries to hold onto his sour expression, but his surprise and delight leach out. "My family will not approve; they want me overseeing our joint ventures."

"Come on you're a big boy," Ahshen says clasping his shoulder in a manly gesture. Tildyn slinks back imperceptibly. "You've earned your rank you are a prince after all. Don't ask, tell them what you intend to do."

"You don't understand my family," Tildyn says mechanically.

"Maybe not, but you do. When I fly back to Bridgenstyl you can join me, and I'll give you your first lesson."

Prince Tildyn swipes at his clipped white hair along his temples and gives Ahshen Owanu a faint smile. "I would enjoy that very much." Queen Ali is surprised by Tildyn's reaction.

SEE THERE I TOLD YOU WE COULD WIN HIM OVER. Ahshen makes the effort to telecommunicate.

"Tildyn, I believe this is the best choice for all our people. I will send an official statement to your father, telling him this is your destiny."

"Queen Ali, first let me approach him myself with the news. I think your letter will be better received once I have talked with him. As you well know, my family still has a strong aversion to being ruled by you." Queen Ali restrains her temper, realizing she may finally be getting Tildyn out of her way.

"So be it." As the words come from her mouth, she feels a rising elation within like a gust of hot air. *At last, I shall be rid of him. They will replace him with another brother but whoever it is will be much easier to deal with than Tildyn.*

36-A Juicy Bit of Gossip

"No one was more surprised than I," Roark says as he delivers the latest gossip to his sister. He is on a furlough to Katara to visit his family. "They met in the Pig Snout Tavern, and she's been following him around like a pathetic puppy dog."

"Mmm, doesn't sound like Alatoi. She is such a vamp!"

"You mean sexual predator? I don't think there is a man or woman in Bridgenstyl she hasn't bedded. I must say she and I nearly had a close encounter."

"Roark do not speak to me of such things."

"She's a temptress and it was a time when I had been away from Faynyl for a while."

"I don't ever want to hear you speak of your temptations again. You need to get your *astil* home more often." The queen shakes her head in disbelief, *but Tildyn? Alatoi and Tildyn?* "It's quite unbelievable."

"If you think about it, they are *two bowds of a bult*."

The queen laughs out loud. "Ah Roark, it is true."

"Ahshen is teaching them both to fly."

"Yes, but I didn't know he was instructing Alatoi as well and he certainly didn't say anything about them being an item."

Roark shrugs, "he may not have even noticed. He is too busy."

"He said the lodge expansion is nearly finished; I will be visiting soon."

"It is and there are several more lodges for our family being built. I am having a house built for Faynyl and Borzok."

"I am aware. I fund these projects, you remember."

Looking awkward, Roark grins and diverts. "The school is coming along nicely. You'll be pleased."

"I am concerned Bridgenstyl is becoming the center of commerce. We discuss this almost daily in the Council chambers."

"Excuse me, Mother," Jaxyl comes into the room and jumps into her uncle's lap. "You forgot about me," she says reproachfully.

"No sweet girl, I had to meet with your mother, last night was my first night home."

"Will you take Borzok and me riding? You promised to teach me the bow."

"But you are already being instructed in weaponry. You can probably outshoot me by now. I'm out of practice. Your old uncle is busy building Bridgenstyl."

"I'm coming with Mother soon. Father misses me terribly. He is going to pick me up in his aerocraft, me and Mother, and he's going to fly us across the sky." She takes her hand and swoops it through the air.

Roark grins at his sister and shakes his head. "Growing up with Galen and you, you would think I would be used to such a clever child, but she makes you both look like *dristils*. She's what? Five revolutions now?"

"Thanks, dear brother. I can't help it if Ahshen and I knock out superior children."

"Will you ever have more?"

Not meaning to, Queen Ali makes a muffled snorting noise rooted in indignation. "Maybe not, the Matong has not gifted us with this knowledge yet, even though I ask."

Jaxyl slips out of her uncle's grasp and gravitates toward her mother. "You don't need another child. You have me." Ali hugs her, kissing the top of her child's head.

"You are right, you are more than enough for one mother to handle."

Jaxyl bows her head slightly. "The Matong has told me, I will not have a sister or brother."

Startled, Queen Ali pulls back.

"What are you talking about? I haven't taken you to the Matong yet."

"Yes, you have many times when I was smaller. You carried me."

"But you've never bonded with it."

"Don't be angry, it lured me with a beautiful songbird. I followed the large red bird and went in there without your permission."

"But it's guarded," Queen Ali says feeling more alarmed with every moment.

Jaxyl shrugs. "It told me to enter, it must have put the guards to sleep. I was afraid you would be angry. It told me many things, some of which I must not share."

Anger, like a steel knife laid across her bare chest, immobilizes Queen Ali.

"But I don't understand. Why would the Matong draw you in? You are a child."

Jaxyl shrugs. "Don't worry Mother, I am unique from you in a way only the Matong understands."

A silence falls around them like a stifling heat. Roark looks at his sister sympathetically. "I've got to go, Faynyl is waiting for me. We will be in the lab most of the day."

Queen Ali gives a furtive look. "This stays between us, Roark. Not even Faynyl is to know."

Within minutes of Roark's departure, Queen Ali calls for Aptala. "May I go with you Mother?"

"What? Where do you think I'm going?"

"To the Matong of course."

Ali smooths the hair on her child's head, feeling the soft silkiness of it. "No, my little one, I must go without you." Rushing down the hallway, Queen Ali is reeling with the bizarre turn of events. *It is not fair to be usurped by your child. I must prepare.*

37-It is Ordained

There is a tiny bead of sweat trickling down Queen Ali's temple. She swipes at the irritating affirmation she is not divine. *Daufffle Matong fights me at every turn.* She nods to the guards and pushes the door open to the sacred chamber a little too gingerly. Despite its immense weight, the tall door, made of thick timbers, bangs against the side wall. *Oopsa!* She looks at the Matong as if to beg forgiveness, but her anger quickly resurfaces. She slaps her palm against the cool hard surface of the orb and is met with a slight jolt of energy.

DO NOT MOCK ME OR MY POWER. YOUR STATION HAS BEEN CHOSEN AND DELIVERED BY THE DIVINE.

"And?" she wants to say but sucks in her breath holding it until the Matong delivers more.

DO NOT ENVY YOUR CHILD. I HAVE NOT OVERLOOKED YOU. I MUST PREPARE HER FOR HER FUTURE BEGINNING NOW. YOU MUST WORK ON YOUR FAITH AND DEVELOP MERTH FOR A BRIGHT AND PRODUCTIVE FUTURE. YOUR LIFE IS FULL.

Queen Ali takes a breath letting it out slowly. *Of course, this is reliable counsel. I need not be so doubtful.* As she is about to let her hand drop from the orb, she feels the pull still in place.

"Is there more?"

YES BELOVED. YOU STILL HAVE BITTERNESS IN YOUR HEART TOWARD ME BECAUSE OF FON-TAR. YOU BELIEVE I SHOULDN'T HAVE PUT YOU THROUGH SUCH LOSS. BUT SOMETIMES WE MUST EXPERIENCE LOSS TO UNDERSTAND OUR GOOD FORTUNE.

That's a load of bult! She wants to scream.

YOUR FATHER HAD MORE HUMILITY. YOU SHOULD DEVELOP SOME. She hears the Matong make a tinkling sound like metal in the wind as it releases her. *Is that laughter?* she wonders.

She leaves the chamber with more questions than an-swers as usual but as always feels bolstered and refreshed by the encounter.

"There you are." Ali's mother Aadya nearly bumps into her as Ali rounds the corner.

"Mother, you won't believe what has happened."

Aadya takes her daughter's hands in hers and tries to still her daughter who is visibly shaken.

"What is it?"

Ali turns to look around to see who might be listen-ing to them. There is no one in sight in the hallway, but she exercises caution anyway. "It's about Jaxyl, let's take a walk."

"It feels like the Matong has taken my child hostage." She says once they are in a nearby garden.

"What do you mean?"

Queen Ali tells the story of her encounter with the Matong and how she came about to know Jaxyl had been lured into the Matong chamber. Aadya practices a blank expression as she had to do many times before when Poma was king, and she was ruling queen.

"I feel like it is no longer my job to be the mother of my child." Aadya pulls her daughter close and hugs her.

"Of course, you are Jaxyl's mother, and you must keep her from harm and nurture her. You can't imagine how difficult it was to raise Galen, our great healer. She has immense powers beyond yours or mine, or her father's for that matter. I was constantly waiting for her to be kidnapped by evil beings who would use her for their purposes. But here she is still healing the faithful people of Merth."

38-A Sister's Touch

"What do you mean my sister is unavailable," Queen Ali demands of the youth standing at the door. "I must see her at once! I have ridden over here from Katara." *I knew I should have sent a messenger for her*. But the queen's impulsiveness and pride had prevailed.

"Your Highness, Galen the healer is leading a meditation group. I am here charged with keeping the noise down so the group will not be disturbed."

Queen Ali bites her lip knowing she has a meeting with council members shortly. "Give her a message to come to Katara at once. The minute she is done with her group." She lets out a sigh, "and tell her it is acceptable to disturb me from my meeting."

"Yes, Your Highness," the young man bows slightly.

Once Ali returns to Katara and goes to her meeting, she is shocked to see her beloved Ahshen, who looks up from the table full of maps and gives her a smile, a smile so inviting to her, she must catch her breath.

"I'm here to pick you and Jaxyl up for an extended stay at the lodge," he whispers into her ear as she draws close to his side. He lifts his face to the group and says "No, this won't work we must have more supplies on hand ready to go, if you want to meet this unrealistic deadline."

As Queen Ali is catching up to what is happening in the meeting, her aide comes to tell her Galen has shown up. "*Flum!*" she mumbles under her breath. She grabs Ahshen's arm gently and tells him her aide will have to take notes to keep her up to date.

"I'll see you tonight," he whispers, and they exchange a brief kiss.

BEFORE DINNER. IF YOU CAN HUNT JAXYL DOWN AND GET SOME TIME WITH HER FIRST. LATER I WANT YOU ALL TO MYSELF.

Ahshen nods toward the corner of the room where Jaxyl is quietly observing. WHY HAVE YOU ALLOWED HER IN HERE?

Ahshen gives his wife an exasperated look. "Because she asked, and she's being good."

The infuriated queen glares at him. PLEASE CAN'T YOU TELECOMUNICATE? SHE DOESN'T BELONG HERE. SHE'S TOO YOUNG AND TOO PRECOCIOUS AS IT IS. Ali elevates her disgust with her lenient husband as she spins around to go. *Ach, everyone makes my life difficult. Why can't they just do as I command?*

When the queen gets to the room where her sister is waiting, it is poorly lit and the unusually dreary weather outside the window is not helping much. "I asked them to dim the lights," Galen speaks softly from the cozy couch she sits on. "I'm having one of my epic headaches."

"Ah sweet sister, you didn't have to come."

"They said you needed me, that it was important."

Ali sits down beside her older sister. She wants to grab her hands as her mother frequently does to her, but she knows Galen being so sensitive to touch, and having a headache, is reason not to. Ali twists to face her sister. "I'm distraught. Jaxyl is barely five revolutions and the Matong is already preparing her for rule."

As she speaks telling Galen the details of her story, Galen nods affirmatively, showing empathy for her sister. "Why Jaxyl told me the Matong is sharing things with her she is not to divulge to me! She's only five revolutions! Is this not absurd?"

Galen reaches for her sister's hand and immediately Ali feels the healer's calmness engulf her. "It is for your own good. As her mother you will be too protective to let her live her destiny. She is young, but it is a signal you need to start letting go."

Like a flood-engorged river, the anxiety flowing inside of her pushes Ali to her limits. "If I weren't under your spell right now, I'd be cursing and shouting." A sisterly smile eases from Galen's lips. "I know. You were always more suited for ruling than I would ever be, even if I did not have my gift."

"Why don't you bring your family to Katara tonight and we'll have only the immediate family to dinner. Ahshen is here to take us to Bridgenstyl for a brief stay, and I haven't seen your kids in quite some time."

"That would be lovely," Galen says.

"I'll tell Mother. She will be delighted to have us gathered. I hope Roark's family can come too."

39-Sing us a Song

Queen Ali is laughing so hard her ribs ache. "Please everyone let my brother speak. He says he has a great accomplishment to share with us."

Roark, still standing with his glass lifted after the family has taken the opportunity to tease him vociferously about his various failures as a scientist, continues his announcement. "Be that as it may. I came into this realm of knowledge late in life."

"My dear wife, Faynyl," he tips his forehead in her direction, "and my extremely gifted brother-in-law," again he nods in the direction of Ahshen who is still grinning from the roast and toast they have been delivering. "Both have been a great influence on my education, but it is my mother who inspired me as a child to question everything and to always try to make Merth a better place to live." And to Adyaa he gives a deep bow lowering his head in respect.

"Are you campaigning for a pay raise?" typically quiet Kandar, jokes. The dishes are being cleared and the children are beginning to slip under the cover of the tablecloth where they are whispering, giggling, and scheming.

"Seriously, we couldn't have done this without Faynyl who took Ahshen's suggestion and ran with it, but she is much too humble to claim this as her own." Faynyl smiles at her husband and lifts the tablecloth where one of the children is pulling at her skirt. "We can't give you a true demonstration until we get our tower built, but experiments indicate we have figured out a way to communicate with our voices through the air." A hush falls over the rowdy group like a fire being quelled with a heavy blanket.

Ahshen is the first to speak. "Can you at least demonstrate from the other end of the castle?"

"Sure. Where's Borzok?"

"Borzok, would you take this and run it down into the kitchen and speak into it like I showed you?" He hands his son a slender handheld instrument.

The kids scramble out from under the table, except for Jaxyl who has taken to stand by her father's chair. "I am going with them," she whispers to him.

"Yes, of course," he urges her with a nod of his head. The four children, Kandar and Galen's Jaru and Olza race after Borzok giggling, while Jaxyl the youngest straggles behind them. Queen Ali's chest tightens as she realizes she hasn't even had a chance to share with Ahshen what is going on with Jaxyl. *I will tell him after I bed him. We already lost our opportunity before dinner. I haven't been with him in at least two moon cycles.* She turns to him. The crooked smile he flashes her tells of his own lust. I AM READING YOUR THOUGHTS AND WE WILL BE TOGETHER VERY SOON. YOU WILL LIKE WHAT I HAVE TO GIVE YOU! Surprised by him telepathically communicating, she cannot fight the flush in her cheeks his message and too much wine have provoked.

I ALWAYS LIKE WHAT YOU HAVE TO GIVE ME.

Suddenly the room fills with the noise of the children running and giggling. "We are here," Borzok claims. Even those expecting the miracle of sound are slightly taken aback.

"It works!" Ahshen shouts. "Good work Faynyl, good work Roark."

"What do you want us to say, Dad?"

"Nothing in particular. Why don't you children sing us a song?"

"Okay, what shall we sing?"

"Sing the song of the little *groat* you like so much."

Borzok starts alone at first. Then the laughter dies down as the other children join in.

"Shalla talla, lontune, you are my little groat.
Please don't bite me, shotu, lofta, alagrote.
I am watching you, softa falna bitty mote.

The room full of adults has grown quiet as they reflect on the beauty of family and the marvels of this invention. "You can come back now children," Roark tells them. To which the dining room erupts in applause and the family stands to congratulate Faynyl and Roark on their creation.

40-Grave Concerns

Ahshen opens his eyes and rolls over to feel the soft breath of his satiated wife sift across his face. He reaches for her in a way only a lover is allowed to do. Her eyes open and her look of pleasure reinforces his satisfaction, but the moment dissipates like a thin vapor as her face twists with concern. "About Jaxyl, I must tell you some alarming news."

"What could be so important?" He strokes her face gently with the back of his hand, scooping her hair behind her ear. "You must tell me now?"

"The Matong has inserted its will into her life. She is already being groomed for leadership."

Ahshen sits up, his dark muscular chest tightens as he leans on one elbow, his iridescent green eyes gleam in the soft lighting.

"Explain."

"The Matong called her to the chamber and is already feeding her information she has been told not to discuss with me."

Ahshen hesitates to speak, allowing Ali to reveal more. "Mother and Galen, both assure me this is to keep me from interfering too much."

"They are wise women. Perhaps you and I could visit the Matong together." Ali stands to pull on her luxurious silken robe with patterns of exotic long-tailed birds woven into the cloth, her still fully alert breasts are the last part of her to be covered. She frowns.

"Even I must not defy the Matong."

Ahshen smiles gently at her. "Those in power must always be wary of becoming corrupted. It seems you have your marching orders."

Ali's lips knot up with frustration. "It is my duty to my people. I must always obey the Matong. I understand the consequences of disobeying."

"And why do you say that?" Ahshen asks as he climbs out of bed, the sight of his muscular body momentarily distracts her, as she fumbles for words.

"I know I'm not responsible for the death of Fontar, but I believe the Matong was exercising discipline, or power, or whatever you want to call it, over me, teaching me. The Matong as much as told me to appreciate what we have we must experience loss." A blast of light spins through the room emanating from the tall window in their bedroom as a rare cloud dissipates. The radiant light highlights Ahshen's muscular body as he stands. "But I don't want to talk about another man while you are here in my bed chamber."

She walks around the massive bed and nestles into him, grasping his seductive body firmly as the thin silk robe she wears loosens and drifts across their bodies. He clutches her chin and lets his tongue loose into her poised mouth, and they quickly forget about their grave concerns.

41-Taking Flight

"Ah, you distract me so!" Ahshen teases his wife when they finally get up to dress "We must get on our way. There is much to do. Are you and Jaxyl packed?"

Queen Ali lets out a muffled laugh. "We've been packing for weeks. A supply caravan left yesterday. All we need to do is take a few items and get in the aerocraft with you." She pulls on a feather-soft tunic over her bare chest. "I must say I'm a little bit anxious about Jaxyl riding in the airship. I know you have improved them." Her voice drops as if to ask a question. He looks at her demurely and continues to dress.

Suddenly Jaxyl barges in. "Mother, Father, I've been waiting for you to get up. I'm greatly excited we are going to Daddy's work! I love it there."

"Come here you little *mooshton!*" Ahshen reels around and grabs his daughter swinging her up into his arms. "You are going to love the surprises I have for you," he tells her as he squeezes her nose playfully. "I want you both to be so happy you will not leave my side."

"Dreamer," his wife scoffs at him. "You know we will have to return to Katara, this is where our life is. At least we will have Matong horses there now for our visit this time."

"Yes!" Jaxyl squeals as they head for the carriage that will carry them to the aerocraft.

As they load their gear into the open cockpit of the plane, Ali realizes how much roomier the new design is. There are two seats in the back now and plenty of room to put their bags. "I want to sit up with you Daddy and help drive the aerocraft," Jaxyl proclaims as she is boosted by her father into the open cockpit. Ali gives Ahshen a worried frown and shakes her head no.

"Little one we must take off first and you will have to buckle up, but I don't see why we can't arrange that," he says giving Ali a questioning look. Ali sighs and continues to frown, but there is a crack in her resolve. He can see it in her face. Ali shakes her head in frustration. *Ahshen's parenting is…he's always pushing me to my limits.*

"You two are always working against me." She complains climbing up and leaning over the back seat to help Jaxyl buckle in while Ahshen walks to the other side to the pilot's seat, checking the propeller and other pertinent mechanical points as he goes. She sits down and ties a sheer silken scarf in a graceful wrap around her head. A gentle breeze grazes her cheek despite the curved glass of the windshield in front of her and she has learned the ride will be windy no matter what. She has chosen a tight-fitting *ferrette* for Jaxyl to wear but she sees it is already in Jaxyl's hand soon to be cast off onto the floor of the cockpit. The festive mood is amplified by Ahshen's joy to be flying with his family. He opens the low door and hops in energetically.

"Now Jaxyl, it's been a while since you have ridden in Daddy's aerocraft. We have designed a more powerful thruster for launch. I want you to stay buckled in until we are in the air and underway."

"But I would prefer to sit up there with the two of you."

"No, honey," Queen Ali says as she turns around to take Jaxyl's hand and squeeze it. "Do as your father says."

"But I can't see back here."

"Jaxyl, do as you are told," Ahshen says in the most severe tone he can muster. With a disappointing huff, the heir apparent settles herself down into her seat, and mentally prepares for the slingshot departure. They can feel the juddering of the craft as the attendants tighten the spring coils of the launch mechanism.

Ahshen revs the engine. "Ready?" he asks her. Ali pulls in a full breath of air and nods yes. He waves to the crew in his rearview mirror. They are signaling him with the 'all go sign.' There is a clicking sound then ZZ-INNGG—they shoot out of the launch pad with a force unnerving to Ali but a rush for her husband and child, who is ready to unbuckle at the first nod from her father.

As soon as they slow to cruising speed Jaxyl is ready to climb into her father's lap. "Now Daddy?"

He turns his head back toward her, the only sound now is the quiet spin of the propeller, the engine is noiseless. "Yes, my little *laciata*, but hold onto your mother. We don't want to lose you." To demonstrate, he gives a gentle jerk to the helm and Jaxyl teeters.

Ali panics and slaps Ahshen's arm. "What are you trying to do you crazy man?" His smile is bold and flagrantly mischievous. "Not to worry my love just giving you a little thrill."

"Stop it. It's not funny," she scowls. Ali turns and puts a death grip on Jaxyl as she quickly slips into her father's lap and takes hold of the helm. A smile of satisfaction spreads across Jaxyl's young face as if she has been waiting her entire five revolutions to partake in this task. "It's fun, isn't it?" Her father whispers into her ear. She giggles.

"We are part of the sky now."

Seeing Jaxyl and Ahshen relaxed and enjoying the ride, Queen Ali breathes a little easier and begins to look around at her kingdom below. *It is even more beautiful from above.* She puts her arm up around her husband's shoulder and they connect with a satisfied glance. Ahshen squeezes his daughter and tells her what an excellent job she is doing of flying the aerocraft. "Look there, you are flying all by yourself," he says as he briefly lets go of the helm.

42-You Have Outdone Yourself

The foyer feels chilly when they enter the newly expanded royal lodge on the 'ledge' but once they enter the great room, where the roaring fire is ablaze in the massive hearth, they are enveloped with its warmth.

"Like it?" With arms spread wide, Ahshen spins around delightedly. Queen Ali's doubts about the expensive expansion are put to ease as she explores the room with her eyes. Above the hearth, which is as tall as Ahshen, is an enormous family portrait of Ahshen, Ali, Jaxyl, and Robic which catches her attention first. "But how... did she do it? We never sat for this."

"Alatoi is an amazing artist. She used separate sketches of us and put them together. The hard part was her time, she is busy with security in Bridgenstyl nowadays."

Ali studies the portrait. "The expressions are captured nicely." *It looks spontaneous, really.*

"Where did you get these beautiful tapestries?" she asks as she crosses the room to place her hand on one of the massive geometric weavings.

"Those are Omi works. Who knew they had a creative side? Well, some of them anyway. Other than their fire-breathing liquors, I had no idea they had an ounce of finesse."

Ali turns to Ahshen. "You have done jwell. We will be very comfortable here."

"Mommy, look! Robic is here." The big dog comes lumbering in with joyous barking which really throws Ali into awe of her husband's talents. He holds an awkward grin. "I had Roark fly him over earlier this morning before we left. There was no room in our cockpit."

"By the One True God, how did he keep him from hopping out?"

"We have a small cargo craft now with a covered cockpit."

Ali shakes her head in amazement and heads for the new bedroom. It is roomy with lots of windows and skylights. An enormous, tall dresser, with a double stack of drawers, lines one wall. It is made of lovely burled *matta* wood. She peers into the bathroom. "Oh, Ahshen this is gorgeous!" He follows her in, beaming, he wraps his arm gently around her.

"I thought you would like it."

Ali's eyes follow the natural stone floor leading to a sunken tub, made of the same stone, but what is remarkable about the generous bathing area is the glass wall and ceiling behind it, which jut out into a natural outdoor garden area sheltered by a rock precipice and carpeted in brilliant green moss. Water trickles down the layers of the stone bluff and wildflowers, scattered like colorful gems, capture the moisture seeping from the landscape. "There's a shower too!" Ahshen turns a knob, and a waterfall cascades out of the indoor stone wall mirroring what nature is doing on the outside. The opposite wall is lined with mirrors doubling the size and the natural light of the room.

"Ahshen this is amazing."

Jaxyl and Robic come tumbling into the room. Her eyes grow wide when she sees the bath. "I wanted to create a haven for you," Ahshen tells Ali.

"Daddee can Robic, and I play in the pool?"

"No, my sweet, you have your own room. Shall we go see it?"

As they enter, Jaxyl and her mother both capture their breath. The room is a smoky green the same color as the cover of *Halpo's Dreams*, Jaxyl's favorite childhood picture book. Pale columns and arches lead to her bath where a mural of colored glass has been constructed with some of the themes from *Halpo's Dreams*. Birds, *busterellas*, and woodland creatures frolic across a starlit sky.

"It's beautiful! I love it!"

"Indeed," Ahshen grins. "I have to chase out gawkers who come to see and then don't want to leave. It is a special room for a special child of mine," he says hugging her as she grasps him around the legs.

"I don't ever want to leave either."

"See," Ahshen says to the queen. "This is my goal, to always have you near." Knowing this cannot happen, she will have to return to Katara to run the government sooner than she would like. Ali smiles gracefully thinking about enjoying the brief respite.

"We will certainly be comfortable. You have outdone yourself."

43-Did You See?

The next morning when the family has risen, they request breakfast served outside on the loggia. As most mornings are on Merth, the air is fresh but mild as if the quiet hours of Merth's two moons have cleansed the air with their benevolence. "I will never tire of this incredible view," Ali says looking out across the valley. A modest fire burns in the outdoor fireplace and Jaxyl and Robic are playing chase.

"Be careful young lady there is a cliff and it's dangerous!" Ahshen warns her. "I guess I need to have a protective barrier built of some sort."

"Yes, I think so. Is there a way to build one without blocking the view?" Ali asks.

Ahshen shrugs, "I'm sure there is but it doesn't come to me at the moment." And then as if the One True God has been listening, Jaxyl trips and stumbles. Before either of them can gasp she flutters up off the ground as if there are wings on her feet. "Did you see?" Ahshen yells as he leaps for his child to grab her.

Queen Ali shakes her head in disbelief. "I'm not sure what I saw." Jaxyl giggles and lurches out of her father's grasp. "Come on Robic, I'll get a stick." In a few moments, what feels like a surreal event vanishes as they watch Robic fetch the stick for Jaxyl.

"Again, you must exercise caution. The dog can't fly like you do," her father jokingly says as he dismisses the moment with the dubious illusion a proud parent has of their child's skills.

A peculiar gnawing feeling is growing inside of Ali when the breakfast appears to distract her. Juicy *qualtal* egg omelets oozing with cheese are served. Spicy *raltar* toasties and *burgon* link sausages, still sizzling, along with trays of fruits and tiny, buttery biscuits are also brought to the table. Queen Ali's favorite honey sauce comes served in a dainty crystal carafe which catches the light. Ali drizzles the sauce liberally over most of the food on her plate, except for the green melon she likes to squeeze *louven* juice on.

"Jaxyl you must sit down and eat, sweetheart."

"Coming Mother!" When Ali turns around to look, Jaxyl is carrying Robic and is aloft in the air beyond the stone cliff face. The dog is big and furry, and all they see of Jaxyl is her legs dangling down.

"AIEEE!!" Ali screams dropping the heavy crystal carafe. Her heart seizes up as if someone has grabbed it and is trying to squeeze the life out of her.

Ahshen leaps to the edge of the cliff only to have Jaxyl swing down and place the dog on the edge of the precipice. As she lands, she tips her head in obedience but is soon giggling. Covering her mouth like a child her age would do to whisper a secret, she says, "Don't be alarmed the Matong has decreed this."

Suddenly Ali has no appetite. She waves the food away to servants who have rushed to her side because of her scream. "Please leave us," she barks and waves her hand.

Sucking in her breath, Ali tries to compose herself. The royal ring on her finger is buzzing with information as it delivers images to her brain. Ahshen sits back down still stunned by the vision of his daughter holding a dog twice her size while hanging in the air. "Come here little girl," he says calmly to Jaxyl. "Come sit on my lap and let your mother and I talk with you a minute." He squeezes her, inhaling the sweet breath of innocence, which wafts from the top of her head. He sets his chin on her head and squeezes. "You understand you gave us both a fright."

She turns around to him, "Yes, Daddy I didn't mean to."

"I want you to listen very carefully to me, honey."

Queen Ali stares at the two of them feeling heavy and useless, like a sword dulled by battle.

"Ahshen takes his daughter's two tiny hands and folds them into his own. "This is quite a surprise to your mother and me. Can you imagine how surprised others would be if they saw you hover like that?"

"I was rescuing Robic."

"I understand honey," he lowers his face to her ear. "But you mustn't let others see you do these things."

"I think the servers saw us."

"They are special people hired to protect the royal family with their lives. They have sworn their allegiance to us to protect our privacy. Still, we do not want you doing these extraordinary things you are capable of doing until you are older, and your time has come."

"That's what the Matong told me, Daddy," she says lowering her head as she begins to squirm in his arms.

"I will restrain myself if I must, but it is fun to fly!" She gives him an irresistible smile as she wriggles loose from his grasp.

Ali shakes her head, still unable to speak. An image of an ancestor she is not familiar with beckons to her in the vision her ring is laying out before her. He rides a Matong horse and leaps across the sky. She shakes the vision off, eager to belong to the present.

"What's wrong?" Ahshen asks her.

She pulls back with a smirk on her face. "You really have to ask?"

He shrugs helplessly. "I'm as baffled as you are. There was nothing like this on Fantu."

"You see I can't even access the Matong here," her voice is stretched thin.

"Do I need to fly you home to Katara?" he offers.

She shakes her head no. "We just got here."

"We could run home to Katara and be back before the day is out."

"No, it is not necessary." She leans into him and places her hand on his. "Just let me catch my breath."

Relieved his wife is not going to take him up on his offer, Ahshen picks up his fork and begins to eat again. When he does servants rush forward to attend to their needs.

"You can bring me more tea." Ali offers. "I will eat later. Please pack us a basket. We will be taking a ride shortly."

44-A Brief Interlude of Tranquility

Jaxyl rides a golden-colored Matong pony she has named Fontsy. Ahshen is astride his dappled mare Terdra, and Queen Ali rides her jet-black stallion Loncifer who is high-strung and edgy. It always makes the grooms skittish about her choice of mount, especially the way she found her father killed in a riding accident impaled on a post, not so many revolutions ago. They start easily, riding along the ridge where they will make their way up to what is known as Pawter's Peak. There underneath the shade of a massive *cotowl* tree, they will spread their lunch Ahshen is carrying in a pack on his back.

Once they have arrived, Queen Ali notices a widespread haze, perhaps smoke on the horizon. "Do you see over there?" She points in the direction of the anomaly. Ahshen squints, he can barely make it out.

"There's a mine over there." He looks at her incredulously astounded at what excellent vision his wife, the queen, has.

"A mine?"

"Yes, we have found more of the precious metals we need."

"You mean like the Targa metals?"

"Yes, I thought you had been informed."

She shakes her head absently. "Of course, I know. There is a whole security risk team at work now. I didn't think operations had begun yet. Speaking of which, I should probably sit in on your meetings while I am here."

He picks up her hand and rubs the back of it against his cheek, inhaling the sweet fragrance of her skin. "Of course, but first we have a few days to ourselves as a family."

"Look Dadee!"

"What is it my little one?"

"Over there I can see a boat on the river."

Ahshen walks over to where Jaxyl is standing and peers down toward the dark green ribbon of water beneath him.

"That my love is a boat. They are carrying cargo to Bridgenstyl. Probably supplies like food and building materials."

"Could we ride on a boat while we are here? I love water. I love swimming. Is riding on a boat like swimming?"

Ahshen exchanges glances with Ali. "What a protected life our child has lived we must take her for a boat ride."

Ali laughs. She has never ridden much more than a small watercraft herself. "That would be delightful. Please arrange it. But now we must eat."

45-No Small Vision

"Simply a superb meal," Ahshen says as he sets his plate down and stretches out his arms. "But I'm thinking I should lay my head down a minute and take a brief nap."

"Sounds wonderful. Lucky for you, I'm inclined to do the same." As he stretches out on the soft quilt they have brought to picnic on, Ali stretches out perpendicular to him, resting her head on his stomach.

Ahshen picks up his head to ask, "But who is to watch after Jaxyl while we sleep?"

Lazily, Ali rolls her head toward him and says, "Oh my, I am used to always having someone with her, but we came out here to have some private family time. The nearest guard duty will be within shouting distance, but they are not accustomed to watching children." Ahshen sighs, always the dutiful father, but not accustomed to the daily obligations, he vows to stay awake. "Here let's move the blanket over here beside this tree. I can lean against it and stay upright to keep from falling asleep."

The afternoon starlight dances through the buttery leaves of the immense tree above them creating a soft flickering of shade and light. As Queen Ali closes her eyes to rest her head on her husband's leg she slips into a deep sleep when she hears the thundering of horse hooves driving toward her. In her dream, she sits up and a streak of light pierces into her vision. The light is so bright she does not see the rider of a white stallion come charging forth and rearing, stopping abruptly in front of her. Looking up at the horse's chest above her she leaps to her feet. "Do not be afraid," the apparition says to her.

Queen Ali shields her eyes from the dazzling light. "Who are you," she asks.

"I have come to you from the future. Do you recognize me now?" The cherry red metallic armor, with black shoulder plates, cuffs, and shin guards the anomaly wears are unfamiliar to Ali.

"I can tell by your confusion you do not see me yet." The figure, encircled by the blazing light, pulls off her helmet and a cascade of golden hair comes tumbling down. "Recognize me now?"

"Jaxyl is it you?"

"Yes Mother," the warrior says softly. "Do not be afraid."

Ali feels a chill run down her limbs. Not one to shrink from the unknown, she inquires. "Why are you here? How is this possible?"

"The Matong has sent me. You will be challenged every day of your life to protect me from my destiny, but Merth needs me." The apparition smiles and looks behind her. "Although a spell has been cast and Father has fallen asleep too. Young Jaxyl is wading in a creek nearby and while she won't drown, she will slip on the mossy rocks and get soaking wet. She will come back to you singing and happy."

Queen Ali lurches forward, but the vision she is trapped in doesn't let go of its grasp on her. "I have a daunting mission ahead. I will be called upon to leave

Merth and assist with vanquishing a great terror that will endanger much of the cosmos. You will have a lengthy reign, and I will be known as the Warrior Princess for my many heroic deeds."

Her daughter envisioned as she will be in a *dacata* of revolutions looks down at Queen Ali. "Remember you must nurture your faith and not smother me with motherly protections. This will be troublesome for you. Please remember I have special skills, and many have not been revealed to you yet."

The glowing Warrior Princess turns and looks behind her again. She returns her gaze to Ali smiling. I must go now, young Jaxyl returns to you with a *froglin* she has captured." The white stallion rears and whinnies and spins upon its hind hooves. Queen Ali awakens with a jerk and the vision is gone.

"Mommee, Daddee, I have a surprise for you."

46-Dancing with Dilemmas

"What is it, sweetheart?" Ahshen asks as he shakes off the restful moments of his nap, not even realizing he has deserted his task of watching his daughter. "Why are you soaking wet? What on Merth has happened to you?"

"I fell in the creek," Jaxyl says wistfully, head bowed. "See?" She opens her hand slightly and two big eyes peer out. "He is ready for me to let him go, but I wanted you to see him first."

Still stunned by her vision, Queen Ali's senses are dulled as if she has been steeped in mud. "I need to get back to the house," she stands and whisks the pollen off her tunic, the tree has dropped while they slept.

Ahshen whistles and the horses jerk their heads up from their grazing. Jaxyl drops the *froglin*. "Goodbye little bud." She sticks her fingers in her mouth and a loud and shrill whistle shrieks from her lips. Fontsy comes running.

Ali can't help but see her daughter in a fresh light. In a way, she is grateful to know part of Jaxyl's destiny. These thoughts keep her quiet on the way home even when Ahshen challenges Jaxyl to race him to the far end of the creek bed. Ali's horse grips the bit excitedly to participate in the challenge, but she holds him back. Her need to process her vision outweighs the family fun. When she does catch up, she receives a torrent of teasing for being a *whoosit.*

"What's wrong with you?" Ahshen finally asks. She shakes her head and says, "I'll explain later."

It is not until they sit by the fire after dinner with Jaxyl tucked in, Ali feels free to tell Ahshen about her vision. "You say it was her? Coming back in time?" He asks. "How is this possible?"

"It was quite remarkable; she was beautiful and menacing-looking at the same time. She said they called her the Warrior Princess." Ali takes another sip of her sparkling wine. "The message is clear; I am not to overprotect her but let her grow like a wild vine. It's like her power lies in the destiny the Matong has laid out for her. She spoke of powers not yet revealed. And she told of a journey she must take away from Merth. I don't know how this is possible. It sounds like a treacherous future is in store for us."

Ahshen studies the fire as it pops and crackles, pondering the mysterious vision his wife has described, wondering if his child's journey to faraway places would be similar to his experience.

"Oh, she did say I would have a long reign. I guess I should be grateful."

Ahshen gives her a warm smile, grasps her cold hand, and squeezes it. "That is something to be grateful for."

They rise early the next day to take Jaxyl on the promised boat ride. There is no pleasure craft yet in the area.

Instead, they take her on the ferry barge still in use even though the bridge has been completed for some time, it has its purpose, mostly to carry pedestrians and their goods who don't want to walk across the heavily trafficked bridge.

"Daddee, we are floating this is fun!" Jaxyl runs back and forth to each side of the barge, so she won't miss a moment of the action. The engine, like the aerocraft engines, runs silent, but the rushing of the water against the hull makes a soothing swishing sound. The boat is empty except for the family and a few royal guards. They have leased the craft for several hours to tour up and down the river. The horses are with them in case they want to stop to ride.

"Ahshen, tomorrow we must return to the real world," Ali tells her husband. "This has been much fun, these past few days, but I really must handle business while I am here."

He nods his head knowing she is right. "Yes, but we will have more of these fun days before you leave."

Book II

The Warrior Princess

47-Coming of Age

"Eighteen revolutions ago, my little princess was born," Ahshen Owanu beams with pride as he stands to address the crowd. "Please raise your glass in a toast to my beautiful daughter! Princess Jaxyl Alexis." He raises his golden goblet into the air. "*Hoosa, Hoosa, Hosonta!*" the crowd roars. "*Hoosa, Hoosa, Hosonta!*" The celebratory cheer throbs through the halls of Katara like a resonating drumbeat.

Princess Jaxyl does not shrink from the adoration. She allows the throbbing of the chant to reverberate for an uncomfortable length of time. Jaxyl knows this helps to bolster her leadership role which will be pivotal to the safety of all Merthians in the coming rotations when she is called upon to fulfill her destiny as prophesized many years ago.

She leaps up energetically, athletically, raising her goblet. She nods to her father and mother while with her eyes she simultaneously works the crowd. "Thank you, all of you who have come to this festive celebration of my birth. I am yours to seek should you need my powers, and I have been blessed by the Matong with many extraordinary gifts." She wears a red tunic and black leggings made from the unique stretchy material woven from the thread spun by *anatong* birds. She is known to carry a silver shield and distinctive sword forged by local metalsmiths from Targa metals and blessed by the Matong. She wears the sword now. At her throat is a heavy amulet encased in whorls of cast sterling and bound by a unique graduated chain which had been blessed by her Aunt Galen, the healer, and given to her earlier in the day by her father and mother.

"As a surprise tonight, I wish to share with you a rare gift which has been bestowed upon me by the Matong. I do not want to frighten you, but I reveal this power so you will have confidence in my ability to lead you to safety in the coming revolutions ahead." She stops there, not wanting to frighten the crowd with the horrors to come. *It will be revealed soon enough.*

Queen Ali holds her breath, *what is she going to reveal? I have told her repeatedly to keep a lid on it!* But before she can allow her panic to fully engorge, Princess Jaxyl begins to rise above the crowd. WE HAVE HAD TO KEEP THIS A SECRET HER ENTIRE LIFE AND NOW SHE FLAUNTS IT! Ali projects her thoughts into Ahshen's head. He turns to his wife, smiles, and raises his eyebrows slightly.

OH WELL, HERE WE GO.

SHE ACTS INDEPENDENTLY FROM MY AUTHORITY.

SHE ALWAYS HAS, Ahshen shrugs his shoulders. NEVER A DULL MOMENT SINCE I WOKE UP HERE ON MERTH.

The boisterous crowd becomes dead silent like a candle snuffed out as they watch the iconic princess rise slowly above them. She floats aloft like a light breeze is carrying her. The miracle is brief as she returns to the podium and shrugs landing lightly on her feet. "It is the same ability our Matong horses have. No different. I am chosen by the Matong to protect the people of Merth when from the Immense there shall come a challenge to our very existence." There is a rumble of voices as the crowd melts into soft discourse.

"Do that again," a husky voice sounds in the distance. Jaxyl smiles knowingly.

"No, I am not here to perform tricks for your entertainment, but I do want to inform you of my extraordinary capabilities and to warn you we are to meet a great challenge. Everyone needs to get back to enjoying themselves, I hear tell there is a cake coming to feed us all."

As she says this a trumpeting sound heralds a white horse who comes prancing into the room, dramatically lifting each hoof high then pausing making it appear he is buoyantly marching. White, feathery plumes, attached to a gold crown upon his head waver as he whinnies. It is as if he is talking to the princess herself. The showy horse pulls an enormous white sled, waist high, on which he pulls a gargantuan layered glazed cake. It towers above the crowd.

The mass of people part letting the handsome horse into their midst. In a dramatic display, the horse nods his head up and down and stops directly in front of Princess Jaxyl.

"There now see I told you!" Princess Jaxyl stretches her hand out toward the horse who whinnies again and looks as if he wants to rear up, but realizing he can't because of the sled behind him, does not.

Queen Ali is seething. She leans over to her husband. SUCH A DRAMA QUEEN OUR DAUGHTER IS.

Ahshen Owanu lets a grin spread across his face. "That's our daughter for you. The Matong has nurtured her until she has become this." Bursting with pride, he stretches his arm out toward his flamboyant daughter.

"While she will be the hero, the entertainer, I will be left with the practical side of ruling this world," Queen Ali grumbles. Ahshen takes her resistant hand and squeezes.

48-Nothing Would Make Me Happier

"Mother you are overreacting again. You just don't get it." Jaxyl comes close to screaming but manages to keep her anger in check. The queen may be her mother, but she is also her supreme commander and a devout warrior such as herself would never dare raise their voice to the queen.

"You do nothing but defy me!" Years of frustration seep into the queen's voice. It is as close to self-pity as she will ever realize.

"Not this again." Jaxyl puts the back of her hand to her forehead, lowers her head, and closes her eyes. "I was told by the Matong to begin introducing my skills to the people. I thought last night, at my birthday celebration, with such a large multitude assembled, I would begin letting the people acknowledge what it is I do, and why they should trust me. They are to follow you, but I am their savior, they must trust me!" Jaxyl's words come spitting out of her mouth. It is a conversation they have had many times.

"You gain nothing by flaunting your gifts. They will see soon enough who and what you are."

"Mother," Jaxyl hesitates. "We are not on opposing sides. We must work together. Do not be jealous of my abilities." Looking at her gracefully aging mother, Jaxyl sees qualities she has inherited: pride, stubbornness, and unwavering strength. She is keenly aware of the privilege she shares with her as it oozes out of the queen like a low-lying mist.

"I'll show you abilities! A smile creeps across Queen Ali's face as she whips her hand across her chest causing a book on the other side of the room to pull away from the bookcase it has come from, and briefly levitate before falling to the floor. Uncharacteristically, Queen Ali giggles diffusing their conversational heat. "I've been practicing. If Matong horses can fly, I can surely levitate a book."

"Oh my, Mother, I had no idea, you were able to do this."

Queen Ali lets humility wash over her. "It's merely a parlor game for me. And it took a tremendous amount of practice. I've been waiting for the right time to show you." She looks at her magnificent daughter and for a moment they connect. "I'm sorry. My pride takes over sometimes. I understand you answer directly to the Matong and not to me. It has always been a thorn in my heart. My only child and you are your own person…always have been."

"We should go see Father before he leaves." Jaxyl reminds her mother to change the subject.

"He promised he would stay for dinner, but he's chomping at the bit to get back to his work. The man will never mellow out."

It was as she thought, he was busy packing when she found him at the hangar. He had grown his hair long again and it was starting to streak with gray. "It's been a good trip," he says without looking at her.

"Coming home is not a trip," she grumbles. "I wish you could see your way to spend more time here."

He stands to face her and stops shoving gear into the aerocraft. "Come here my Queen," he opens his arms, and she walks into his embrace. As he folds around her, she feels a sense of comfort, the only time this happens anymore is when he is there. "You may not age, but I do. Someday I will not be able to keep up and build all the projects I want to."

"Don't be absurd. I do age." She takes a breath and searches for the words to express what she is feeling. "I love you because of who you are, not because I need you by my side constantly. I wish we weren't always both so busy." He turns back to his packing.

"Jaxyl is no longer a child, you must let go of her."

"That's something I've never heard before," she scoffs.

"I mean it. Don't drive her away, you will need each other in the coming revolutions."

His words are like the weight of a heavy stone. She lowers her head. "I'm afraid the doom the Matong has predicted is upon us. It will take all our resources to survive."

He throws another duffle through the cargo door. "You would be safer at the ledge, and I would be there." His green eyes still effuse a vibrant sparkle stirring her passion.

"It may come to that. You must prepare for me to run the country from there."

His smile breaks further across his face. "Nothing would make me happier my love."

49-Deluge

Queen Ali was a young girl when the Great Targa storm disrupted their society with its clashing of fantastical sky fires and the dumping of millions of pounds of metals and other materials, from the Great Immense. Looking up on any clear night, and most nights on Merth were clear, you could see a jagged, jet-black tear looking as if someone had ripped the sparkly fabric of the sky.

But the metals dumped upon Merth's surface turned out to be a blessing. With Prince Roark's scientific team, swords were developed that homed in on the enemy leaving the warrior only having to hang on, and the sword itself would engage terminal blows. Another metal, while lightweight, was particularly suitable for shields as it was impervious to attack. Still another metal, because of its reflective properties, was assembled for mirrors to blind the enemy, even in the weakest of light. A fourth material was ideal for its elasticity and could be sewn into protective clothing, which looked and felt like supple, copper-colored leather.

Ali's mother, Queen Aadya, the Peasant Queen had been injured long ago in a similar precursor to the Great Targa storms when she was pregnant with Ali. That was when the family became convinced of her Aunt Galen's healing abilities. Just a child, Galen had healed her pregnant mother by removing the alarming shard in her back and sealing the injury with her healing touch.

Queen Ali thinks of these distant memories more and more as the Matong continues to warn them of the impending danger. It is one afternoon, late in the day when the shadows of the afternoon star grow long, when she feels compelled to bond with the Matong. With reverence but not much humility, for it is not in her nature, Ali visits the Matong chamber for guidance. *Show me how to prepare for this ordeal, what is my role? What is my daughter's role oh masterful Matong?* The warm, undulating orb latches her palm onto its curved surface and transforms her thoughts. KATARA MUST BE DEFENDED. YOU MUST DEPART FOR BRIDGENSTYL WHERE YOU WILL BE SAFER. YOU MUST LET GO OF THE PRINCESS JAXYL AND LET HER DO WHAT SHE WAS BORN FOR. PREPARE THE PEOPLE WITH PROTECTIONS AND DEPART. THE STORMS WILL BEGIN BEFORE TWO ROTATIONS ARE UP.

Ali stumbles and nearly falls when the orb lets go of her. It is her least favorite part of bonding. She always has an irrational sense of abandonment when the Matong lets go. Reeling with her instructions, she searches for her aides. "We must begin packing for Bridgenstyl and someone must be put in charge of poor Robic he is barely able to walk without pain. And tell Jaxyl to come at once."

When Queen Ali sees her daughter, the Warrior Princess, enter the room, she is struck at how well the sobriquet suits her. The tall physically strong woman shows no resemblance to the child she raised. And her demeanor is now on full alert. "We must waste no time; I am to depart for Bridgenstyl immediately. Your father has put in place many security standards for my protection." Ali falters, "And supposedly I am to leave Katara in your hands. You must defend the Matong. Galen will be by your side as your physician as we have discussed and thank the One True God, we at least have reliable communications we can count on for keeping in sync with each other. Our first obligation is to keep the people safe, but there will be looting and riots. You must also police the darker element of our people. The Omi in particular. They will challenge your ability to protect the Matong."

Jaxyl shrugs, "The Matong is capable of all things, we must show our gratitude by protecting its sovereignty."

Ali reaches for her daughter's hand, but it feels more like she is trying to coddle a nameless soldier rather than her own daughter. "Please stay safe. A great responsibility to lead our warriors is upon you."

"Yes Mother, now please do as you have been told and get yourself to safety."

50-Preparing for Targa Storms

When Queen Ali awakens in her sumptuous bed at the lodge, Ahshen has already departed and is probably miles away attending to his work and the lockdown preparations.

A restrictive curfew has already been set into motion, and soon the streets will be empty for the safety of the people, except for emergency troops on patrol. Experience has taught them; people need to stay indoors to avoid severe health complications. And despite strict mandates on looting, there will always be a selfish element alive and well in the stream of life, those citizens who will take advantage of the situation.

The past rotation feels like a blur. Ahshen had picked her and Robic up in the aerocraft. And now Robic lays at her feet breathing raggedly in his sleep as his chest visibly rises and falls. She thinks longingly of the rambunctious puppy he once was. How she would awaken to him licking her face while gracefully hunching over her partially so as not to crush her, but those days are gone. His once fluffy fur hangs in limp ribbons from his sides even with the extra care and brushing, he gets as the "royal dog."

As she looks around in the safety of her lodge, Queen Ali feels a pang of regret her daughter will be charged with such a massive burden of responsibility, defending Valtar, the Capitol of Merth. *But this is as the Matong has decreed.* Readying herself mentally for her day, she hears the bathwater being drawn. *So much to do, I must get out of bed!* She slips from under the luxurious quilts and tries unsuccessfully not to disturb Robic who whimpers with the wistfulness of the aged.

When Queen Ali finishes her breakfast, she is met in the receiving wing of the house by Alatoi, Chief of Security in Bridgenstyl. Alatoi dips at her knees in a showy display of respect as she often does. "I have asked Tildyn and Prince Olafar to join us, King Brechnole is not feeling well," Alatoi pauses. "In fact, he has been confined to his bed for more time than we had hoped." Alatoi gives Tildyn a sympathetic touch on the arm, and for the first time, Queen Ali is alert the rumors must be true. *Alatoi and Tildyn have become intimate but, she's been intimate with nearly everyone on Merth.* There was no doubt an unspoken understanding floated between them. *Wouldn't it be something to see her settle down? Is it possible?* Prince Olafar, bulky in girth and slightly off-smelling, nods his respect to the queen.

Queen Ali remains standing, fidgeting nervously, but still managing to exude authority. It is as much of her personae now as a physical crown. "If I have understood the Matong correctly. The catastrophic deluge should begin sometime later this evening. Lockdowns are imperative for everyone's safety. I will be here in Bridgenstyl for the foreseeable future. Jaxyl is in charge of protecting the Matong and any disruptions in the city of Valtar." She spins on her feet for emphasis, "Alatoi you are in charge of managing any outbursts. The people are afraid, but I think we are sufficiently prepared." She notices Tildyn's unusual silence.

"We are here at your direction," Prince Olafar, bows his head.

"I need you to be on the lookout for damages, people hurt by the deluge. It is not possible to have the healer, my Aunt Galen attend to everyone, and she is at Katara anyway." She looks at Tildyn her long-ago suitor and one-time friend, still pale and thin with his unusually white hair looking like harvested *crosen* stalks atop his head. "Tildyn you are in the best place to see our aero fleet is in great shape and can be deployed at a moment's notice. We will depend on you to expedite travel between here and Valtar. Only no one is to take to the air, until we are certain the deluge of metals and fire are over." Tildyn says nothing but a thin satisfied smile grows on his lips.

She tries to bite her tongue, but the queen cannot resist. "Is it true what they say you and Alatoi are together?" She whispers.

As if glued in place Tildyn's expression does not change as he looks to Alatoi. "We are to be wed," Alatoi explains.

The announcement feels like someone has dropped a heavy stone onto her foot. "Ah, surely you have thought this through?" She looks to Alatoi for an explanation.

Alatoi is unable to suppress her smirk. "It seems the prince delights in having more than one woman in his bed, and I am more than willing to accommodate him." It takes every bit of Ali's hard-earned discipline of royal stoicism to suppress her from laughing. Even Tildyn blushes and Prince Olafar turns away from the conversation in silence. He is clearly embarrassed by his brother's choices. *Alatoi never ceases to shock us.* "Then it will be a most unusual alliance," the queen says without skipping a beat. "But now we must stay focused on the immediate problems at hand."

51-Trouble Descends

Jaxyl tugs at her tight sleeves and peers into a full-length mirror encased in a heavy and ornate metal frame. She looks into her own eyes and steels herself for the battle to come. Her instincts tell her most Merthians will obey the edict to stay indoors during the event, but afterward, *what will happen?* When her handsome aide comes in with the wine she has requested, she asks him to disrobe. This is not the first time they have been together, nor will it be the last. She is prolific in her dalliances. And openly objective about her choices.

"I want a man who is physically stronger than me, but this is hard to find," she once told her Aunt Galen who gave her a potion to protect her. "I'm not into romance or love, just the physical nature of the act. It gives me a most interesting boost, both physically and mentally," she proclaimed coldly. Respectful of her niece's unusual role in the order of things, Galen does not judge and it is never questioned Jaxyl's unusual conduct in this regard should be brought up by anyone as long as she and her chosen partners are discreet.

Jaxyl and her consort are in a knotted disarray and soundly asleep when the pounding of metal on the roof above them, a clashing of metals so vociferous, awakens them and they both leap up out of bed. Instinctively Jaxyl grabs for her sword always within her reach. The guards stationed at her door pound loudly to be heard above the roar. "Princess Jaxyl, the terror is upon us!" She hears one soldier shout. "Are you all right?"

"Yes, wait a minute, I'm getting my clothes on." As she pulls on her undergarments, she looks out the window. As foretold by others who had lived through the Great Targa Storms before, there were great flashing and spiraling lights pinwheeling across the broad expanse of the sky, and chunks of exotic metals falling from the abyss of the Immense. The light display is mesmerizing but there is no time to waste.

"Round up the troops for reinforcement of the Matong and get my horse." Jaxyl commands.

She is met with opposition by the soldiers now massing in her room. "But Your Highness, there is no way we can do this. You will be instantly killed," a familiar soldier tells her.

She peers out the window again. "Perhaps you are right. The importance of staying indoors makes sense, more people fell ill from the lights than were harmed by the falling metals. But this is insane!" She says shouting over the noise, which continues for what feels like an eternity. *Why didn't I think to arm the men with helmets?*

"Order the men to remain inside until the flashing light subsides." She continues to watch as the kaleidoscope of colors cascades across the night sky while fighting the compelling urge to jump on her horse and secure the safety of her people.

It feels more like a work of art than a harmful array of toxic tymas. The assembled troops at her side are also hypnotized. Suddenly they hear a shriek, a distraught, ear-piercing scream by a woman on the street fills the air with an ominous aggression. "Stop them, they are taking my baby!"

Heroically, despite the harm to themselves, the troops rush to the aid of the woman outside holding their shields above them for protection. They surround the woman for her safety.

"Creatures, horrible creatures. They came and took my baby straight out of my arms!"

"Please calm down, ma'am," the officer tries to calm the panicked woman. "Can you describe them for me? You shouldn't have even been outside."

"I was just running across the street where my other children are when these two strangers approached me. It was dark, but when the lights flashed I could see how strange they looked. Their skin was leathery and in places, they had what looked like the bark of a tree on their neck and shoulders. They just snatched the baby out of my arms."

"Could you be imagining these creatures?" someone in the crowd of growing soldiers asks.

"Absolutely not. You don't forget something like this. It was horrible, just horrible." The woman begins to tremble visibly as if suffering from a high fever, and burying her face in her hands sobs uncontrollably. "My baby is out there with those monsters."

"Scouts, we need to get scouts on the roads and check this out," Jaxyl orders her men who scatter in a frenzy of activity. She jumps on her pure white Matong stallion Flodynhelm who towers above her, and heads in the direction of the woman's waving hand. She can smell a peculiar stench even at the great distance they have already traveled. It is like nothing she has ever smelled before, a dozen soldiers follow, hooves pounding on the hard clay surface of the road.

52-A Wild Chase

The wind howls in her ears as Flodynhelm instinctively dodges the falling metals, occasionally leaping into the air to avoid darting fires seeded by the swirling fireworks in the sky. It takes fierce discipline for Jaxyl to even stay astride as she races toward her prey, The Warrior Princess yanks at a swath of cloth used to wipe down her horse which she carelessly stuffed in a crease of her saddle. She wraps the sweaty rag around her head, hoping this will be enough protection from the toxic rays of light.

As the horsemen race toward their prey, they are blinded by a flash of light so great it makes their skin burn with pain. Jaxyl pulls Flodynhelm up abruptly and the warriors behind her quickly are at her side. "We need to take shelter." She looks around and sees a large tree with enormous branches. "Over there, quickly."

As they crouch and gather their wits, Jaxyl realizes the horses are not protected. "Jawtal, you will come with me. The rest of you get back to some sort of shelter as fast as you can, this is not over yet." She is confident the young warrior is someone she can count on.

"I can smell them," she tells Jawtal. The stench is sinister and like nothing she has ever encountered before even with her heightened sense of smell. "They are not far away. Perhaps the light was a distraction they initiated to confuse us." She looks at their two horses, wondering how badly they will be affected by the toxic air. "Do you have anything to cover yourself up with?" Jawtal laughs as he pulls out a robe from his saddle bag and hands it to her.

"Put it on." She tells him.

"No, Your Highness you must wear this, I have something else." She looks at him curiously and he pulls out a sweater.

"Oh, okay," she laughs. "You may be the best-dressed soldier we have." She slips on the robe not knowing for sure how much protection any of this will be. "I think we need to secure the horses and walk from here," she says in hushed tones. "They're close I can even smell the baby."

Jawtal shoots her a peculiar expression but doesn't say anything. They begin to stealthily walk toward the abductors when Jaxyl hears the baby crying. "Shh," she turns to her companion. "I can hear them now; we are nearly upon them." They continue creeping toward a low outcropping of trees. "I think they are over there," she turns and pulls her sword out without a sound. In the darkness behind them, the sky still lights up with an occasional flash which helps them to find their way.

Peering behind a thick branch Jaxyl gets sight of the baby's abductors. They are completely foreign to anything she has ever seen. In the arms of one of the strange creatures is the baby who frets as if its cries have been stifled somehow. She looks at the tiny red face twisted with frustration and holds her breath before she bursts through the bushy branch of the *crandor* tree startling the creatures. Their eyes bulge when she does. Wielding their swords before them, the two warriors approach cautiously, but it is evident the two strangers are not willing to put up a fight because the one holding the baby quickly surrenders it with awkward unfolding appendages. The smell is becoming intolerable to Jaxyl, she nods to Jawtal to grab the baby while she keeps her sword drawn. The transaction takes place in silence, and the creature handing off the baby stumbles and lets out a piteous sound. There is a flash of light, and the two peculiar figures are gone.

"Holy flum!" Jawtal shouts, and there is another flash of light that blinds them as a large sheet of metal crashes to the ground very close to where they are standing.

"Take shelter!" Jaxyl shouts and instinctively ducks. They both race to a nearby tree with large outreaching branches.

Jawtal juggles the baby to shelter it under his arm as he runs. "I have nieces," he says to Jaxyl who looks at him with surprise as they land at the foot of the tree like it is home base in a game of *kottles*.

"I can't believe that was so easy," Jaxyl shakes her head and gathers the roomy robe around her. "But they have escaped…such strange creatures."

Jawtal takes a minute to check the baby out who is beginning to whimper. He pulls off his leather glove and lets the infant suck on his knuckle. "I hope they have not harmed the little one."

Jaxyl reaches for the child and Jawtal hands the baby off to her. "We must keep it covered." She bundles the child in the folds of the robe and heads for the horses. "It should be safe; the sky has quieted, and we need to get this little one home to its mother."

"I'll gather the horses. I think that peculiar pair has returned to wherever they came from." Walking through the thick undergrowth with the long robe is a nuisance, but Jaxyl is more than glad to have the coverage for herself and the baby.

"It was a stroke of luck I brought the best-dressed warrior with me," she laughs at Jawtal, who grins back at her feeling closer to his leader than when she had invited him into her bed not long ago. The male troops were strictly forbidden to discuss their liaisons with the Warrior Princess, but there was knowledge amongst themselves who came and went.

"Yes, and with my experience as an uncle, too." He grins proudly.

With the storm over, they walk their horses gently home careful to not disturb the baby who sleeps in Jaxyl's arm like a limp puppy. "I am curious about her captors. I wanted to take them back to my uncle Prince Roark who could study them and figure out where they came from. We may never know now."

53-Curious

When word gets back to Queen Ali, still at Bridgenstyl, of the troubles encountered at Valtar she immediately shares the news with her husband Ahshen.

"They surely came from somewhere else," Ali muses. "We have no living creatures like the ones Jaxyl described. Their appearance here must have had something to do with the Targa storm."

"Perhaps, but not necessarily," he shrugs. "There was no such event when I arrived here from Fantu. Of course, anything is possible. What you need to understand is, there are many millions of planets and people out there. It's a miracle there haven't been more visitors here already. It is curious what they were doing though, it's as if they wanted the child and then realized it was too much for them. We'll never understand the logic behind the event."

"I need to get back to Katara, and to the Matong. I need some answers."

Knowing it was not advisable, Ahshen gives her that loaded look he often does when disagreeing with his wife. "It's the Matong that told you to come here and stay out of danger. And as you experienced, we didn't have nearly the severity of the storms here they had at Valtar."

Switching topics because the conversation is not going anywhere, Ali asks him how the progress is going on the improvements to the communication system. "If I can't communicate with people in Valtar, especially Jaxyl, you will need to fly me back and forth frequently."

"It's a good thing they are nearly finished with the new relay tower because that's not going to happen my dear."

Ali frowns looking at her handsome husband. "Those eyes may still be irresistible to me, but you must do what your queen commands." Her words are hollow for if there is one person on Merth who can test her authority, it is Ahshen.

"When will this tower be completed?"

"I'm guessing in a couple of rotations. You will be amazed at how much better our communications will be."

Ali looks at her hands. Her royal ring tells her to be wary of events to come. "For the most part. things are going well here," she justifies to her husband. "The clean-up is underway, but I need to check on Valtar, I need to see my family and bond with the Matong. I'd like you to take me over early in the morning, and we can return before nightfall." She thinks for a minute. "Actually, *Sout-ou* will be occurring. We needn't rush back, both moons will be in the sky together early in the evening and there will be plenty of light to land." A quiet peacefulness falls over her as she considers her plan. But this will be quickly changed later in the day when she meets with Alatoi.

"Your majesty we have a problem," Alatoi blasts into the room. "We have havoc in the town. Everyone was obedient about staying protected and indoors, but now the people are scavenging the metals. Our metals we told them were off limits."

"Give them a chance to return the materials, and if they do not lock them up."

"The jails are already full. We have increased our number of protective forces, but we need more help."

"If the people go back to work, it will help. Send out an edict and get everyone back to work." Queen Ali considers it is unusual for Alatoi to react like this. *Perhaps Tildyn is rubbing off on her.*

"Is there something I need to know about?" The queen asks her.

The typically defiant artist turned spy, turned head of police at Bridgenstyl stares down at her feet for a moment. "I am no longer happy in this position. I feel at odds with the Omi, and I am an Omi. I'm about to marry an Omi. I understand it's not an ideal time to quit, but you need to find someone to replace me. I want to get back to being an artist again. As Tildyn's wife, I should be able to come and go as I see fit and enjoy the benefits of my position. I've never experienced leisure, but Tildyn assures me it will be beneficial for my soul."

"And you have a soul?" Ali suppresses her smile and regrets her sarcasm, but she has known Alatoi, ever since the eccentric artist painted her when she was an adolescent. *This alliance with Tildyn now, and resigning from her post? It's a bit too curious.*

54-The Rumors Are True

"I love it up here! I don't know why you are reluctant to fly me home more often." Ahshen grins. He loves to see his wife be joyous and free, something she rarely allows herself to do.

"I'm doing my best to protect you." He pats her on her arm affectionately as a devilish grin blossoms on his face. "So, hold on." Ali braces and checks her seat belt realizing he is up to something. The plane twists and turns and she has the sensation she is going to lose her breakfast.

"*Ditzu*, would you stop it?"

The light aerocraft swivels, righting itself and her husband reaches to touch her cheek. "You know you love it!"

"You are being a complete *baltoff!*" She scolds, wiping back her hair that has fallen like a sheet across her face.

When they land, they are met by Jaxyl and three warriors they are unfamiliar with, who stand as stiffly as if their spread feet have been cemented to the ground. The light mood of the ride dissipates like the fragrance of *sookletoes* on the wind. "What is it?" Ali strains to read her daughter's thoughts, but the Warrior Princess will not allow this invasion of her psyche under the official circumstances.

"We're here to escort you to Katara. We have a situation on our hands."

Queen Ali looks at her husband. "You'd better come with me."

"Are you certain the thefts are being committed by these strange creatures?" Queen Ali questions her daughter.

Jaxyl nods. "We almost captured one, but they can disappear, often in a burst of blinding light. The people are terrified of them. Few have seen them yet, but rumors are spreading like *shizle* syrup on a hot day." She adjusts her tunic and touches the amulet around her neck. "I am at a loss how to fight a foe I cannot see."

"What does the Matong say about this?"

"The *fluming* thing speaks in riddles to me."

"I must go at once. You two come with me." She looks to Ahshen and Jaxyl who follow her to the chamber.

THESE SPECIES ARE NOT OF YOUR WORLD THEY ARE NOT EVIL, JUST CURIOUS. BUT THEY COULD DO HARM IF ALLOWED TO CONTINUE THEIR RESEARCH. YOU MUST LAY A TRAP AND CAPTURE ONE SO YOU CAN COMMUNICATE. LOOK TO WHAT THEY SEEK NEXT.

"That's baffling, any ideas?" Ali says to Ahshen and Jaxyl.

"Unfortunately, I think thefts are happening by our people as well, and they are being blamed on these creatures. It's hard to tell what is really going on." Ali looks at her daughter and is fascinated to see such power in her physical appearance, *the way she stands erect and official. She has transformed once again before I am ready as it has always been with her.*

"This certainly isn't what we prepared for," the Warrior Princess complains.

WE MUST ENHANCE OUR SCOUTS. QUESTION EVERYONE. I THINK WE NEED TO ENGAGE ROARK IN SOLVING SOME OF THESE MYSTERIES. Ahshen, who rarely places his thoughts in others, projects to Jaxyl and Queen Ali.

ALATOI WOULD BE HELPFUL NOW TOO, ONLY SHE HAS LOST HER INITIATIVE, the Queen adds.

Jaxyl gives her mother an inquisitive look. Ali shakes her head. "It's unbelievable her association with Tildyn has turned her to mush. Perhaps he has even orchestrated her retirement to take advantage and get her out of the way so Omis can do what Omis do best."

"The rumors are true then?" A smile spreads across Jaxyl's face.

"Yes," her mother tells her with a look of disgust.

55-Looking to Set a Trap

Roark is sent for immediately, but it takes him some time to show up. While they wait for him, food is brought to the Queen and Ahshen. "I love it at the lodge, but the food doesn't compare to the kitchen here, pass me some more of those *gartu pasters* would you?" Queen Ali eats the pastry-covered pâté eagerly. Ahshen makes a mental note to improve the food at the lodge, while Jaxyl pulls out a sketch of the creatures which she slides across the table to her mother.

"My they are peculiar," Queen Ali stares at the likeness. They are gangly with thin arms and legs, wide shoulders, squarish heads, and what look like paddles where hands might be. "How accurate are these drawings?" She turns to Jaxyl. "Is it true they have bark on their shoulders?"

Jaxyl laughs. "I couldn't say for sure, but I think that may be their clothing. They have a peculiar stench though. Nobody seems to be able to smell it except for me."

"Yes, you do have a heightened sense of smell."

Roark bustles into the room slightly out of breath. "Sorry folks, I was consulting with our metals team. We are working on finding other applications for the metals, now we have an even more bountiful supply."

"I'd like to call a full council meeting, but we don't have time. Ahshen and I are trying to return tonight, and we have lots to cover." Ali signals for the food to be taken away and the room vacated of any unnecessary persons. "First, we need to make a list of the thefts committed by our strange little friends. We must be cautious. Unless they were seen or seen disappearing, we won't count the theft. The Matong says we are to make a trap based on what they might take next. What do we have so far?"

Jaxyl passes around a list. "If we are to stick to actual sightings by people we trust, we can probably eliminate half of these."

"*Frap!* There are hundreds of thefts here," Roark groans as he looks at the list. "We need Alatoi. Someone send for her immediately. Tildyn can fly her over."

"No, I'm not sitting here waiting for her." Queen Ali protests. "Let me handle Alatoi, we do need her though."

"We've got to act swiftly. And we must use force, if necessary," Roark adds.

Jaxyl, still standing, observes the group. "Have we asked ourselves where they are taking these things? Some of them are rather large. We do know they typically travel in pairs, another pattern."

"What are your thoughts Ahshen?" Ali asks. "You are the only one here who is from another planet. Do you have any insight for us?"

He clears his throat. "You know how we can fly back and forth to Bridgenstyl?"

"Yes, what is your point?"

"It was a long-held belief, where I come from, species should be able to travel from one planet to another. These creatures as you call them, are distinctively different than us, they are surely not of this world." Ahshen had finally said out loud what most of them feared.

"This could be true," Jaxyl says to her father. "If it is, it will be much harder to trap them and communicate."

Queen Ali's finger tingles as her royal ring sends a message telepathically. She sees a vision of some peculiar visitors to Merth many generations ago.

"Our ancestors have dealt with this before according to the ring." There is utter stillness in the room as the elite group awaits her explanation. "I'm sorry that's all the information I received. Perhaps you, Roark, you are the one most familiar with the sacred library of the past, perhaps you can discover more."

"I've got students I can put onto this."

Ali sighs, "I guess there is no room for secrecy in this."

"No, the people are spooked and rightly so," Jaxyl says allowing her concern to carry on her voice as if it is somewhere in the distance.

Ahshen tosses the list on the table casually and grins. "They seem to have a fondness for sweets. Whenever they steal food, it is some sort of cake or baked goods."

Jaxyl perks up. "This is a good point. And maybe we should pay attention to how they travel in pairs. Perhaps if we were to separate them."

"I think you are on to something," Roark agrees.

"Perhaps we should consider their disappearing act could be upset if we were to interfere with their process somehow, like throwing water onto fire."

"Hmm, we've been doing some more tests on the Targa metals. I am curious if we might interfere with their getaway flash by intercepting it somehow."

"I like your thinking," Queen Ali says to her brother.

Ahshen breaks in, "Something to consider would be to lure them into a cave, this might also be a simpler way to block their transmissions."

"Hmm, I like it."

56-What I Wanted to Hear

"They have gotten more cautious," Jaxyl tells her warriors. "They have stopped stealing until after nightfall." She looks around the room at her tall, muscular chosen few. Eight men and two women, now wearing carefully crafted, fluid Targa cloth with special armor metal shields in strategic places. "We still don't understand their intelligence level, and we know little else about them except they have a predilection for sweets. They attempted to steal a baby, but now it is mostly an array of curious equipment and even a few peculiar artifacts; an antique Merthian ware bowl, a hand-cranked generator, some old coins, and a rare knife. Does anyone have an idea how to trap these curious beings?"

"What do we do with them once we've caught them? How do we connect or communicate with them?"

Jaxyl nods, "All good questions Plauto, but let's capture them first."

"It sounds unconventional, but perhaps we could lure them with a child, not a baby but a child," one of the warriors interjects. The idea sparks some mumbling, but no one comes out and endorses the questionable notion.

Jaxyl's eyes swipe around the room looking for answers. "Any other ideas?"

"What about going large? What about a small aero craft? We could put *dosey pasties* on the seats and if they take the bait, throw a tarp over them." The group laughs.

"No idea will be dismissed. We must work together on this plan."

The meeting is interrupted when a guard comes crashing into the room. "We have an incident; there's a fire and people are shouting in the street." Jaxyl nods and waves three fingers, three warriors cut out in a run as the guard leads the way. The others mingle jitterly, and Jaxyl realizes she has lost their attention.

"Princess Jaxyl, I have an idea." She looks over at Lorthian, one of the brainier of the crew. He is the smallest physically of her elite warriors, but fights like a poison *snarkle*, snapping and lurching aggressively at his opponent, until his unpredictable motions deliver a fatal blow. His tenacity has landed him in this position. "What about the Targa cloth? What if we had a tarp made from it? It has great properties we don't even understand. Perhaps this might defer their ability to disappear."

Jaxyl turns to him as she starts for the door, signaling her warriors to follow. "Sounds like a great idea, but we need to quell this fire immediately and whatever else it is." Lorthian bows his head slightly with a humble pause.

"We will get these creatures, most revered Princess."

Turning away from him, Jaxyl cannot contain the smile creeping across her face, but her mood quickly blooms into outrage as she sees the flames leaping up into the sky from the street below.

The fighting is intense at first, but the warriors are joined by other guards and peace officers, and the thirty or so *hanigalans* are rounded up before long and their hands bound behind their backs. Several of the men are wounded, mostly the disrupters, as the warriors now wear the copper-colored Targa cloth uniforms that protect them. Only one person does not rise, a boy not fully grown. The fire, started in a nearby store, partially extinguished continues to flare up occasionally.

Jaxyl paces angrily in front of them, shouting her displeasure. "What have you fools done? An innocent boy has perished. Have you no sense?" There is mild chuckling amongst the beleaguered men. "The boy is no innocent, Maxxon, is one of the craftiest of thieves."

"Tend to him, see if he is still alive!" She shouts suddenly realizing he may not actually be dead. Two men go to pick him up and one gives her a disparaging look. "Send for Galen the Healer now!" she barks. "Take these men and lock them behind bars," she grips the knife at her waist menacingly and snarls at the perpetrators "You will regret your actions today."

Ideas have been mulling around in Jaxyl's head the entire rotation like stones caught in a landslide. Even a fast ride to clear her thoughts does not produce peace and a visit to the Matong is counterproductive and maddening because she gets more questions lobbed at her than answers. With no clear solution to the complex task at hand, she finally lays down in a hammock in the shade of a giant *mullen* tree in one of the many outdoor gardens at Katara. She is about to doze off when she hears the soft voice of her Aunt Galen. Galen's flowing white tresses fold over her shoulders, giving her a mystical aura as she approaches with the sunlight to her back. "The boy will live. He had a moderately severe blade wound in his chest, but it was clear of any major organs, and I was able to heal him."

"Where is he now?" Jaxyl asks sitting up in the hammock.

"They have him under guard in one of the kitchen maid's rooms. He's resting now."

"I'd like to ask your opinion." Galen perks up, surprised the great Warrior Princess is asking her advice.

"Sure," she says pulling up a chair near to the hammock. "What is it?"

"You are the healer, but is there anything else you can do with your gift?"

"What do you mean?"

"These creatures have come to Merth. We're not sure what or who they are exactly except they are thieves. It is my duty to capture them and I'm struggling with how to accomplish this. They are slippery, like an *eelta* on a bed of moss, and they disappear in a flash of light. It has been suggested we make a tarp from the soft Targa cloth we now wear to shield us from wounds. If we were to capture one, do you think you could hold it in a trance?"

Looking intently at Jaxyl, with her famously deep purple eyes, like two iridescent *tõramalli* gemstones, Galen pulls in a full breath. "I'm not sure, I have calmed wild animals before, and perhaps this would be similar."

Jaxyl clamps Galen on the shoulder. "That's exactly what I wanted to hear. Now I must visit a thief!" Galen looks around bewildered as her impressive niece leaps up out of the hammock and disappears in a flurry to go speak with the youthful bandit and enlist him to her purpose.

57-We've Got Them

The hunting party has dutifully remained silent and deadly still as if waiting to club a *phowdal,* but their bones are beginning to ache in the clear, cold night air. Jaxyl is about to call off their vigil for the night when they hear a rustling at the mouth of the cave and she smells them. They hear a soft noise as if an animal is sniffing the air. As her pulse tightens, Jaxyl calms herself with trained proficiency and sends a minute vibration to her subordinates to warn them to be alert. There is a soft glow of light as the two gangly figures approach. *Could it possibly be this easy? No,* she reminds herself this is their twelfth attempt, and coordinating with Galen, a mother with children at home, *has been challenging, to say the least.*

The four warriors holding the special cloth leap forward and throw in one coordinated swoop. There is a sharp whining sound as the cloth falls across the expanse as if someone is letting air out of a *coval.* The dense cloth begins to bounce and sway. Galen comes forth and bravely reaches underneath not knowing what kind of peril awaits her healing hands. But the object she touches is lifeless and a small object falls to the floor.

"We've got them!" Someone shouts and Galen backs off realizing she is of no use. Someone else reaches underneath, while another warrior ignites a torch so they can see.

"Son of Gaskell!" the brave but foolish warrior says. "I think the thing bit me?"

Laughter, fueled by the uncertainty of their tedium now released, breaks out among the group. "Wrap the cloth around them like a babe in arms, scoop it up, and quit sticking your hands in there," Jaxyl orders. "I would bite you too."

Several warriors place their hands on the bumping blanket while two others lower themselves to wrap the tarp around the bottom. Galen looks on in disbelief trying to quell her horror at the strange sensory phenomenon she has experienced.

"They are not alive," she mumbles while Jaxyl laughs at her jest, watching the tarp bounce and cavort madly beneath the outstretched hands of the crew. "No, really, it's not alive. I think they are some kind of machine."

"Get the crate we brought," Jaxyl shouts above the uproar. "Shove them into there, but keep the blanket on, it could be what's keeping them from blinking out on us. Do we have another one we could throw over the top?" Instinct is guiding her now as she shouts her orders.

Oddly there is another tarp available. "Always prepared," Lorthian grins. "It was the kid's idea. Smart to hire a thief to catch one." They drape it over the large cage and shove the bumping mass in.

It feels like the tedious journey home over an endless jarring road takes forever. Jaxyl assigns Lorthian the task of keeping the cage covered until they can build a larger, buffer space.

"But I don't understand, they love sweets," Jaxyl says to Roark as they secure the room where the two creatures will be kept. "That's how we caught them."

Roark pushes his dark curls aside affectedly from his forehead. They have now allowed the tarp to be pulled back on one side of the pen where the gate is. "They must be machines. We think they were processing the sugar into fuel, much the same way we do. They were fading like a child's windup *solvar*, so we gave them sweets and they shoveled them in with those paddles of theirs. It was quite a sight."

"Any progress on communicating with them?"

"Only through their love of sugar," Roark shrugs. "I've asked Ahshen to come over in the morning and see what he has to say. He'll bring Ali with him, I'm sure."

"Good," Jaxyl says placing her hands on her hips.

58-Yech! Let's Hope Not

"We haven't dared to take the tarp off because we didn't want them to escape like they have so many times before," Prince Roark tells his sister, Queen Ali, when she arrives on the scene.

Ahshen is still mulling thoughts around in his head as he peers at the creatures who look as deflated as a child's water toy. "So, when did you give them their last sugar treats?"

"Yesterday afternoon. We thought about giving them straight sugar, but I didn't want to do anything differently until you arrived." Roark looks pointedly at Ahshen. "So, what is your best guess about this curious pair?

"We set some water out for them, but they don't seem to be interested."

Ahshen paces outside of the cage as he assesses the slumped-over figures.

"We don't want to mistreat them, but we don't want them to become so strong they escape."

"Here's what you might try," Ahshen cautiously points out. "Keep their energy source limited. Like you said, don't enable them to escape." He takes a thorough look around the room. "You have them below grade here, cover those light slits up there with Targa cloth." He points to the two grates high up on the wall. "Let them out when you feel secure, and your work can begin in earnest."

"I know I can't see them in the cage. I think there is a lot to learn here," Queen Ali says to no one in particular. Turning to her husband she asks him if they had anything like this on Fantu.

"We had robots and drones, but they seem a far cry from these specimens. Their grayish green exterior suggests they might even be an amalgam of bio and machine, especially seeing they have been able to refuel with sugar. We aren't sure what their optimum fuel is." He looks at Roark sharply. "I wouldn't change anything about their intake until you are more familiar with them."

Over time the two mysterious figures grow used to their surroundings. They express gratitude with a nod of the head every time they are fed. Their piercing eyes, like shiny black beads in their face, soften when spoken to, but their freakish lack of a nose of any kind, makes it difficult for their captors to consider them with compassion, although they have strict orders from the top, to be kind to their prisoners. Roark comes to visit them every day to study them, and Jaxyl, still battling unrest within the Valtar community comes less and less.

One morning when the changing of the guard comes into check on the creatures, they have nicknamed, "Bird" and "Testor," a large pinkish crystal is found lying on the floor. "Oh, my have they finally taken a clort?" One man says to the other.

His surprised partner laughs and shrugs. "Got me, mate. Somebody needs to fetch Prince Roark."

"Yeah, but what if it is really their clort?" To their surprise "Bird" picks up the large crystal and tries to hand it to them with his clumsy extended paddles.

"Yech, let's hope not. Quick send someone to fetch the prince."

Roark shows up nearly breathless, having run most of the distance to the underground chamber, where the captives are being held. "What is this I hear? We have something new to look at?" The two guards look at each other quizzically, not brave enough to come out and tell him their theory. Bird picks up the crystal again and makes the motion to hand it to Roark. "Mother of the One True God look at this! It's the first time they have tried to interact with us." And just like that he takes the stone from Bird's outstretched paddles and disappears in a vortex of brilliant lights as the two guards stare with their mouths hanging open.

"Holy *flum,* what has happened.?" The guard charges the two fugitives with his knife. "Wait. Stand down!" His partner leaps between him and the captives. "Stop! What are you thinking you fool?"

"Go now and send for the Warrior Princess."

59-I Haven't the Faintest Idea What to Do

"Disappeared? What the *flum* do you mean he disappeared?" The Warrior Princess asks the runner. "By the One True God, you say they handed Roark a pink crystal and he disappeared in a flash of light?"

"Yes, Your Royal Highness? The runner lowers his head in respect. "I did not see it for myself, but they told me it looked like the same flash of light the creatures themselves disappeared in."

"He's gone? And they are still here?"

"Yes, Your Highness," the young man's voice wavers like a *flowsal* leaf. The Warrior Princess is so distraught she is not mindful she has levitated above the floor. The boy bows his head even lower trembling before her.

"Run like the wind, tell them not to touch anything!"

With clasped hands he crouches before her. "I don't think it is something to worry about. They are terrified of the creatures."

"They'd better not let them escape." Jaxyl grabs her sword and races down the hall gliding upon the air beneath her feet as if slipping on the fine oil made from the wings of the *petral tong*. There are three staircases between her and the cell where the creatures are kept. But she arrives before the runner has a chance to blink much less deliver her directions. In her haste to arrive, it feels like she has sucked the air out of the room and the guards, still dumbstruck by the peculiar disappearance of Prince Roark, are pointing their weapons defensively at the two odd creatures who appear ill at ease with their newfound predicament. Bird makes an uneasy chirping noise as Jaxyl approaches. Testor bends down as if to reach for the crystal, but before he can, Jaxyl blocks his movement with her sword, careful not to touch him, or the stone.

"I think not you *sorpontine*! Now return Prince Roark or I shall torture you within an inch of your life." Bird begins to chirp uncontrollably louder, his arms tremble and Testor shrinks back childlike and remorseful. Jaxyl takes her sword and beats it loudly against her shield. Sparks fly and the two strangers slink back even further away from her.

"Pick that thing up and put it over there away from us," she commands. But it is like talking to a fencepost. There is no recognition in their beady little eyes. She whips around toward the guards. "How long have they been here? And we have made no progress with communicating with them?" Their hapless shrugs make her even more frustrated.

"Prince Roark spent many hours with them, more than anyone, but even he was frustrated by how little progress we have made in understanding them," one guard says.

"Where could they possibly have transported him?" A rare combustion of panic rips at Jaxyl's chest as she realizes for once she has no solutions. An internal struggle within her mind rages. *I must seek out the Matong, but that useless orb usually has more questions than answers.* She clears her throat and is startled to hear Galen's voice as she and Grandmother Queen Aadya make their way down the hall.

"We came as soon as we heard," Galen says softly. Jaxyl shakes her head like someone offering condolences at a funeral.

"He was the one who knew the most about them. I'm afraid we might have lost him permanently." She turns to the two creatures still slinking back in the shadows of the room. "I haven't the faintest idea what to do."

"We must go to the Matong immediately," says Queen Aadya. "We must get my son back. The longer he is missing the less likely we are to get him back. Has anyone gotten word to Ali?" She says absently.

As the three of them make their way to the Matong chamber. There are two believers and one skeptic, who has more confidence in her abilities than the Matong, but once they bond, Jaxyl is slightly more optimistic.

THERE IS ONLY ONE WHO HAS THE POWER TO TOUCH THE CRYSTAL. THIS IS GALEN THE HEALER. SHE CAN RESIST THE PULL OF THE STONE.

The three of them waste no time returning to the cell. Jaxyl yields her powerful shield and sword to protect her as her Aunt Galen the Healer, kneels to grasp the stone. As she does a pink haze surrounds her and she appears to be struggling with a force they cannot see. It is all her mother, Queen Aadya, can do to not reach for her, but Queen Aadya's faith in the Matong is strong and she does not stray from its warning.

When Galen is released from the stone, she falls back on her heels, looking startled and apprehensive. Slowly she returns to the physical space surrounding her as if awakening from a vivid dream.

60-It's Another World

"Are you all right?" Aadya rushes to her daughter's bent-over body to help her up. The two alien creatures shuffle in the background and Jaxyl brandishes her sword at them.

Galen looks completely drained, but she manages to stand. "It is another world they are in; he has been taken, but he is unharmed. I saw him conversing with his captors."

"Who? Who are the ones who have taken him?" Jaxyl demands. Galen turns to her with a face slack of any emotion. It is unnerving to Jaxyl, who has never seen her so devoid of her healing grace.

"They are on a floating ship, maybe inside the Immense. It is much different than our world, The beings talking to Roark are more like us than the creatures we have caught. They have snatched him to study and communicate with him. I don't think he will be harmed." She looks directly at her mother and her niece. "But I don't know if they plan to return him. They seemed to understand I was watching them and I have the power to resist being captured."

Aadya uncharacteristically wrings her hands, wondering if she will ever see her son again. "We must get word to the queen."

"Yes, but right now I want both of you to leave for your safety." Jaxyl turns to the guards. "Post more sentries and you are sworn to secrecy. Do you understand? And do not touch that *flowkin* stone!"

Queen Ali wastes no time returning to Katara and announces she is finished with her Matong-imposed asylum. "I'm done hiding," she tells her husband who has been the joyful recipient of her presence on the ledge these many rotations. "The Targa storm was not nearly as troublesome as the Matong has led us to believe, but these strangers in our midst and losing Roark, now that has been a nightmare!"

When Roark has still not returned after the moon cycle has completed and begins anew, the Royal family is irreconcilable. "Send someone to touch the stone Alatoi half jokes one day at a council meeting. Now she has broken it off with Tildyn, she has been invited back into the council. No one trusted her during her time of regression. Queen Ali had to bribe her with a title of her own and a modest fortune, so she would not marry Tildyn, an Omi Prince who could never be trusted.

Jaxyl perks up at the queen's suggestion. "The key here is how we shall ask for volunteers. We have failed to keep Roark's disappearance a secret anyway. If someone was willing to take the journey of the pink crystal, perhaps they might return or help release Roark."

"What if we made our little captives return?" Prince Bonder suggests.

"But they've been able to touch the stone at any time, why would they do so now?" Alatoi asks.

"They were coming and going before the stone appeared if you recall," Jaxyl says. "It wasn't until we put up the Targa cloth, that they remained."

"There's something to be said for allowing them to return," Ahshen speaks up. "I think if we let it be known to them that's our desire. I think we could fill them up with sugar, take down the Targa cloth, which seems to have some detrimental effect on them, and assure them they could leave. They would do it."

"What if they disappear and we never hear from Roark again? They are the only leverage we now hold." Queen Ali argues in a rare public display of discordance with her husband.

"So, we let one of our own touch the stone? Who would do such a thing?"

"I'd do it in a heartbeat," Jaxyl says, pushing out her chest, her shoulders erect in a heroic gesture.

"NO!" Queen Ali's resounding voice echoes throughout the room. "You are our most valuable warrior. It is out of the question. We ask for volunteers. We have many brave warriors in our midst."

Ahshen folds his arms. "We put the word out and see who shows up to play."

"It's settled we will select our hero through a series of challenges, both physical and mental. By competing for the honor and reward of finding Prince Roark, we will select the most qualified candidates," Queen Ali proclaims.

"Hold on I have a better plan," the Warrior Princess protests. "I already know who the elite-class warriors are. I propose I will lead a team and we will touch the stone together and see where it takes us. We have no idea what we will run into and there will be strength in numbers."

Queen Ali stares at her daughter and understands the value of her plan. A voice from the recent past echoes in her head. It is the voice of the Matong. YOU MUST LET GO OF THE PRINCESS JAXYL COMPLETELY AND LET HER DO WHAT SHE WAS BORN FOR. IT IS HER DESTINY.

"Oh *flum!*" she mutters softly to herself.

61- Andival, Conto, Forciful, Drose

The Council's plan worked. The next morning when the five warriors return to the cell to touch the stone prepared to travel to another world, the two alien creatures are gone. The prison guards are embarrassed but have no recollection of their disappearance.

"We did as instructed, we took down the cloth. I think they somehow stunned us. One minute they were standing over there in the shadows, the next minute they were gone. It was the middle of the night, so we didn't see any need to awaken anyone. We knew you'd be here early for your departure, and the stone is still here," one of them explains.

Jaxyl enters the stale cell not able to smell the strange creatures anymore. As she does so the large crystal begins to pulsate with light. One of the crew, Jayder Lawster, laughs. "It's calling to us mates!"

It is then Queen Ali and Ahshen show up. "We wanted to come say goodbye," Queen Ali's voice drops off, but everyone in the room recognizes what a difficult time this must be for her.

"We will be back my Queen." The formal response is Jaxyl's way of distancing herself from her mother and carrying on with propriety. Queen Ali hugs her anyway and she and Ahshen look directly into the eyes of each warrior giving them the honored fist to the chest and a slight bow of the head.

"I have consulted the Matong, and your protection has been guaranteed," Queen Ali lies. Jaxyl, knowing the Matong rarely promises anything, sucks in her breath.

"Warriors ready? Armed and fed?" Jaxyl asks. They each nod and circle the stone still pulsing with light. "On my count," she kneels, and the others follow. "*Andival, conto, forciful, drose!*"

In one swirling flash of light, the five warriors vanish. A sour taste erupts in Ali's mouth, but she doesn't flinch. *Will I ever see her again, my beautiful and amazing daughter?* Without projecting her thoughts to Ahshen, he realizes by the rare uncertainty in her face, she is terrified, and she may have let her daughter go on a fool's errand. He pulls her close and squeezes. The gesture is comforting but doesn't stop the dry knot in Ali's throat from gagging her.

"I can't…" the words won't come, Ali shrugs, but lifting her shoulders and straightening her spine as if raising a flag to a stiff breeze, her royal highness shrugs off her personal feelings for the good of her people. Jaxyl's legendary skill as a warrior and leader outweighs any personal favor she might have for her own daughter.

Without prisoners to guard, the staff look around awkwardly waiting to be dismissed. "Would you like to wait a while to see if they return," her husband asks.

"Yes, a little while, though this will likely take some time." There are no chairs in the room or hallway of the cell. The only seat is a thin board hanging from the wall. "I want guards posted non-stop until they return. No one is to touch the stone. It should remain where it is, and the cell shall stay locked for precaution in case any other creatures use it to return here."

"Yes, Your Highness," the guard says.

They wait in uncomfortable silence until finally Ahshen looks at Queen Ali. WE NEED TO GO MY LOVE. THE GUARD DETAIL WILL INFORM US IF ANYTHING CHANGES. Resignedly Queen Ali turns to leave.

Book III

The Talvoc

62-First Contact

"Watch out!" Jaxyl ducks and swings. Sparks fly from her shield as large whizzing bolts of light attack her and her party. They find themselves in a large room with no cover to hide in. Her four compatriots quickly place themselves between her and the array of projectiles barraging them. She glances behind to ensure they won't be attacked from the rear. "Let's retreat to the wall until we can get our bearings," she commands.

An observer would concur this is a prudent idea, but the warriors' every instinct tells them to advance.

The team, made up of the most elite warriors, gently eases into a semi-circle around their leader, backing as they go, while the onslaught of fiery ordinance dances around them. Suddenly Jaxyl receives an inspirational thought.

HALT WE COME IN PEACE! Her words, mind-projected rather than spoken, elicit an immediate response. The onslaught stops abruptly, but the warriors do not relax and let their shields down. The unexpected silence infiltrates their senses like the absorption of sound in a cavernous space, but this room is bright as if natural starlight illuminates it. Almost to the edge of the room Jaxyl peers behind her, where giant windows expose the heavens. WE MEAN NO HARM. WE ARE HERE TO RECOVER OUR MAN ROARK. WHAT HAVE YOU DONE WITH HIM?

"Your Highness, are you in contact with Roark's captors?" One of her team shouts. Jaxyl nods but does not respond verbally. Her instincts are on high alert, and she wants no distractions.

At first, there is no response then a thunderous reply fills the silence like flood waters. WE ARE THE TALVOC WE HAVE YOUR PRINCE ROARK.

"Where is he?" she says aloud mostly for the benefit of her crew.

"By the One True God, it is good to see you." Jaxyl jerks around to see her uncle walking through a filmy opaque section of the wall in the vast room. She takes a deep breath and approaches him. The others stand their ground ready for anything.

"Are you okay?"

"Yes, it's been both enlightening and exhausting. But for the most part, these people are just curious. I've learned a lot."

A sudden panic, like cold water poured on a hot stone, unleashes inside of Jaxyl as she reminds herself there has never been a viable plan for returning to Merth.

"Why haven't they allowed you to return? And where are they?" she says looking around warily.

"Don't worry, they are watching us. They are consummate observers."

"Everyone has been worried sick about you."

"I'm sure, it took a great deal of time before we could even communicate although they have many linguists on board. They've been good to me. I wanted to get word to Merth, but I became so absorbed in what I was doing."

YOU SHOULD HAVE TOLD US YOU WERE SAFE. NOW WE HAVE RISKED OUR LIVES TO BE HERE. AND I'M WONDERING IF WE WILL BE ALLOWED TO RETURN.

"Oh certainly, Jaxyl. No worries the Talvoc are a good people."

HAVE THEY CAPTURED YOUR MIND? YOU ARE NOT MAKING ANY SENSE.

"You'll see," he assures her.

"Will I?" She looks around. "Where are they any-way?"

"Welcome," a strange voice exuding strength echoes behind her. Jaxyl whips around again surprised to be caught off guard in this way. "We thought we would give you a minute to become reacquainted with each other."

The figure, taller and larger than Merthians, seems non-threatening despite his towering stature. "I am Othniel, captain of this ship. We are on an exploratory mission. We come from Ulthea." Othniel points, and an image appears before her, of stars in the sky Jaxyl is un-familiar with so it is of no use. Eager to get out of there in one piece, Jaxyl begins to survey the landscape of their location. She has no information yet about how they will return to Merth's surface.

"Thank you, Othniel for this enlightening experi-ence, but I must return Roark to his people." She decides to omit the fact he is a high-ranking official of impor-tance on Merth even though it is insulting to him not to precede his name with his title. "We must return imme-diately," she says with authority.

"Really won't you let us welcome you with a feast of your favorite foods? Thanks to Prince Roark here, we know how to prepare your nourishment, although it is much different from ours."

SO, HE KNOWS YOU ARE A PRINCE?

I HAVE SHARED MUCH WITH THEM. I TRUST THEM.

"If we truly are your guests, why did you fire upon us when we first arrived?"

"Were you not armed?"

"Yes of course. We didn't know what to expect."

"Were you using stealth?"

"I grow tired of this. Answer my question," Jaxyl demands.

"We met you with our stun array only because you were armed. It's standard procedure. Please don't take it personally. Our stun array does not cause permanent bodily harm."

WHAT A CROCK OF *SHWIZA* Jaxyl projects to Roark looking at him with disdain.

"Warrior Princess, please understand I can hear your thoughts when you project them."

"Okay as a show of faith, return us now, all of us. If you truly are our friends, we can return under better circumstances. The people are worried about our Prince Roark. And what about those creatures you sent to steal from us, and they even took a baby!"

"We owe you a huge apology for the unfortunate glitch." The tall captain shifts his gaze and gathers his thoughts obviously chagrined. "Those are first generational *flibions*. We use them to scout because they are partially biological and can be self-sufficient. Regrettably, they reacted adversely to your atmosphere and became somewhat rogue. Our timing was further complicated by the trash storm. We didn't detect it until after they were deployed. I greatly apologize for the thefts, especially the *litzle*. It was a terrible introduction to our good intentions."

"You mean the baby? Someone's child?" she says scornfully. Othniel sighs, "Again, I so regret we got off to a bad start."

"And what about the Targa Storms are you responsible for those too?

"Oh no, they are caused by the tear in your atmosphere which you call the Immense. It is an unusual rip, and this exacerbates the severity of a trash storm. A ship probably crashed or met with disaster near enough to cause a concentration of debris. When galactic trash gets drawn into your gravitational pull, you have these storms or we call them dumps, which unleash the materials onto your planet, and most of it gets burned up. Only the strongest materials make it to the surface of Merth, and they have proven beneficial to you in the long run according to my new friend, Prince Roark." Othniel claps Roark on the shoulder in a friendly gesture.

The information so readily shared puts Jaxyl somewhat at ease. "But I don't want to make the same mistake in keeping you too long. Our time flows differently here than on your planet. So, I want to make sure you return quickly, and we don't worry your queen."

Othniel nods his head, and an aide brings forth another large pink crystal and sets it on the floor. He carries with him a pair of glistening yellow gloves with strange markings on them.

"The gloves are how you handle the traveling stone," he explains. "Use them to touch the stone once you are on Merth. We have programmed it for travel back and forth between Merth and our ship." Othniel points toward the stone. "You may leave at any time."

Jaxyl still holding her sword at a defensive angle, nods to Roark. "You first."

With resignation, Roark steps closer. "You don't have to go one at a time. You can all go together if you like," Othniel tells them.

"Then we will." Jaxyl nods and the whole crew huddles in. "Everyone place your toe on the stone at the same time. On my count, *andival, conto, forciful, drose!*"

63-Roark's Return

"Tell me everything!" Queen Ali embraces her brother who still looks a little ragged from his ordeal. They have gathered in an antechamber on the first floor of Katara. In addition to the rescue party, other high-ranking members of the family are there, including Galen the Healer, Princes Bonder and Parsa, and of course Ahshen. Roark has already put on the sui generis gloves and carried the 'traveling stone' to a locked closet nearby.

"Again, I am sorry I was unable to get word to you I was unharmed. I kept telling them this was a priority, but apparently the time frame for me was much different than for you. I felt like it was a couple of busy star rotations, but they were so curious, and they shared so much information with me. They sent me with this," he says holding out a small tablet to his sister. "I'm not sure what's in it, but I think it is an invitation for us to return to the ship and get to know them better."

"And why can't we see their ship?" Queen Ali questions her brother.

"The Immense is completely dense and black. There is no light there as we have always suspected. And they are very far away. We couldn't fly one of our aeroships there."

"From what they have told me so far, they have traveled from a great distance. I shared with them the mystery of how Ahshen came to be here on our planet, and they seemed to have an understanding of how this could happen although I don't understand it myself. They called it cosmic transference."

"Great!" Ahshen speaks up. "I have never understood the miracle of my presence here, but I'm grateful," he flashes his wife a smile meant only for her. "But it's *flowkin* crazy." Queen Ali gives him a condescending smile. I DO WISH YOU WOULDN'T SWEAR BEFORE ALL THESE PEOPLE. He just looks at her and grins. Language on Fantu was much more casual than on Merth and he had never really gotten used to holding his tongue as much as she would like.

"They are quite a spiritual people." Roark defends the Talvoc. "Unlike our culture where only our family has contact with the Matong, they each meditate with their higher power, they call *Divonia* who guides them on their individual paths."

Queen Ali taps the missive in her hand absently and finally decides to take a look at it. It has strange lettering on it, but when she taps it, the written language of Merth surfaces through a pearly backdrop. It reads:

We the Talvoc people come to you in peace and gratitude. We respectfully request your presence for a welcoming feast at your earliest convenience. Please speak into this parcel for your response and time of attendance.

Queen Ali's lips draw tight across her face. She passes the tablet to Roark. "Do you think they are listening to us?"

"Let me see it. No need to take chances," He takes the screen and scrutinizes it but can't tell if anything is awry.

"They do have a view of dominion in their culture. We should assume they are."

"Perhaps it would be safer to invite them here. They might try to hold us hostage again," Prince Parsa says.

Jaxyl shakes her head. "I don't think they will, they have given us a 'traveling stone' of our own ostensibly for us to come and go. Why don't we send a warrior team back and forth a few times before we allow heads of state? Get a feel for their intentions. For what we know they gained mind control over Roark while he was there. He said time was at a separate level for him."

"I'm not suspicious of them, but I like your ideas Jaxyl. We need to build trust with them and not rush into a compromising situation. They are far more advanced than us," Prince Bonder says.

"This is a sound plan," Queen Ali agrees, and it is decided Jaxyl will take the same team and a few other specialized scholars, as well as Roark.

"I'd like Faynyl to go, but she won't because of the children, but maybe in the future," Roark mumbles mostly to himself.

"No, it is too dangerous," Faynyl wails when Roark finally gets home to his family. "You are not going back. I thought I'd never see you again! And you are already planning to return? What about your children? What of me? Don't you care about us anymore?" Never good at smoothing things over with Faynyl, Roark looks at her helplessly.

"I'll delay the return for another star rotation if that will make you happy. You are right I've been missing for a much longer time than I realized. I will send word to Jaxyl and the Queen about the delay."

"One measly rotation? You've got to be kidding me?"

"You don't understand how important this is," he says to his wife through gritted teeth. "You once were a scientist; you should be understanding of my position."

Faynyl straightens herself, "Yes, but we are parents now."

Roark looks at her helplessly. "Of course, we are but we don't know how long the Talvoc will stay here. We must learn everything we can from them. Why don't you get someone to care for the children and come with me?"

"And leave our children completely without parents? I think not. What the *flum* has happened to you? Have you lost your mind? Did they wash your soul from your body?"

Roark braves her wrath and reaches for her arm. "Faynyl, you don't understand. Their technology is so advanced; they have methods for creating instant pictures and machines that do drudgery work. You would be astounded by their capabilities."

"No, leave now. I don't want you here in the house, you have forsaken us."

"I shall not! We will have Ahshen fly us to the Ledge and have some time together as a family. We must not let this destroy us."

Faynyl's shoulders drop, "Two rotations, I want two rotations of your undivided attention."

64-Hard in Pursuit

"That's fine Roark, take the time you need but, I'm taking a crew up there tomorrow," Jaxyl tells her uncle.

"Have you cleared it with your mother?"

Jaxyl gives him an annoyed look. "Don't call her that, it's degrading."

The smirk grows on Roark's face when he sees he has hit a nerve with his proud niece. "To you or her?"

Jaxyl glowers at him for his snippy remark. "She may be your sister, but you really should always refer to her as the queen, especially when dealing with me."

"Oh, I do in public, I'm harassing you, Warrior Princess. You know that's what they call you don't you?"

Jaxyl rolls her eyes at her irritating uncle but is proud of this unofficial sobriquet. She wants to say something spiteful back to him but decides it's not worth it. "Which of your scientists should I take with me?"

Roark shrugs, "Take all of them. I will follow in a few rotations. I must give Faynyl some family time or she might leave me and take my kids with her. Or so she threatens."

They walk outside together. There is a strong wind blowing, which is unusual for Merth. "Ah, it's going to be a *bitchyl* to keep the aeroplane from pitching. Faynyl is not going to like the ride. But she'll be happy once we get to the ledge."

"Before you go, please instruct your guys on what to look for. Any words of advice?"

At first, Roark seems blank about her question, but does answer. "Yes, the Talvoc will be truthful with you, but unless you ask them specific questions, like how long you have been away from Merth, they will immerse you in their world making you easily distracted. Take Malteu's timepiece; it should not get scrambled by their optics." Roark's attention is drawn inward as he continues to contemplate her question. "Get my team to ask incessant questions about this 'cosmic transference'. It's way over my head, but maybe my team can decipher it and come to an understanding if they ask enough questions."

To quiet her mind from the anticipation of tomorrow's visit to the Talvoc ship, the Warrior Princess goes to the stables to take an evening ride. Her horse, Flodynhelm, was presented to her with great fanfare a few years ago, by her father and mother. The majestic stallion is a descendant of her grandfather's legendary steed Brodynhelm. The pale light of 'Asunder', those few nights before the two moons wane completely, has always held a fascination for her, and she wants to let off a little steam. When she arrives, she is met by a handsome, but unfamiliar grom, who leads the impatient horse to her. Jaxyl is captivated. "I've never seen you around here. Why are you handling my horse?"

The strapping stranger, whose dark hair falls to his shoulders, suddenly looks caught off guard. "Forgive me Princess Jaxyl, I was told by a friend you might want someone to ride with you."

Despite her immediate attraction, Jaxyl is suspect. "Who put you up to this? You are not supposed to approach a royal like this."

"It's okay, I should have introduced you first," Pulo Twenton approaches from the barn with another horse and hands the lead to the mysterious man. Pulo grins good-naturedly at Jaxyl whom he has known since childhood. "I can ride escort, if you'd like, staying my distance of course."

Jaxyl continues to look perplexed and finally, the stranger looks at her and introduces himself as Clouton Flaxst. "Forgive my friend's impertinence, please, Pulo suggested you might enjoy companionship. I didn't mean to offend." His piercing eyes gleam with tinges of gold and she is pulled in by his muscular build and broad shoulders.

"No, Pulo knows me too well, I'm afraid, I have a big day tomorrow and he is familiar with my ways." She looks at Pulo and scolds him. "Being that Clouton here is a stranger to me and is not a warrior from our ranks, you certainly should ride escort, but stay your distance, your friend and I might find some amusement along the way." She mounts Flodynhelm and pulls off her leather shirt with only a minimum of clothing left on her chest, she says, to Clouton, "It's a warm evening feel free to take off your shirt and let the breeze cool your skin."

Clouton gives her a knowing smile and a slight nod. When his shirt comes off Jaxyl has one destination in mind, and she rides hard toward it with Clouton firmly in pursuit.

65-Swoosh

The pink crystal transport stone has been elevated to a chest-high table for convenience when the team gathers to travel to the Talvoc ship. A special chamber has been built for the stone to keep it safe from chance contact. Jaxyl has requested they use the tablet to let the Talvoc know they are coming, still, there isn't a member of the crew who doesn't hold a bit of reticence in their heroes' hearts. She gives them a gallant grin to inspire them. "On my count, *andival, conto, forciful, drose!*"

The five men and two women disappear with a vociferous swooshing noise filling the small transport room; this being somewhat of a surprise as a new sound possibly caused by the confined space versus the open cell where they had transported before. Jaxyl and another warrior are the only two in the group who are not scientists. There is no one to witness the early morning exit. They have chosen this privacy for their departure.

"Stand ready," Jaxyl commands once their bodies reformulate on the ship. They are greeted by Othniel, his first mate, Oscara, and Gemfolden, the ship's commanding security officer. The Talvoc in general are substantially taller than Merthians, a fact which frustrates Jaxyl who is used to being the most physically commanding person in the room.

It is their first exposure to Oscara and Gemfolden and it is Oscara with her visibly fluctuating aura that startles them. Some might describe her as beautiful. Others might be fascinated by the clarity that emanates from her despite her softly yielding aura. "It is as if her soul is not tightly contained in her body," Jaxyl would describe to her father later when they returned to Merth. Gemfolden has a more straightforward appearance with a dense body and fierce black eyes he flashes commandingly toward them. His gruffness and solicitude are everything you would expect in a security officer.

"We invite you to come this way," Gemfolden motions to an anteroom nearby. When they are seated refreshments are offered. "The first thing we need to address with you for your understanding is the time discrepancy experienced by your comrade Prince Roark."

"Yes, why did this happen? It is not acceptable if you are playing mind games with us. We insist you stay in truth with us." Jaxyl taps her fingers on the table authoritatively.

Othniel smiles, "This was not our doing only a naturally occurring event due to the time travel involved caused by the distance of our ship from your planet Merth."

"If this is truly the case, we must address it. Do you have a quantification of this anomaly?" Gingeryl Crossana, one of the scientists, asks.

"Of course." What I suggest is in this brief meeting, we discover your areas of expertise, and we peel off separately to immerse you in individual studies." Othniel looks up and peers at a nearby screen. "In what feels like a short time here, say a simple conversation, is a half-rotation of your home planet. We have programmed a device for you to codify and translate the difference. You may keep these communication devices to continue working with us after your departure."

Oscara nods and the devices are brought out. "These tools are easy to use," she says, "but I am going to have an instructor demonstrate the fundamentals." Jaxyl holds the device in her hand as the instructor walks them through the basics.

"The device shows you the relative time here and on Merth. You can also communicate with them. See look here," their instructor points to the screen on the hand-held device. Once the group looks comfortable with their communicators, Othniel offers to take them on a tour of the ship.

"We'll break off into smaller groups afterward, please this way." A door opens automatically before them, and they enter a small rectangular room that silently begins to move horizontally catching everyone slightly off guard as seen by their puzzled expressions.

"Our ship, the Ursula Weir runs on harmonics," Othniel explains. "Much of what we show you, well, I won't go into great detail about everything, but ask questions and this will give us a platform for connecting with you on an individual basis."

The group remains cautiously silent, but one of the Merthian scientists, Osaval Packard, begins to take visual notes with his communicator. He is one of the younger scientists and is known for his quick learning skills. "What do you call this object?" He waves his handheld instrument at the captain, but it is Oscara who grins and replies.

"We call them vims. But my first finger here holds the same properties your vim does. We are assigned this alteration as children when we prove responsible enough to handle it. We have a ceremony when we achieve this level of competence."

She demonstrates by pointing at a nearby wall and projecting an image of a tiny animal onto a transparent screen. "That is a picture of my pet *cafter*. She is much like one of your *huny botes*."

There is laughter and someone comments. "We don't have them as pets, they spit."

"Really?" Oscara looks surprised, "My Cotilla is way too civilized to spit."

"So how is it you can communicate with us?" Osaval asks abruptly changing the subject.

"We adapted to your language when we first met your Prince Roark. We are an exploratory ship. This is an important aspect of what we do. We have visited many planets before Merth. We use a combination of technology and a group of experienced translators to develop our language skills rapidly. We are near the communications center so we can show you that next. If you wouldn't mind stepping back into the transport tube, we'll continue."

66-Harmonics

The room where they stop next is huge, and there are many terminals where a variety of beings are busy at work. Some are huddled together but most are in little booths with their screens before them. The sight of this diverse collection of beings is shocking to the Merthians. Even Osaval is tongue-tied. He leans over and whispers to Gingeryl, "By the One True God, can you believe this?"

Gingeryl is surprised too. She nods her head no. Jaxyl looks to Othniel and projects her thoughts I HAVE NEVER SEEN SOMETHING LIKE THIS. WHERE DO THESE CREATURES COME FROM?

WE TRAVEL ACROSS THE HEAVENS. THESE TRANSLATORS ARE HERE VOLUNTARILY. Seeing the distress on the faces of the Merthians, he looks toward Oscara, "Let's move on to the engine room."

"Okay but first, I think they would benefit from a demonstration," she signals to a stout being wearing a brightly covered head scarf whose arms are a pale pink. "Sharif, can you tell us a joke in *Chabatin*?" Sharif giggles and shakes her head no.

"Please?" Oscara persuades her.

A melody of words spews from Sharif's unusually full lips. "And in Merthian?" Othniel, looking uncomfortable for fear of what the translator might say, scowls at Oscara, but it is okay because the joke is a common one on Merth and the Merthians smile. The humor is lost on Othniel.

"Well," Othniel says, "let's get on down to the engine room. I don't want to keep you too long on the first visit."

They step back into the transport chamber and Jaxyl peers at her vim. They have been away from Merth for over three rotations. "I need to communicate with our people. They have the tablet you gave us. I want to let them realize we are, okay?"

"Surely," Othniel says. "Do you need help with that?"

"No, I think I've got this." But what Jaxyl doesn't know is Roark has taken the tablet to the Ledge with him. And it will be several rotations before Queen Ali becomes aware of their message.

"I'll send word," Roark messages back.

The whisper-quiet transport chamber takes them to the entrance of the engine room where they are greeted by an imposing hum. "Not all ships run on harmonics, but we find this source of energy the most versatile, we can use almost any fuel to create the energy for the frequencies we need to propel a ship of this size. We can burn dirt if we have to." Othniel says with some pride in his voice. "It is the harmonics we create with a minimal amount of fuel, that gives the ship its power and agility."

There are colossal metal arches that span the tall, massive room. "These tensile structures are tuned specifically to create a specific harmonic resonance."

"We have nothing like this. Can you share your technology with us?" Asvar Cantole asks.

"Surely," Othniel pats the scientist's shoulder in a friendly gesture.

As Jaxyl assesses the information, her world becomes especially inconsequential. It is as if by letting in these new experiences and sensations, she has become smaller and less significant. This rare emotion manifests as a sharp pang in her chest.

As the tour continues, the Talvoc begin to identify which Merthians should be escorted where to get the most out of their tour. "We understand this is a lot to absorb," Othniel says to Jaxyl. "I would like to invite you to the ForeSat where you can view for yourself the ship's operations, while Oscara can manage the guides to carry on with individual tours." He looks apologetic. "We don't let just anyone on the ForeSat deck, I think you'll understand why."

67-The ForeSat

It takes quite a while to get from the engine room to the ForeSat. Othniel motions for her to step off the tube and enter. "This is where it happens, this is where we conduct the steerage of our ship." Walking into the ForeSat of the massive ship is like the first gulp of air at birth—raw, gasping, and spectacular. Jaxyl is completely astonished by the serene display before her. A soft blue lighting engulfs her as she gazes upon a myriad of colorful screens and consoles where Talvoc are stationed. "It's rather quiet here now as we have been immobile for quite some time with our mission to your planet. When we are in motion this place is alive with activity. Come let me show you what I'm talking about." But Jaxyl cannot stop staring at the massive window to the skies. Othniel, sensitive to her reaction slows down to let her take it in. "Impressive, isn't it?"

"Yes," she responds, surprised by her own astonishment. Finally, she admits, "I never realized how incredibly huge the sky is." She thinks about the Immense and how it had always puzzled Merthians.

Othniel laughs softly like a father with a child. He wants to tell her Merthians are living in a class Xi-0 tier culture with a class 14 technology level boosted by the Queen's husband's cosmic transference, but he knows this will make her feel like she is the subject of a lab experiment and alienating her is the last thing he wants to do. He is already considering how to convince her to join them and leave Merth behind, but a lot of groundwork will have to be accomplished first.

"Are we located in the Immense now?" She asks. Othniel looks puzzled. "Oh yes," the light comes on in his face. "We understand through our contact with Prince Roark, what you see from Merth, the *Tolquial Resonance*, is what you call the Immense. He says it looks like, from your perspective, a rip in the sky. Yes, that is something we can explain to your scientists, as time goes on. They have enough to absorb at first though. The *Tolquial Resonance* is an anomaly with complex algorithms. We'll get into it later."

She doesn't say much as he tours her around the ForeSat and invites her to sit in the captain's chair. "This area over here is called the helm. It is dedicated to the operation of our speed and direction. We have a whole crew of navigators who determine where we are and where we are going. Over there is the communications sector." Othniel then begins to introduce her to everyone at their station.

While they are polite, they don't engage with her except for one of the navigators whose attraction to her is discernable, and while this is nothing unusual, for the first time she thinks about what it would be like to become one with a Talvoc. *They are so tall.* Othniel's voice returns her thoughts to the room temporarily. "The Fore-Sat, by necessity, is restricted to everyone who doesn't have a level 6 security clearance. There are over 400 crew members on this ship," Othniel explains oblivious to the flash of desire passed between his crew member and the fiery Princess Jaxyl.

The spark of attraction transports Jaxyl to thinking about yesterday and riding Flodynhelm, racing through tall grass naked and bareback with her latest dalliance, Clouton. Suddenly weariness overcomes her, and she finds herself exhausted as if she had been slashing her sword endlessly in battle. *I've had enough of this. I want to be back on Merth soil.*

"Yes, sir. You have been most gracious, but I am overwhelmed, and I'm sure if I am, my team is also. It is probably time for us to return and regroup."

Othniel looks down at her with understanding. The glazed look on her face is telling "Yes, I understand. Let me round your crew up." He lifts his 'vim' finger to his lips and calls Oscara. "How are the others doing? Their leader is ready to go."

"Yes, I'll gather them up," she replies.

68-I Have Led Warriors into Battle

Osaval Packard surprises everyone with footage from their visit. While she had seen him recording, Jaxyl was astonished at how much he captured on his vim. Queen Ali and Ahshen Owanu are stunned by the images and ask to watch several times. Once Roark sees the visuals, he starts planning a return visit to the Ursula Weir, but it will be another rotation before he organizes the next expedition. Jaxyl tells him she is "going to pass on this one," and spends the next couple of rotations in a desultory state. The normal distractions fail her as she becomes further entrenched in her foul mood. She gets so angry she punches her fist through a *solto* board used by warriors to practice their fighting skills.

"I don't know what you are talking about," she quarrels with her mother the queen when it is suggested maybe she should consult with the Matong because of her ill temper. "I'm fine." She says with gritted teeth.

"No, no you are not," the queen tells her. "I'm worried about you."

Finally, after Jaxyl can no longer stand her own company, she enters the chamber and places her hand on the glowing orb. The room has an unusual chill to it, but Jaxyl's long-sleeved, red leather tunic keeps her warm. When the Matong delivers its message to her, however, a pulsing radiant heat overwhelms her. YOU MUST

LOOK TO CHANGE AND ACCEPT THERE ARE MANY THINGS YOU DO NOT COMMAND. YOU ARE A MIGHTY WARRIOR, BUT NOT EVERY WISP NEED SWAY IN YOUR WIND.

BUT THAT'S NOT THE WAY IT IS SUPPOSED TO BE. THEY CALL ME THE WARRIOR PRINCESS BE-CAUSE I AM FEARLESS, I AM THE BEST. MY DESTI-NY IS TO LEAD AND CONQUER.

THIS IS TRUE BUT DON'T BE SHORT SIGHTED.

Suddenly Jaxyl is released from the orb. She cusses inside her head for an extraordinary length of time while facing the massive sphere. Her frustration makes her head throb. Finally, she tries to bond with the Matong again, but there is no pull from the orb, and she sighs heavily lowering her head in defeat. *Flowkin pistoid!*

Moping around does not improve Jaxyl's attitude but when she learns the Queen and Ahshen want to visit the Ursula Weir she insists on leading the mission. "We must have more traversing stones," she warns Roark, "and we must expand our security measures. Perhaps we should take Ahshen there first and the queen can go another time."

"That's a great idea. In fact, why don't we host the Tal-voc here before we take her up there? I trust them, but I want to proceed cautiously."

"Agreed, it's a good plan, but you will have to be there when I tell my mother. She is not going to like it."

"Don't worry, I will back you up."

"That is absurd!" Queen Ali shouts. "I will not be treated like some *souble* weakling who must be shielded from harm's way. I have led warriors into battle."

"Yes, and you were captured, remember?" Only Jaxyl would have the *catonas* to say this to the queen making Roark have to subdue his grin.

"Let's do this my way," Jaxyl says firmly. The queen glares at her daughter in a most perfunctory way but her shoulders slump subtly as if to resign herself to her daughter's decision.

"You could consult the Matong, but you know I'm right." As she says this, she regrets it. *The Matong probably would tell her it would be fine.* "Really Mother, my instincts tell me to proceed with caution, the Talvoc are much more advanced than us, if they did capture any of us, we would not have recourse. No one is going to judge you for prudently proceeding. Ahshen needs to go, he is our technology expert. He has a greater understanding of these things than any other Merthian."

"I suppose you are right. He will interpret his findings for me anyway."

69-Transformation

Jaxyl accompanies her father Ahshen for his entire excursion aboard the Ursula Weir and learns more about the Talvoc and their advanced technology, because of his astute questions, than she did on her first visit. Roark had warned her they operated this way. His words echoed in her mind. 'The Talvoc will be truthful with you, but unless you ask them specific questions, they don't volunteer the information.'

When they stop for a meal, Jaxyl takes the opportunity to quiz Othniel on this issue. He smiles warmly and pushes his tall drink glass around a little, not wanting to offend her in any way. "This is a good question, we have found on our many exploratory missions, it is best not to present information before our guests are ready for it. By waiting for their inquiry, this signals exactly where they are with knowledge absorption, as we call it. Does that make any sense?"

Jaxyl's doubts are tempered by his explanation which allows her to understand and trust Othniel and his crew a little more. "I suppose," she acquiesces.

Jaxyl looks toward her father, Ahshen, who meets her gaze. I TRUST THEM. He shares with her.

It is on this visit Roark informs Jaxyl and Ahshen he is going to 'take a berth' on the ship temporarily so, "I can be immersed in my education here." Jaxyl doesn't have much opinion on the matter.

"If Queen Ali is okay with it, and I'm sure she will be, we will leave you here when we depart."

"Yes, Gingeryl would also like to stay and assist me with recording our sessions. She is a whiz with her vim," he adds. It is hard not to grin when he says this, Roark is known for his roving eye. There was gossip, but Jaxyl was relatively sure he had always been a faithful husband to Faynyl. She shrugs as if to say, don't bore me with your details.

When they get to the ForeSat, Othniel offers to take them for a short ride. "I want you to get a feel for what it is like when we travel, how fast we can go." The pride in his ship and crew can be perceived in his voice. Still, Jaxyl is wary.

"We'd love that," Ahshen beams. "What do you have in mind?" Othniel ushers Ahshen to the First Officer's chair. "You sit here," he tells Ahshen. "And you sit in my chair," he tells Jaxyl. "Don't worry; it will be handled for you, but I want you to enjoy the' rush of the crush,'" he says. He nods his head to signal the pre-planned flight. "Place your hands on the apex of the armrest, right here," he shows them. The shape of the chair encourages them to lean slightly back. "Yes, you should let your body fit into the chair until you are comfortable," he encourages them. "And don't be surprised by anything, this is routine and safe."

Jaxyl and her father exchange glances. Ahshen shoots her a big grin. He has been grinning the whole time they have been on the ship. Suddenly she feels as if her body has splintered into a thousand little pieces. This strange feeling only lasts for a few seconds, but the tingling sensation accompanying it stays with her for considerably longer.

The sky before her appears to move, although imperceptibly. Jaxyl finds the sensations mesmerizing. I COULD GET USED TO THIS. She shares with her father.

"Nice, right? We will travel a distance of 309 OTZs, then shoot back to where we came from for optimal transporting to Merth and back."

"I hardly feel like we are moving now," Ahshen observes.

"Oh yes we are moving," Othniel flips up a screen with his finger to show them the path of their flight. It doesn't mean much to either Jaxyl or her father who, for the first time since they have transported aboard, have no questions. Jaxyl is transformed by the star's hypnotic appearance and the foul mood that has followed her since her first visit to the ship erodes in soft waves of acceptance.

70-A Not So Idle Threat

As they ready to depart, Othniel pulls Jaxyl aside and invites her to also spend a more extended time with them. She studies him to read him with her kinetic sight, but there is still no clear path to his thoughts. Unless they project their thoughts, all she can read from any of the Talvoc is sort of a dim buzz as if they are blocking their minds although she can project her thoughts to them.

She nods her head negatively, stalling for the words. She wants to get back to Merth, she wants to ride Flodynhelm, and mostly she wants to get back to Clouton, her latest dalliance. She moves through men like water, a fact that is beginning to weigh on her. *It's just my nature* she often justifies, until the next flare of lust when a man turns his head her way, his muscled shoulders diverting her rational thoughts until she can have him, never allowing herself to stay with anyone enough time, to form a cerebral connection like the other women in her family enjoy. Because Clouton is somewhat of a mystery man, he is not one of her warriors, she wants more of him. All this goes through her head as she tells Othniel no, she won't be staying this time. WE HAVE MANY MEN HERE WHO WOULD SUIT YOU. He pushes his thoughts into her mind. The shock of realizing he has read her thoughts startles her. She is speechless as she tries to shut down her mind and the invasion of her privacy.

Nearby Ahshen is busy talking to Oscara, for whom he has openly shown a degree of fascination. "Explain to me again," he waves his hand circuitously toward Oscara, "this aura surrounding you. I hope I'm not being rude."

ON MERTH I AM PRACTICALLY A GOD. MY GLORY SURPASSES THAT OF MY MOTHER THE QUEEN! Jaxyl scolds Othniel with her thoughts. Again, he smiles at her with a familiar compassion.

I DID NOT MEAN TO PUSH YOU. PLEASE TELL ME YOU WILL RETURN AND I WOULD LIKE TO MEET WITH YOU ALONE. I HAVE A PROPOSITION FOR YOU.

SURELY YOU DON'T MEAN A SEXUAL INVITATION?

Othniel's expression reveals his chagrin, and he lets out a soft chuckle. "I'm sorry, I think something was lost in the translation." He has difficulty hiding his amusement which pridefully seeps into his face. Jaxyl's imagination briefly explores the idea of a sexual encounter with him. *No, he is too old for me.*

Later when Jaxyl has returned to Merth and the comfort of her bed, she quizzes Clouton. "Why have our paths not crossed before this?" She sits up and disturbs his position with his head in her lap. He kisses her hand and smiles an indulgent satisfied smile. Instead of answering her, Clouton turns over and begins kissing her sporadically across her body.

"I'm too easily distracted, you really must explain your background and why you are not a warrior, you are more fit than most of them," she says allowing him to continue with his exploits.

He grins and pauses. "I'm an Omi spy of course."

She playfully puts her knee between him and his advances. "That's not even funny."

Clouton does not hesitate, realizing Jaxyl could flatten him in an instant, to turn her playful rejection into a heated game of pursuit and resist.

"Get out!" She says playfully to him once they are done. "You may not stay the night. In fact, you may not see me again until I have found out who you are." Clouton grins and backs up holding his clothing to his chest.

"Okay, but the help will talk if I walk out of here without my clothes on." Jaxyl throws a pillow at him. "They already talk. Now get out if you won't tell me who you are."

He shrugs, his silky long hair sliding off his broad shoulders. "And take away the mystery?"

And then he does what he has threatened to do, he leaves the room carrying his clothing.

71-A Mystery Unraveled

"He's what?"

"You heard correctly Your Highness. He's one of King Brechnole's grandchildren."

"I don't believe you. He doesn't look like an Omi."

The young aide shrugs, "That's what I was told."

"Get Pulo in here right away to speak with me. Tell him I am in a foul mood, and he should drop whatever he is doing and get here immediately!"

When Pulo Twenton arrives, her mood has not dissipated. "What were you thinking you fool? What possessed you to bring to me an Omi, a grandson of Brechnole? By the One True God you are killing me here."

Pulo is unable to hold back a triumphant grin. "Surely you didn't sleep with him?"

"Are you kidding? That's why you brought him to me."

Pulo shrugs. "Calm down he's not actually Brechnole's blood. He is Prince Tildyn's half-brother's son. His grandmother was married to Brechnole, but he is not of Brechnole's blood. His father was born to a different father before Brechnole married his mother.

"What's the difference? I have slept with the enemy!"

Now Pulo's grin surfaces full-fledged. "I'm certain this is not the first time." There it was the insidious guilt creeping into her mind as of late. "Besides the Omi are technically not our enemy."

"Oh please, we have known each other practically from birth and you've never introduced me to anyone before. What is going on here?"

"Actually, I have, there was Drado and Balfer, and oh yes, I think you were vastly enamored with Quandyl."

She gives him a chagrined look. "Well, that was back when we were adolescents. What is this pay back for something I did when we were kids?"

"You dumped me. They were my friends."

"We were all friends together."

With the memories of his middle years brought into focus, Pulo drifts into melancholy.

"Look I didn't mean anything by it. He was at the stables that day. Call it my little prank. Besides haven't you been enjoying yourself?"

Jaxyl laughs, "too much so. I can't get enough of him."

"Nice." Pulo looks into her eyes. "But we both know it won't last long between you two."

Jaxyl rolls her eyes, "My mother has hinted at marrying me off. But she's a little scared of me, and the Matong has said nothing about my involvements, nor marriage."

Pulo Twenton studies his childhood friend. "You have got to be the most privileged person on this planet." His words were still ringing in her ears like a pleasant melody when she meets with Othniel as requested, later the next rotation.

But first, she sends for Clouton.

"I have found out who you are," challenging him with her defensive body language, hands on hips and slightly spread feet. "No wonder you didn't want to tell me."

Clouton meets her gaze with a subtle smirk. "Now, my Princess, you can see why I kept my secret. I knew you would find out sooner or later anyway." He pulls her close enough she can smell his breath, sweet and salty and pungent as if he has just eaten sausage. At first, she doesn't resist but finally, she pulls away.

"We have to have some ground rules."

"Of course,"

"If you disobey, I'll cut your head off myself."

"I'm sure this is no idle threat." He meets her gaze with steadfast resolve.

"First my privacy must be maintained at all costs. If I hear rumors, you have been loose with your tongue," they both start to laugh. "You understand what I mean, keep your *flowkin* mouth shut." She pauses and draws closer to him staring directly into his eyes. "No other women while you are with me."

He grins. "Now you are just taking the fun out of it."

"And remember," she scowls at him meaningfully, "there are no guarantees how long this will last."

"And?"

"When it is over, no remorse and keep your *flowkin* mouth shut."

"Is that all Princess?" He pulls her closer again taking her arms, strong and hard into his hands, and kisses her with a lurid passion she revels in.

72-Time is of the Essence

"I'm curious as to why you asked for this meeting?" Jaxyl doesn't hesitate to get to the point. She has finally returned to the Ursula Weir as Othniel had requested the last time he saw her. She is escorted to a conference room below the ForeSat known as the Portal. It has the same impressive view as the ForeSat deck but is more private for mission planning.

Once the door is shut, he points to a chair and responds. "Yes, of course. I wanted to inform you we will soon be leaving Merth and I wanted to invite you to join us as we venture on to our next destination."

The idea is startling at first and rests heavily on Jaxyl. "I'm sorry why would I want to leave Merth? My destiny is with my people."

Othniel fidgets nervously and sits down awkwardly facing her while meeting her eyes. "This is why you should go with us." He waves his vim finger at a blank wall and a picture appears on a transparent screen of thousands of giant warriors outfitted in heavy black armor marching across a vast parched expanse, and when they come to some buildings, they crush them with their massive boots. They are that large. "These are the giants of Escobar. They are not so far away, and we want to make sure they don't make it here to this beautiful, mostly peaceful place you know as Merth…as home." He flips his finger again and another screen appears with the picture of a space vessel.

"They travel in threes. They hook together and transform to make a vessel that is both fast and efficiently devastating. They only have one weakness."

"Yes?"

"They were created as a robotic system, no living being resides within and they are somewhat blind. They roam without any sensible strategy. We don't understand who sent them out into the Expanse, but their program is to search and conquer. They do this through a systematic approach and once they have subjugated a society, they plunder it for whatever they find valuable. They show no mercy and are anathema to all living beings. They are easily destroyed, but sometimes, and we don't understand why, when we blast them with our weapons, they multiply, not always, but we seek to understand this phenomenon."

"I don't know how I could possibly be of any assistance if this is true. I need to be with my people to protect them."

Othniel looks deep into her eyes. "I need for you to consult your Matong. The answer lies there, I'm sure of it."

Othniel visibly struggles with how to convey the urgency of the situation. "You have to understand, your people, your technology, the many advancements you have made rather quickly will not be enough. You will be annihilated once the Escobar giants stumble upon Merth."

A dark mood settles on Jaxyl like the enveloping heavy blackness when both moons, Ava and Duna, disappear periodically from the sky. Nothing is appealing about Othniel's proposal.

"We have enjoyed our stay here but are anxious to get back on track with our mission."

Jaxyl's thoughts race. "If this is true, why did you stop here?" Othniel doesn't answer immediately.

"I'm not saying this isn't a huge sacrifice for you and your people, but I need to show you more evidence of how imperative our mission is." With that, he flicks more screens up across the wall with his vim finger. Each one is filled with devastation and destruction. People are screaming, fireballs burst across the sky and forceful booming sounds infect the room with the disturbing chaos.

"Would it be possible to meet with your Queen Ali, to share with her this information?"

Jaxyl's stomach turns, and she feels slightly weak in her legs as if she has ridden Flodynhelm for a long time and has not stopped once to let her feet touch the ground.

Is it possible they came here just for me? She gives Othniel a long and discerning glare. "Why me? Why Merth? Why did you come here?"

"Obviously, there is more to this."

"And?"

"What first alerted us to Merth was your father Ahshen's cosmic transference. These are rare occurrences. But when we got here, I must admit you were the one we knew we were seeking."

"And how is that?"

"You have inherited qualities of *flowzo* essence from both your mother and father. You are of a rare genetic make-up indeed. We believe you may be the key to communicating with the Folotor."

"And who are the Folotor?"

"They may be the only answer to putting an end to the Escobar giants and their destruction. You see with our hundreds of translators on board…you saw them."

"Yes,"

"Not one of them has been able to crack the mystery of communicating with the Folotor. They are a god-like species whose only form is a spirit body."

The topics are intriguing to Jaxyl but leaving Merth, leaving her beautiful world, leaving her horse behind, and most of all leaving the complete freedom, she enjoys every day of her life, feels wrong.

"Will you set up an appointment with Queen Ali and Ahshen Owanu? I need to move forward with this. I wish I had more time to let you acclimate to the idea, but time is of the essence if we are to protect Merth."

73-I Don't Want to Leave Merth

Even last night's exploits with Clouton had not calmed Jaxyl's mind. They had not slept a moment, instead, she pushed him to the edge of physical prudence, challenging him to meet her own physical strength in several acts of dangerous foreplay. *It scared us both, but the deeper we got in the more we both enjoyed it.* She had bruises to show for her flagrant debauchery which she wore like badges of honor. "See here, look what you did to me, she points to several spots on her thigh and one on her breast."

"*Shwiza,* I thought you were going to break my *flowkin* leg." They both grin at each other. "But I've never had it better," he confesses.

She tries to hide the smirk on her face and shoves off the vulnerability she is feeling. "I have a lot on my mind. I thank you for the diversion." She says pulling on a fresh tunic. "I'm going to ride down to the river and take a swim. Don't be here when I get back."

"Wow, really?

She turns to pull the tight tunic over her breasts. "Yes, really."

But before she leaves the castle, Jaxyl decides to bond with the Matong, and in what is one of the strangest encounters she has ever had with the monolithic orb, she discovers it is her destiny to travel with the Talvoc to destroy the terrifying Escobar.

I DON'T WANT TO LEAVE MERTH.

YOU WILL RETURN. The orb tells her. YOU WILL RESTORE THOSE WHO HAVE BEEN CONQUERED. YOUR DESTINY IS TO BE THE VESSEL FOR RE-BIRTH. A thin, moist mist percolates from the orb with a slight hissing noise. Jaxyl falls to the floor and dozes. When she awakens, all she can think about is the night before with Clouton, and her body throbs for more. She has overslept. There is no time left to ride as she must meet with Othniel and her mother and father concerning Othniel's request.

Oscara accompanies Othniel and strangely the meal brought in for the meeting with the Talvoc is spicier than normal. The taste of the *jotal* is sweeter and more pungent but with an extra kick of the *leesal* herb. Jaxyl is so hungry she wants to scarf it down, but royal decorum is ever present in her mind. She nods for the server to bring her more wine and is still completely preoccupied with the performance of Clouton the night before. *We inspire each other.* The thought brings an inappropriate smile to her face as Othniel begins to make his case with the three most powerful people on Merth. Oscara's aura glows more intensely in the dim candlelight of the intimate dining room porch where they are seated. Ahshen is giving her too much personal attention and will pay for it later when he and Queen Ali are alone.

Jaxyl hears the veiled bartering going on, but she hasn't been quite the same since she was swallowed by the mist in the Matong chamber. "Bring me a writing tablet," Jaxyl tells the nearest server, and when he does, she pens a quick note to Clouton, *I was wrong to be dismissive to you this morning, please forgive me and please come to my bed tonight and surprise me with your lust. I want more.*

Jaxyl's body warmth increases to the point she is close to perspiring. *I put in two pleases how very humble of me.* She gives the aide another nod and whispers in his ear to take it to Clouton.

"Are we boring you, my dear Jaxyl?" Her mother's tone is sharp and critical, but Jaxyl is in such a relaxed state of being she merely smiles politely.

"If you think about it, they could have abducted me, but they took the time to show us their ways. I will leave in the morning after I have had a good night's…" She shoves the word out. "sleep." She straightens herself in her chair. "As I understand it, they plan to return me, but by then you may all be dead."

Oscara's aura flares with more intensity and she tips her head down slightly. Othniel squirms in his chair. Ahshen is the only one not seemingly bothered by the awkward moment. "I would go myself, but I belong here by my beloved Ali's side." His comment lightens the atmosphere of the room and Queen Ali gives her husband a rare look of approval despite his flirtatious demeanor with Oscara.

"Now, if you'll excuse me, I have some things to do before my departure." Jaxyl gets up and shoves her chair under the table. The four of them look rather startled but nobody challenges her.

74-One Last Ride

What Jaxyl does with Clouton on her last night on Merth goes beyond anything she has experienced before as if her depravity might subdue her unease. When they have exhausted themselves, she has the servants fill the enormous sunken tub with the finest aromatic herbs which float on the surface like lilies on a pond. Afterward, two massage artisans come and work on their depleted bodies on tables in the open air, soothing their spent muscles with the finest of oils. The birds sing provocatively and the early morning starlight filters through the trees.

The next morning Jaxyl ignores the alerts the ship is about to leave. She ignores the remonstrations from the servants advising her, her mother and father are waiting to go to the Matong Chamber with her in a final blessing, or that the last meal she was supposed to have with the reigning royalty in her honor has been served, eaten, and the table cleared.

"Go fetch my Aunt Galen and bring her here to my chambers. And pack my clothing and armor, for I have not prepared," she tells a trusted servant. Clouton grows quiet, but she doesn't dismiss him, instead, she shuts his presence out of her mind as she looks around her chambers for anything she wouldn't want to leave behind.

When Galen the healer arrives, there is no judgment in her voice for leaving the family expectantly waiting at the dining hall, until they ate and left. She touches Clouton first and as the tingling sensation of her healing touch fills him, he bows his head in reverence to her.

With Jaxyl it is much different, the energy is sharp and bright and Jaxyl is filled with an uncanny sense of energy flowing through her. Galen smiles and wants to counsel Jaxyl, but she holds back and merely hugs her as she leaves, saluting her with the most intimate of gestures by placing one hand on her heart and the other on Jaxyl's.

When Jaxyl goes to meet Othniel and Oscara, who are both there to escort her to the ship, the family is gathered to say goodbye, realizing they may never see her again. She is uncannily quiet and her heart burns for her beloved Flodynhelm. "I'm sure this is an inappropriate request, but I would like to take one last ride on Flodynhelm."

Othniel gives her a fatherly gaze, and sensing her regret, volunteers she might even consider bringing the horse with her. "What? I could do that?"

"The horse would not be the only animal on the vessel, but he would certainly be the largest. It wouldn't be like here where you can ride him in the fresh air, it would be somewhat confining for the horse, but considering we are taking you away from your home…"

Jaxyl wastes no time in signaling an aide to get her magnificent horse. "Bring him saddled." Othniel and Oscara swap confused looks and Oscara murmurs something under her breath.

Galen and her family, Roark and his, her mother and father stare in disbelief as they follow Jaxyl outside and watch as she mounts her horse, spinning around and urging Flodynhelm to make a mad dash away from the castle, leaping over a clumsy *closttlewat* that has wandered into the street. Her father Ahshen chuckles and gives Othniel and Oscara an embarrassed grin. "Let's hope she returns. Do you still want her?"

As shocked as anyone there, Othniel shrugs, "Considering the circumstances, she hasn't had much time to process this. I think it will be okay to wait on her a little more."

Disgusted but patient, because he forces himself to be, Roark tells Faynyl she should take the children home. Finally, the rest of the family dissipates, and it is not until much later Jaxyl shows up ready to go. Othniel, discouraged she is going to ever show up, has delayed the departure of the Ursula Weir because there is much weighing on her joining the expedition, more than he has told her.

"I'm sorry to have delayed you. I had some unfinished business."

Othniel chokes back his frustration. "You understand the concept of discipline, I'm sure. This kind of conduct will not be tolerated once you join our ranks."

Giving him a grin without the smallest hint of humility, Jaxyl nods. "I had to have one last goodbye with my courtesan, certainly you can understand?"

There were many things Othniel wanted to say, to scold, to shout, to let the Warrior Princess recognize how arrogant and selfish she had been holding up the entire mission! But he controls his tongue and wonders how difficult it is going to be to manage this *incorrigible vixen.* Instead, he nods and joins her to transport to the Ursula Weir holding onto the horse's reins as well, his way of preventing her from slipping away.

75-This Ship is Huge

Jaxyl looks around the room on the ship where they have been transported. It warms her heart to see Flodynhelm there standing by her, but it also provokes thoughts of guilt, something she rarely experiences. *This was an impulsive decision. What was I thinking?* But when she touches her forehead to his and feels his warm breath against her face, Jaxyl is comforted by his velvety soft muzzle she caresses with her palm. Flodynhelm jerks his head up and whinnies softly. "He will be stabled near your quarters You can ride him every day if you want," Othniel assures her.

"But how?"

He gives her an understanding smile. "You will be amazed by our reality deck. It even has a moving track where you can run him…for hours if you want. It won't be like racing through the woods of Merth by any means, but it will be a quality experience."

"Have we left Merth yet?"

"Yes, we have. We departed the minute we were transported aboard; we have a great distance to traverse."

"Could you have someone escort me to Flodynhelm's stable? It's been an exhausting day and I'd like to get him settled and get some rest."

"Yes, of course," Othniel nods to his aide. "Please take these two to their quarters."

"Will you please join us for a welcoming dinner? I will have someone come to escort you in about 40 *jotules*. That's about one-twelfth of one of your revolutions on Merth."

"That will be fine," Jaxyl agrees hoping she won't have to be civil for much longer,

"We'll get started in the morning with your orientation. But tonight, we relax." His smile is kindly and inviting. Now she is away from her father, Othniel reminds her more of Ahshen.

Jaxyl is impressed with how spacious and luxurious her quarters are. There are two massive windows where she can view the skies as the ship hurtles through space. Her clothing has been delivered and even put in closets and drawers. *This is not home, but it is comfortable.* Her guide shows her how to use the "regenerator" where she can select from almost anything she might need for nourishment and refreshment. She is shown how to use the screen for communicating with anyone on the ship, but also, she can check on Flodynhelm. She is even happy with his quarters clean and comfortable, more of a suite than a stable for animals. It's located adjacent to the reality deck and not far from her quarters.

The aide also shows her the bath area, spacious and accommodating with several ways to bathe including a supersonic method for decontamination or quick uniform changes. "If you have any questions, open the screen and ask," the aide tells her. She is too tired to be polite and the minute he leaves she falls back on the huge bed and tests it for comfort. *This will do!* She would love to fall asleep but is too weary for rest.

She experiments with turning the screen on and it is still set to watch Flodynhelm which brings a faint smile to her weary lips. She has been shown how to start the tub filling – most things in the room operate on her voice control. When the big shiny black tub is filled, she instructs it to turn on the jets and she sinks into the luxurious tub letting out a guttural murmur of fatigue.

Dragging herself out of the tub she crashes on the bed and doesn't hear the knock on the door until she hears the aide pounding. "Excuse me Princess Jaxyl, but it is time to report to the captain's quarters for dinner." She pulls on a sumptuous robe she finds in the bathroom and opens the door. "I will wait outside the door, Your Highness."

Jaxyl has absolutely no idea what to wear to the welcoming dinner and decides to wear one of her dress uniforms. And as soon as she dons it, she opens the door and asks the aide to come in. "Will this be acceptable at the party?"

The youth is unable to disguise his clueless expression but does his best to assist. "Some will dress in evening attire, but most will be in formal dress uniforms."

Satisfied with his answer she asks, "I'm sorry I didn't catch your name earlier."

"Scorzo," he says stiffly. "I have actually been assigned to you as your permanent aide."

She examines the awkward fellow and fluffs her silky blonde curls which she is wearing much shorter these days and closes the door to her quarters. Standing in the hall, Scorzo does not move.

"What?' she asks him.

"The door locks behind you automatically and only opens to your voice command. I'd like to test it now to make sure it is programmed properly. Sometimes these locks have an annoying glitch. I don't want you to be locked out in case you return without me."

"I don't know how I could possibly do that yet; this ship is huge."

"You can always flip up a navigator screen with your vim."

"Oh, I didn't bring it with me, should I?"

"Yes, until you get one installed in your finger, you should carry it at all times."

This idea of having something placed surgically in her finger is extremely unappealing. *There is much I must learn! I am like a child here.* She turns away from him and faces the door. "Open," she says.

76-First Encounter

The evening turns out to be rather enjoyable, everyone is friendly, and the food is fantastic. The chef has gone to the trouble of preparing foods familiar to her on Merth, and it is an interesting conversational topic as the servers bring trays of tasty morsels bearing the distinct flavoring of her planet's own soil. In a special effort to make her feel at home, the kitchen staff had stocked up on Merthian produce during their stay.

The group is made up of mostly higher-echelon officers and at first, they mingle in the spacious dining room, adjacent to the captain's quarters, sipping on exotic and colorful cocktails served in glasses that look as if each is created individually by an artist. And as it turns out they are products created by crew members who have taken the master class in crystal blowing.

"I'll have to get used to the idea most of you Talvoc are taller than me," Jaxyl tells one of the first crew members she meets. He is a striking man sporting a red beard and a welcoming smile.

"Yes, but we are not all Talvoc, surely you have noticed some of our more unique-looking crew members. We have an assortment of species on our ship."

"I have, and this will take some getting used to."

"Keep an open mind and you will appreciate the varied skills of our crew."

Othniel approaches the two and sweeps Jaxyl away from her companion. He doesn't seem to want to let her wander on her own. "You must meet everyone here tonight. We will soon be working together, and they need to recognize the great Warrior Princess for who she is." Othniel's praise is more potent than the cocktails, especially when he alludes to the special task for her ahead.

But something is missing. Here she is merely one of the crew and very green. The burden of being heroic is temporarily dissipated and it feels good. *Perhaps this is what I need. I'm not exactly invisible and yet no expectations are weighing on me by everyone in the room.*

"We hope you are enjoying the *apersoff*," Oscara greets her.

"Oh, you mean these things?" Jaxyl is about to open her mouth and put in another tidbit. "We call them *botsoi* on Merth. Oscara's aura flutters slightly and she smiles softly. The dinner chimes sound and everyone is called to sit down. The lights are dimmed and a conflagration of lit tapers flicker in the dim light.

"You sit over here at the center table," Othniel motions. I want you to get acquainted with our Master at Arms, Joesla Cruuws. You will be working with him closely in upcoming time."

"How do you do?" Joesla places his hand over his heart, a sign of greeting and respect. "On your other side is Lorta Enzel." He gestures to the woman on her right sporting a helmet-like haircut but with long, tight ringlets cascading down her back. She has a grim determination on her face as if she has already judged the Warrior

Princess and she has come up short. "Lorta is our head translator. You'll be working closely with her."

"My pleasure to meet you," Lorta puts out her hand in greeting but Jaxyl, unaccustomed to being touched defers to her own ways and returns her gesture with her fist over her heart. Lorta shakes her head slightly embarrassed and mirrors Jaxyl's hand over her heart. "Of course, I forgot royalty on Merth are not to be approached physically."

Feeling Lorta's awkwardness, Jaxyl laughs, "It depends on who it is wanting to touch you." *This woman is not a good fit for me. She has already proven herself to be incompetent at her task.* She turns back toward Joesla. "When do we begin our work together?"

Startled by her abruptness, Joesla adjusts realizing Jaxyl is used to leading. "I should say I will give you a thorough tour of our vessel in the morning. We are scheduled to meet the captain for a luncheon meeting, but if we get an early start, we shouldn't have difficulty meeting our schedule.

"Excuse me," Othniel stands. "I hope everyone here tonight has taken a moment to greet our newest team member. If not, please do so after the meal. We are greatly pleased to welcome Princess Jaxyl Alexis of Merth. We have great hope she can assist us with connecting with the Folotor and eventually defeating the Escobar Giants." To her surprise, everyone stands and applauds.

Instinctively, Jaxyl stands, raises her glass to Othniel, and bows her head slightly. "Thank you for the warm welcome." *No more is needed. You are not royalty here.* And she sits down. As the evening drags on, she succumbs to the tiredness she experienced earlier in the day and as soon as she can duck out, she makes her exit with Scorzo.

"Do you think we could stop by and check in on Flodynhelm?" Scorzo gives her a baffled expression. "My big white horse? Can you take me to his quarters before I go to bed? I don't want to get lost?"

"Oh yes, of course."

"I'd like to reassure him everything is okay. I don't want him to tear the place down looking for me." As they make their way through the maze of corridors, doors, and turns drawing closer to where Flodynhelm is stabled, they hear a piercing whinny as he senses Jaxyl's presence nearby.

"Oh, I'm glad to see you, big boy, she lets her hand graze across his belly and his back, finally burying her face in his. "His stall must always be clean, or he will cause a ruckus if he has to stand in his own muck."

"Yes, he will be well taken care of."

"Jaxyl grabs his mane at the withers and swings up effortlessly with her floating abilities to mount him. She leans over and hugs him and Flodynhelm wickers softly tossing his head. Forgetting Scorzo is even there, Jaxyl takes in the smell of her majestic horse and is transported back to Merth in her mind. *I am grateful you are with me.* Flodynhelm's silky mane flops as he tosses his head. "How and where can I ride him?" She asks.

"Ah, your schedule is filled until later in the day. I'm not sure how long the captain will detain you. I will have him saddled and ready to go. The nearest reality deck has a moving track. You will be able to have a real riding experience."

Jaxyl's weary body tells her it is time to go, but she doesn't want to leave. She can feel Scorzo's impatience and acquiesces by dismounting.

When she gets back to her luxurious accommodations she goes to the window and peers out feeling unusually insignificant as the universe races by. "May I fix you some hot *auso* tea before bed? It is very comforting." Scorzo asks.

"No, I think I can manage the regenerator on my own. Thanks much for your assistance, good night." As soon as the door slips closed behind him, Jaxyl undresses and curls up naked in the luxurious sheets. She stares at the whirring of stars as they skim past her window and is snoring softly within minutes.

77-Chain of Command

"May I be frank?" Jaxyl asks Othniel. They have been talking and eating a mid-meal in the mission portal, just her, Othniel, and Joesla. Othniel has given her the rundown on the Folotar and their importance in vanquishing the Escobar Giants. Othniel pauses, frustrated by her interruption as he is about to make an important point.

"Yes, of course, what is it?"

"I don't have a good feeling about your head translator."

"You mean Lorta?"

"Yes, I'm sorry I couldn't even remember her name. I don't think she and I will make suitable collaborators."

Othniel stares blankly at the Warrior Princess in a manner to squelch his frustration. "Would you please elaborate?"

"It is not fair to discount my ability to work with her at this point of course, but she…I can tell you we will not be successful collaborators. First, I won't be her underling, and she will have difficulty with this."

"And you know this how?"

"I can't say my kinetic sight is as strong here as it is on Merth. But she disapproves of me, and she is not going to be easy to deal with."

Othniel twists in his chair, weighing his options. His eyes meet Joesla's in a brief and wordless conversation without even a transfer of thoughts as Jaxyl might be able to read them.

"I realize this makes you uncomfortable, Captain, and no, I do not think getting to know her better will help." Jaxyl points out.

A swift recall of hundreds of missions throughout his career and Othniel can think of dozens of times when adverse working relationships blossomed into lifelong friendships, but he sees no wisdom in arguing with the Warrior Princess about this. "I see." There is a silence in the room Joesla finally fills.

"We must get past this. I'm sure you grasp how to work with others?" He turns swiveling in his chair and stares at Jaxyl straight on.

"Of course, when I command them. This is a different situation altogether."

Othniel lets out a heavy sigh. "Okay suppose we re-structure how this works. I'm not making you command-er of the translators, but perhaps you can view them as collaborators Lorta leads. She will be instructed to deal with you in the same way. And I must firmly state you will do your best to work together. Much is at risk here."

"Of course," Jaxyl is unsure of how loyal to this con-cept she can be, but for now she might as well feign com-mitment.

"This afternoon you will have your mandatory phys-ical examination, and tomorrow we get to work. Scorzo has indicated you would like to have a ride scheduled every day. I suggest you do this early in the day before operations are in full throe."

"I was under the impression you had me medically scanned for physical imperfections back when I was a visitor for the first time on the ship."

"Well, er yes, that is true, but every new crew member must undergo a complete physical exam."

78-One Wild Ride

It was early when she got up and headed for Flody-nhelm's stable, but you couldn't tell by normal standards. "I hate not having any natural light!" She grumbles to Scorzo who had, at her request, come to her room to wake her up and set up breakfast for her.

"It takes a bit of getting used to," he says sympathetically.

Flodynhelm is already groomed and saddled to go when they get to his stable. He is visibly anxious to see Jaxyl and whickers loudly when she shows up.

"Yes, my sweet friend, this is new to both of us," she says stroking his forehead and ears. He pushes toward her eagerly.

"I suggest we start slowly. I don't want you or the horse to get hurt," Scorzo warns. "We can keep you running for hours if you want. Today I will stay and run the equipment for you, but I will teach you how to operate it once, you get your vim installed into your finger."

"Will they do that today at my medical exam?"

"Possibly, it's up to Doc Sandral."

"And how do we get to this reality deck?"

"Follow me down this way." He points to the lengthy corridor they have reached. Flodynhelm's hooves make sharp, clipping sounds on the floor of the ship. When they reach the door, it slides open, staying that way until they are fully through it. "I have taken the liberty of programming some scenic pastoral scenes from Merth for your enjoyment." Jaxyl isn't quite sure what he is talking about but doesn't let on. "It would be best to start at a walk until you and the horse get your 'sea legs.'"

Jaxyl shoots him a confused look. "I'm sorry it is an odd expression I picked up from one of my fellow crew members. It means you need to get accustomed to the floor moving under your feet. I will stay here until you are ready to go or until it is time to escort you to your medical exam. I will start by slowing the treadway down. As you cannot operate the speed yourself yet, put your thumb up or down to signal to me what you desire."

Jaxyl swings up into the saddle effortlessly, she can feel Flodynhelm trembling with energy, and they start with a flash of his tail as he flips his head up nervously. *Oh, okay big boy let's go.* And they take off with a blustery start. When the treadway picks up speed automatically to match the pace, Flodynhelm prances and whinnies, rising slightly above the floor. Jaxyl relaxes and laughs realizing the treadway is not a concern for a horse who can fly. *By the One True God, I'm glad I brought you with me! We will meet our challenges together.*

They race through what feels like real Merthian terrain until they are both exhausted, but the allotted time before her medical exam comes too swiftly. Scorzo has the stable attendant come and take Flodynhelm back to his stable. "He's wet will you walk him down?" She hands the reins over to the attendant. "It's most important he is not put up wet."

The aide bows his head. "Yes, certainly Officer Karda, I have read up on his needs to take proper care of him."

"Excellent," she gives the stable hand an appreciative smile. *It's going to take some getting used to, my new title.*

Jaxyl looks at Scorzo, "Do we have enough time to swing by my quarters? I'm a little wet myself," she says to him wiping her brow with the back of her red leather sleeve which does not absorb the moisture to cool her.

"I'm afraid not, and it is not wise to keep medical staff waiting, they serve the whole ship." He pauses, they do have a supersonic stall you can cleanse with."

"I'm not sure how safe those things are, I tried the one in my quarters. It didn't make me feel clean."

Scorzo does not allow a smile to form on his lips, but he is tickled by her superstition. "I assure you Princess Jaxyl there is no need for concern."

79-An Unlikely Surprise

"Oh, and when you get back from my quarters with clean clothing, would you please bring me my vim? I need to begin to learn to use it. So, you don't have to hold my hand all the time."

Scorzo gives her a confused smile. He can't imagine how she could possibly function without her vim he thinks, when the humorous reality hits him. For the foreseeable future, he is her vim.

"Maybe the doctor will install that today also." Scorzo does not leave until she is ushered in to have her blood analyzed and get her exam.

"Ouch, that hurts!" Jaxyl complains.

The nurse smiles at her compassionately, "I'm sorry this new method is supposed to be pain-free, but back when we stuck a needle in your arm, a skilled technician could be done before you even noticed they had punctured your skin."

Doctor Sandral comes in and begins her examination. She is quietly efficient, but not overly friendly, the experience is distinct from dealing with her Aunt Galen the Healer back on Merth, who is spiritually dynamic and exudes a selfless attitude of healing. *This woman looks like she might blow over in a stiff wind.*

"I am going to go ahead and install the vim into your finger today if you are ready for this. It will require you to attend a brief orientation on how to use it immediately following."

Jaxyl shrugs. "Can it be taken out again, after I have served my time?"

Doctor Sandral chuckles despite her grim facade. "You make it sound like a prison sentence to be here on the Ursula Weir."

"In a way it is," she says wistfully.

Doctor Sandral backs away from her slightly to take a studied look at Jaxyl's facial expression. "Well, I hope someday soon you will understand what a great honor it is to serve on this ship, and especially your part of the mission is so critical. If successful, you may save quantosands number of lives."

"That's what I've been told, but my real objective is to protect my people. I was born for this."

"Yes, what is it?" The nurse who took her blood joins them in the sterile exam room.

"Doctor Sandral, I'm sorry to interrupt, but there is something you need to be aware of."

The doctor stops waving her medical recording device at Jaxyl and looks up at the nurse who brings her an electronic document reader. She studies it and a frown settles across her face. "I see," she says. "I will handle this. Get back to your analysis and let me know if there is anything else."

Jaxyl hardly notices the intrusion until the Doctor starts asking her some strange questions about her sexual history. She sits up erectly, no longer willing to be submissively studied by this woman with pale skin and milky eyes.

The doctor lets out a frustrated exhalation. "Officer Karda, I believe you might be in vitreous."

Flum that flowkin baltoff Clouton has given me something! I've heard of this. He had me fooled I thought he was loyal to me. If I were home now, I would rip his limbs from his magnificent body and let him bleed to death and feed his carcass to the glotor birds.

Reading the anger on Jaxyl's face, the doctor suggests she will have to run more tests for conclusive results. "I'm not terribly versed in your species, but we gained a lot of knowledge before we left Merth."

Jaxyl looks puzzled. "My aunt the Healer would cure me with her touch, but I presume you have to give me something for my condition, that pistoid Clouton, I could kill him for this!"

Realizing for the first time Jaxyl doesn't understand what she is telling her, Jostal Sandral regroups. She places her hand compassionately on her patient, knowing the importance of touch in the healing process for this fearless warrior from Merth.

"I'm not sure who Clouton is, but based on what you have shared, he must be your latest sexual partner. He has not given you a disease if that's what you are thinking, Officer Karda, you are with child."

80-Impossible

"**B**ut that's impossible, my aunt protected me with her skills."

Doctor Sandral lets out a heavy sigh, choosing her words carefully. "I will run more tests, but the blood test is what we need to confirm."

Suddenly the memory of her last bonding with the Matong floods Jaxyl's mind as strongly as if she were re-living it. *There was the mist. I fell on the floor and passed out. Is that what happened? Did the Matong intend on me becoming pregnant even with my important mission ahead?* It was as if a *mustophiel* fueled by rain, had swollen in her brain, she can't think. Jaxyl looks helplessly at the doctor. "I must go back to Merth."

Before the doctor even has time to respond, Jaxyl stands up from the exam table and tears off the thin sheet they had given her to wear during her exam. She stomps out of the exam room without a lick of clothing on causing a minor skirmish as patients in the waiting room are shocked to see the newest arrival on the ship striding through the room completely naked. Before she can make it to the door someone shouts behind her, and everything goes black.

When she wakes up, Oscara is beside the bed she is lying on with an apprehensive smile on her face. Jaxyl struggles to sit up but when she does there is a grinding, torturous pounding in her head. "What have you done to me?" She scowls at the doctor who is busy giving directives to her aides.

"Jaxyl, listen to me, you are electronically restrained. We are worried you will harm yourself."

"Ha, the only ones I am going to hurt are you *pistoids*. Let me go now!" But every word she says is like a nail being pounded into her head."

"We don't have much time. I'm sorry you have been given such surprising news," Oscara looks back at Doctor Sandral, glaring at her. The timing is bad as we have recently become aware of an Escobar giant, and we need to destroy it. Captain Othniel wants you on deck now!"

Jaxyl groans, fighting off the pain. "Listen to me, Officer Karda, you have a responsibility to meet. I will have Dr. Sandral release you if you promise to pull yourself together and perform your duties."

"Where are my *fluming* clothes?"

"Do you promise to comply?"

Jaxyl rolls her eyes and even this small motion causes her pain. "Yes," she stammers.

"Give her clothes back to her," Oscara commands and nods to the others to give the Warrior Princess some privacy. Doctor Sandral waves her medical instrument at Jaxyl, and the pain subsides. "I had to give her double strength sedation," the doctor mumbles at Oscara as she exits the room.

Oscara closes the door and hands Jaxyl her clothes. "Now listen to me, I am here to support you, we all are. If you want to save your beloved Merth, we need you to focus. For now, let's just put this personal matter aside and we'll figure it out together."

"You don't understand the meaning of this child, it is the physical union of the royal Karda family and the Omi royalty. Something that shouldn't have happened. The Matong intervened, I need to return to Merth."

"Did your Matong tell you to go on this mission?"

Jaxyl backtracks her thoughts, "Maybe, the *flowkin* thing can be absolutely obtuse."

"What did it tell you exactly?

Jaxyl pulls on her underclothing and searches for the recall of her memory which has been stunned by her recent dose of sedation. "It said I will return," she recalls as if she were bonding with the Matong. "YOU WILL RESTORE THOSE WHO HAVE BEEN CONQUERED. YOUR DESTINY IS TO BE THE VESSEL FOR RE-BIRTH."

The message suddenly makes sense. Oscara's aura surges purple and Jaxyl's mindset, like a scale reaching equilibrium floods her with peace as she realizes what her directive is. "This was conceived by the Matong."

Oscara, not trying to make Jaxyl feel rushed, gives her a tentative smile, pushing her thoughts into Jaxyl's mind. SEE THERE IT IS ORDAINED; YOU NEED NOT BE CONCERNED.

Ha, you are not the one who is pregnant!

81-Attack

The ForeSat deck is abuzz with activity when Oscara and Jaxyl arrive. Captain Othniel gives Oscara an irritated, quizzical look as if to say *it's about time*. "We are keeping our distance until you can be present, Officer Karda. I want you to see what we are up against. Their vessel is currently traveling at a tremendous speed of *louzo quantums*, but we are tracking it, preparing for battle in the meantime. See the tiny dot with the red circle around it?" He asks Jaxyl and points to the immense ForeSat screen next to the massive, curved space shield window. "That's the ship."

Jaxyl nods in acknowledgment. "For now, sit over here, with Officer Grundel, and learn. It is going to be a while before we catch up." Jaxyl does as she is told. She met Vola Grundel the night before and found her to be friendly but for now, she is all business. As they silently follow the images on the screen, Jaxyl thinks about battle. Her sword and shield would have no meaning here. There would be no hand-to-hand combat. The screen before her is like starlight on water back home on Merth, translucent, quickly fading in and out. But there is one constant, a looming black object that keeps growing on the screen.

"All stations ready?" Oscara asks, her aura is now lifting straight up and is a bright luminous red. She looks as if you were to touch her, your flesh would burn. "Command Central is now ready to engage captain, on your mark," she says.

"We wait for the optimal distance for engagement, not a second sooner, but not so close we don't maintain an edge for their counterattack. How near are we to it Officer Grundel?"

"Sir I'm posting now on all screens." Jaxyl watches as the countdown begins.

"Go ahead and set your mark and firing range. Don't leave any room for failure, we've still got time to let the weapons perform the first blast as a surprise attack. It's the follow-up that will be tricky as the Escobar Giant will disperse into pieces. First Officer, give the command to fire when ready," Othniel says tersely.

Jaxyl watches as the descending numbers on the screen disappear and there is a whisking blast of energy released from the ship. Moments later the flash reaches the target causing it to explode in a fiery array of fragments. There is no sound, but a shock wave finally hits the ship, causing it to jerk and pitch. Following the disturbance, they can see a functional Escobar giant swoop in their direction, latching onto the surface of the ship, just above the ForeSat.

"Cameras?" The captain barks.

"Working on it, sir," someone says behind her. There is a groaning sound and the entire ship shudders eerily.

"Get that *flowkin shwiza* off my ship now!" Othniel, barks.

"Yes sir, we'll have to use heat combined with bursts of firepower or we may damage our hull."

"Wait a minute there is another loose giant headed toward us. Maybe we get two birds with one stroke."

"How do you mean sir?"

"I want you to use a *magnetletto* beam from another part of the ship, and when this *jakletogg* attaches to its other part we will have them both caught in the beam, and we will send a *trasbown* particle stream down it to obliterate them. As soon as we are rid of this piece of *flyxtcal*, we need to track to see if there are other functioning giants still out there."

"Beam ready sir."

"Now son, now."

A camera shot from another distant location pops up on the screen. The *magnetletto* beam is too high. "Lower the beam now!" Othniel shouts and just as the beam comes down, the other giant slips into sync with the section already attached to the Ursula Weir.

"But sir we might hit our ship!"

"Now son, now!" There is a loud zinging noise and vibration, then an enormous explosion and a fireball blows past the ForeSat space shield window. The released tension in the room is palpable as everyone takes a big gulp of air.

"Excellent marksmanship Officer Kedlo!" Othniel beams. "Excellent indeed."

The strategic firearms officer responsible for the risky shot looks as if he might normally be a little cocky, but at the moment is humbled by his amazing good luck.

"Okay the clean-up crew will now take over and make sure all parts of the giant are destroyed I will be below in the Portal debriefing." He looks toward Oscara. "First

Officer Oscara, and the defense team please join me. You too Officer Karda."

82-Another Shock

With the chaos of the battle over, Jaxyl finds herself still in a state of mental confusion, but she manages to report as requested. She slips a note to Scorzo to get her set back up to get the vim installed. *I need that out of necessity. I am handicapped without the ease of functioning the others have.* She sits in the only chair left and tries to concentrate on what her captain is saying.

"We will make it to the home planet of the Folotar in about 40 *drexls*. Then, we will initiate a request for a visit. Since we have previously been unable to communicate with them, we will have to fly cold. We hope..." he stares at Jaxyl, "Officer Karda will be able to reach them before we attempt to put a landing party on their surface, but it is not a given. We need to spend our time, before arrival preparing for this event which means you, Officer Enzel, will be working non-stop with your translators to come up with answers. With the help of Officer Karda of course, we believe it is her genetic makeup that will make her be able to connect with the Folotar, and not so much her language, but we are covering all bases. I want to remind everyone this is a diplomatic mission. Through countless sources, we have been led to believe the Folotor hold the key to vanquishing the Escobar giants. Questions?"

Lorta Enzel stands. "If this is true as you postulate, the connection is genetic, not lingual, will our efforts as translators be in vain?"

"Good question, the answer is no. We need you to understand how to speak with them in the future I suggest you use this opportunity to avail yourself of finding solutions now."

"Sir," she looks nervously over at Jaxyl. "If this truly is a genetic resource, we need to understand Officer Karda's genetic makeup thoroughly. This will require her consent."

There is an imperceptible pause as Othniel turns directly to Jaxyl. "I see no problem with that do you Officer Karda." *I hate being put on the spot like this! I am coming to despise that pistoid Enzel!*

"Up to a certain point, I'm guessing this means working with the medical team. I won't endanger my physical body if that's called for."

"I won't mince words Officer Karda, we believe your Matong was a gift from the Folotor many eons ago." The captain's words, so unexpected, burn in Jaxyl's brain almost as intensely as her recent news she is to have a baby. *The Matong came from the Folotar? How is this possible?*

Jaxyl pulls herself up in her chair feeling adrift. Emotions swirl through her mind. *This is so curious. Why would he say that? I must say something but what? A warrior does not yield to weakness! I want out of here how do I make that happen?* Using her handheld vim under the table she signals for Scorzo to come to take her back to her room. She searches for Othniel's eyes and pushes her thoughts to him. I MUST BE EXCUSED. I DO NOT FEEL WELL.

Realizing something is going on with Jaxyl, Othniel shuts down the meeting. "That's it for now, let's adjourn, your orders will be sent to you soon."

Thank the One True God! Let me out of here. Jaxyl stands and goes through the motions of saluting her fellow officers mechanically. *I need training, not just for the vim but for protocol here on this ship. This has been overlooked.*

Othniel looks as if he wants to speak with her, but Oscara gives him a subtle nod and places her hand on Jaxyl's back to escort her out. ARE YOU OKAY? She asks pushing her thoughts into Jaxyl's head.

NOT REALLY, I NEED SOME TIME OF SOLITUDE. I HAVE NO MATONG TO CONSULT.

I UNDERSTAND. I AM AVAILABLE IF YOU NEED ME.

Jaxyl smiles warmly at Oscara realizing how busy she must be.

Thankfully Scorzo is at the door waiting for her. "Would you like to go back to your quarters?" He asks her.

"*Holzo* no! Let's get this vim thing done, and I need some training about protocol on this ship. I'm currently clueless."

"Yes, of course, the captain didn't want to rush you, but I can see where it would be a, er issue for you. I will have some training visuals sent to the screen in your room."

"That would be most helpful."

83-A Maelstrom of Inner Chaos

Finally, Jaxyl has time to get to her room and rest. According to her newly installed vim, a passage of time similar to a rotation on Merth has passed and she has had nothing more to eat than a few *bostiles* left from this morning. *They were tasteless then and tasteless now. Maybe I shouldn't have sent Scorzo off so quickly. But shwiza I am exhausted. Maybe I will test the regenerator out.*

"Gen," she says as she has been instructed. "Fix me a generous chunk of *Androsa* cheese and *posta* chips like on Merth and look up recipes prepared for the royal Karda family and prepare me a feast. I'm starving. And I'd like some wine, comparable to what I am used to. I don't know vintage dates, just surprise me with something wonderful." The cheese, wine, and chips come almost instantly, but the Gen tells her the rest will take some research and she should be ready to pick up each dish as the chime sounds to avoid a backlog.

Jaxyl closes her eyes as she pops the succulent cheese on a crisp posta chip into her mouth and takes a swig of the wine. *Amazingly good! Maybe there are some redeeming qualities to fake food.* She dozes on the couch while waiting for the rest of her meal, but the chime begins to ring as warned and she jumps up.

'I replicated the feast created for you on your eighteenth birthday, making single portions of course,' the machine notifies her. 'Please take them out and place them on the table as I release the dishes.' Jaxyl is flabbergasted as dish after dish comes rolling out of the Gen but taking her time, she finishes it all, amazed at how much she has eaten. Licking her fingers, she decides to have a luxurious bath. She takes the bottle and flute with her into the bath. *Finally, time to consider the extraordinary events of the day with all its shocking revelations.* As she settles into the turbulent water, letting it massage her warrior's hardened body, she lets her mind wander to her puzzling predicament,

I have never considered being a mother. It's not what I'm trained for, and it's certainly not who I am. I always thought I would spend my days in combat. Sure, I would have eventually taken a royal consort, but who would have ever thought I would end up on this ship? I would find some way out of this predicament if it was possible. How ironic the child will be half Karda and half Omi. And now I realize, thanks to Oscara's astute observation, it is the Matong's divine plan.

With her difficult day behind her, and her heavy, satisfying meal weighing her down. Jaxyl climbs into bed and dreams about Clouton whom she is entwined with, his hard rock muscles embracing her as he grips her breasts. Suddenly she is interrupted by the distinctive voice of the Matong.

WARRIOR PRINCESS DO NOT BE ANXIOUS I HAVE NOT ABANDONED YOU. WATCH AND LEARN.

"*Flum!*" She mumbles in her sleep and rolls over, sleeping soundly until her door chime awakens her the next morning. Standing in the doorway is Oscara.

"Did we have an appointment?" Jaxyl says pulling on a comfortable caftan.

"No," Oscara's aura flutters slightly. "I was worried about you after yesterday and I thought I'd come have breakfast with you before I have to report to the ForeSat."

Oscara doesn't wait to be invited in but begins to make commands to the Gen explaining to Jaxyl she needs some strong tea. "That was some encounter yesterday, who would have thought they would have latched onto us like that?"

"Is it unusual?"

"It certainly is. A good strategy too as it turns out. We just barely were able to defend ourselves."

The conversation fades like the non-stop succession of stars and planets they pass incessantly by and Oscara's aura flutters and spurts. She giggles awkwardly, especially for her status as the ship's first officer. "I'm not very competent at this, my aura gives me away."

"I'm not sure what you mean?"

"Emotional stuff."

"Oh," Jaxyl takes the steaming cup of tea Oscara hands her.

"Me either. I think I would have rather been pierced through by an arrow than this."

"I need you to tell the captain. He needs to know."

Jaxyl lets out a forceful breath. "The doctor's office has been sending me messages to report back in. This gestation timing is not going to hinder me. I am still a warrior first. I will have this baby, but it is incidental to my mission here on the Ursula Weir."

Oscara sips her tea and pushes an *almonde et chocolat crisple* toward Jaxyl. The Warrior Princess grins and takes a bite, the pastry crumbs spill onto her lap, and she waves her hand to scrape them off.

"Listen to me, may I call you Jaxyl," Oscara asks her,

"I need you to cooperate with the doctor. She is only looking out for your best interests. We need you to remain physically strong. Once we reach the Folotor realm, we need you. It's why you have sacrificed so much. It's why you are here."

Many thoughts of the women she would normally be sharing this time with, her mother Queen Ali, and her aunt Galen the healer, these women were *quantotillions* of miles away now. Jaxyl looks at Oscara and realizes she is reaching out to her as a friend. The irony makes her laugh. "You don't know anything about children or giving birth, do you?"

A chagrined smile crosses Oscara's face and her aura turns yellow. "No, I guess I don't but I'm willing to stick with you and see this thing through."

If only she knew the chaos, I am swimming through, she would understand how much this means to me.

84-Jaxyl's Prickly Predicament

"Yes, First Officer Oscara has told me you wish to share some personal news with me." Captain Othniel has become more fatherly with her than ever, and Jaxyl pines for this conversation to take place with her real father, Ahshen Owanu. She would love to see his face glow with the news he was to be a grandfather despite the complicated issue of the baby's father. *I may never see him again, my wise and kind father.* Her acknowledgment produces a sharp stabbing sensation in her chest. *I have never appreciated my wonderful parents or my status as the royal heir. Royal heir! Who will replace me if I don't get home in time?*

Jaxyl's thoughts unhinge her like a sword twisting into her chest. This feeling of anxiety is completely unfamiliar to her.

"Officer Karda, are you okay?"

"What?"

"I said are you okay? Do we need to have your report to the ship's medical lab?"

Jaxyl shakes her thoughts loose as if she has plunged into a frigid pool of water and is coming up for air. She gasps, her breath catches in her throat. "I'm sorry sir. I am here to report a most unexpected situation." She throws her shoulders back and breathes fully as she pulls herself together. Her golden curls swish softly against her red leather tunic.

"And what is it, Officer Karda?"

"Captain, I have recently found out I am with child. I want you to understand this changes nothing. I am prepared to carry out my mission."

This is one of those moments for Othniel when he recognizes he must hold his emotions in check and walk the fine line between Commanding Officer and sympathetic listener, but his head is pounding with surprise encased in a hard shell of anger.

"Are you sure?"

"Sir," Oscara interjects. "Doctor Sandral has confirmed."

Jaxyl stares at him blankly. "To tell you the truth, I wish it wasn't so, but I'm afraid it is wishful thinking at this point. I'm as shocked as anyone, but I think there was divine intervention on the Matong's part. I was supposedly protected against such a situation as this."

Othniel clears his throat. Thinking of how his departure from Merth had been delayed by Jaxyl for her to indulge in one last dalliance. It was too ironic. He looks down uncharacteristically groping for words, carefully framed words, and not the harsh scolding he wants to lambast her with.

"I'm without words." His tone is transformational as he pushes forward through anger to issue the appropriate response. "I guess I understand how this happened I have three children myself, but Officer Karda this is beyond belief. Why would you allow this to happen now?

"It shouldn't have," she stammers. "I was supposed to be protected. Believe me when I say there is no one more perplexed than I am sir."

"Going back to Merth at this time is not an option."

"I understand sir, I think you recognize my abilities and my strengths by now."

"The question is what is the length of your gestation period? We should reach the edges of the Folotor realm with the next *quadforth*." He looks over to Oscara, who gives him a slight nod.

"I have checked with Dr. Sandral. We should reach the mother planet of the Folotor before her time comes."

This is the first time Jaxyl has been aware of the time-table and how she is affected by it.

"Ah sir, may I change the direction of the conversation for a minute?"

Othniel's eyebrows curl upward a visible sign of surprise on a Talvoc. "Certainly."

"I understand it's been hectic since I arrived, but I need some instruction as to protocol on the ship. I now have my vim installed," she raises the artistically engraved and featherweight prosthesis on her hand as evidence. She had chosen a design with the royal Karda seal on it.

"Yes, we wanted you to have some breathing room, but yes, this got overlooked in our recent scramble with the Escobar giant. Tell Scorzo to help you work out a schedule and arrange it any way you like. I understand riding Flodynhelm daily is a priority for you."

He mentions Flodynhelm by name. This is impressive. "Will do sir," She notices Oscara touching her ear tab.

"Excuse me sir I am needed on the ForeSat."

"Of course, you are both dismissed."

Book IV

The Folotar

85-First Vision

When Jaxyl first sees the Folotar mother planet it is through the soft cloud of sleep. The gentle but persistent chime on her communication screen awakens her and Oscara appears, filling the space. Her closest friend now, the First Officer's aura flutters with gold and white, Jaxyl has come to recognize this as a sign of calm balance in her demeanor. "I realize it's late," Oscara says, "but I thought you'd like to see it." Jaxyl turns over to sit up, her belly has grown enough she has to be more careful with her body. Which at first perturbed her but since she has spent time with the child growing within her, she is more understanding and loving, a surprise to all who have come to know the Warrior Princess since her arrival on the Ursula Weir.

"Oh, no problem. Yes, put it on the screen please."

The planet is a pale purple with a soft haze surrounding it. "Oh my, it's quite beautiful," Jaxyl says pushing her curls back which have now grown to shoulder length again.

"Yes, it's more colorful than I imagined it."

"What are those pulsing spots?"

"I'm not really sure, they may be energy cycles or a density of population."

"When do we reach it?

"In about four more watch rotations."

"Ouch!"

"What's the matter?"

"Oh, the baby gave me a sharp kick in the ribs. Caught me by surprise."

"Have you come up with a name yet?"

"No, I probably should. I have a little more time though."

"Get back to sleep."

"Okay, I'll check with you after I ride in the morning."

"You're still doing that?

"Of course, it's fine." *It's the only thing that keeps me from plunging my sword through my chest!*

Jaxyl lowers herself back down into her bed thinking of her new sparring partner, Taldon Tornall, as the little bundle of energy in her womb begins to do somersaults. *Aach, I'll never get back to sleep now. I wonder what Taldon thinks about fluming a pregnant woman. He doesn't seem to mind sparring with me as long as we only use touch swords.*

"No," he tells her gently "as much as I would love to I can't." Taldon lunges and his aim is a near miss.

"I'm sturdy." She thrusts back effortlessly.

His clever smile surfaces and the light in his golden eyes shines. "That's not the point," he says laying down his touch weapon momentarily. He wipes the sweat off his brow with his sleeve.

"I don't understand. I've been with other men since I've been pregnant. Are you going to let a baby bump get in your way?" She nods to him to pick his weapon back up, but he doesn't.

"Yes…no, that's not it."

"Well, what then?"

"I'm involved. It's complicated."

"Oh, you never mentioned anything."

"I know; besides, you and I are friends."

Jaxyl looking perplexed says, "I don't believe I've ever been turned down before."

Taldon laughs, his face crinkles in that charming way when he does. "That I can believe."

He picks his sword back up and they go back to their exercises. "I tell you what, after we are done, let's go get a massage and fission bath, we can relax and talk, I will tell you everything," he says brandishing his sword playfully. *He turns me down but continues to flirt. Flotzal!*

86-Secrets

"**W**ell?"
Taldon nods his head slightly in a negative fashion. "You must wait a minute. We must have complete privacy."

The silent pulsing water in the tubs has a delightful lavender scent as they have both selected this herbal additive for their treatment waters. The attendants lift a white sheet for privacy and because of her condition, two attendants help Jaxyl into her tub despite her protestations. Once they are comfortable and ensconced in the pulsing waters the sheet is dropped.

"Isn't this nice?" He grins.

"Yes, I don't know why we haven't done this before?" Jaxyl lets the conversation fall off deliberately growing silent as she sips on her chosen nectar, a multi-berry concoction, chosen for its high-intensity flavor and restorative properties. The silence between them goes on for some time as they enjoy the pleasure of relaxing.

"I trust you completely," he says turning to her, "but still I hesitate."

She meets his gaze and can read his growing apprehension, but not his actual thoughts. "I admit I am curious, but if it causes you shame, don't tell me."

"No, it's nothing like that, but on this ship when one is in a relationship with another and there is concern by either party the knowledge of such a relationship would hinder their duties, well, there is often secrecy. Especially when it concerns a high-ranking officer." He takes a sip of his spicy *cherrilia* nectar and setting it down nervously waves his hand. "We have our married couples, but even when on duty they will be perfectly stoic with each other out of a sense of commitment to their jobs. As you are aware quarrelling amongst crew personnel is strictly forbidden. But the person I am in love with holds her feelings close, she has to." Suddenly it hits her, and it all makes sense. *Taldon and Oscara are together.*

"But how does she do it? Hide her emotions toward you with her aura?'

Startled Taldon jumps visibly in the tub. "Are you able to read my thoughts?"

Jaxyl cups her hands and squirts him with her tub water. "No, don't worry, if I were able to do that, I wouldn't have made such a fool out of myself."

He grins, "I kind of like it you did."

Jaxyl flashes him a disapproving look. "No, really how is she able to control her aura around you?"

"Being she is the only *Dosvle* on the ship, most people are ignorant of what the color of her aura signifies. Except I guess for you. The funny thing is I usually bring out a soft green glow, which signifies calm. She doesn't get the purple of passion unless we are, you know about to do it. And then…Oh, how I love purple."

"I bet you do." She turns away from him and slides lower into the tub letting her head submerge and when she comes back up, she asks. "But why must relationships be kept secret?"

"I guess it's about a confidence level." He shrugs but she can't see because of the bathtub rim. "On this ship, it's what everyone does."

"Does anyone else know your secret?"

"We've been together for some time now, and I don't believe anyone does. If they do, they've been quite discreet."

"I'm curious what people say about me, about the baby?"

A grin spreads wide across Taldon's chiseled face. "Everyone is too afraid of you to judge you. Besides you're sort of like this Messiah everyone is putting their faith in the hopes you can deliver this sector from the Escobar giants."

"But what if I can't?"

"We'll know soon enough, won't we?"

87-Folotar Bound

"Be prepared for anything," Othniel tells her. "Your escort team is comprised of our brightest and best."

"Yes, we've trained together endlessly, but I'm not sure what makes you think the Folotar will communicate with me once I'm down there if they wouldn't do it over the communication system when we tried."

"They've let us come this far, no one stopped us at the outer ring of lesser planets. That's an excellent indication they will welcome us." Captain Othniel turns away from her briefly to suppress his troubling doubt about this most important mission. "They are sensory beings; my guess is they will deliver their thoughts directly to your mind."

"I know the atmosphere has been tested extensively, and it is not toxic to us, but Dr. Sandral has requested I carry supplemental air, in case I need it for the protection of my child."

Captain Othniel nods. "Yes, we've been over this."

"And if the landing party coms malfunction, we revert to the emergency departure plan."

"Yes, if you are unable to check in with us periodically. You will be brought back immediately. This is our protocol." He hesitates briefly letting his hand slide down his chest.

Thoughts roil in her mind like seaweed caught in the back-and-forth pulsing of shore waves on Merth. *I have my baby to protect now. Should I be doing this?* But she relinquishes such thoughts to the terror of the Escobar Giants. The indoctrination she has been subjected to since joining the mission has been compelling. *They could reach Merth and destroy my people along with multitudes of other planets, and other civilizations being wiped out like gnatxles on a leaf. Everyone on the ship is aware of this to be true. Something must be done.*

"You are not the leader of this mission. Your role is most important, but the safety of the entire crew lies with Officer Cruuws," the captain reassures her.

Jaxyl sighs. *I am not experienced at being subordinate. I must be careful to listen.*

"You'll do just fine. You've been training with your landing crew for some time, and I know you are prepared, but do you have any last questions for me?"

"No."

"I'll escort you to the transport room and deliver my last orders to the crew."

The rest of the crew is assembled there waiting for the Captain and Jaxyl to arrive. They are standing on a round platform with a stand in the center. The large pink transporter crystal, emanating a slight pulsing light, has been programmed specifically for the eight of them.

"You have your orders. You understand all contingencies. Correct?"

Each crew member nods affirmatively.

Jaxyl turns and nods saluting with her fist to her chest toward Captain Othniel. Turning again, she joins her comrades on the departure platform where she salutes her commander Officer Cruuws, who nods and begins the countdown. They all join in with three arm gestures by bending their forearms at the elbow. On the second count, the baby turns and spins within Jaxyl, but she does not flinch. And on the fourth count, they touch the transporter crystal with their fists, disappearing from the Ursula Weir.

88-Purple Haze

A purple haze permeates her mouth with a peculiar, sweet taste. At first, it makes her want to gag, but then she gets the feeling it is something like amniotic fluid, a life support system of sorts. She looks around and the landing crew has been frozen in the same circle they transported in. Only Jaxyl is mobile, and it is treacherous as her body floats mysteriously and randomly. The weightlessness creates a playfulness in the baby inside of her as Jaxyl spins gently in place. She instinctively reaches for her sword, but there is nothing to slay.

Like a sensuous whisper of dozens of lips, she hears the voice of the Folotar.

WE ARE PLEASED YOU HAVE COME DEAR DAUGHTER.
DO NOT BE FEARFUL FOR THE CHILD YOU CARRY IS SAFE WITH US.
WE LOVE YOU BOTH WITHOUT LIMIT.

By the One True God, I can hear them! Her thoughts spin like her body, swaying in the emptiness. She looks around at her comrades and is alarmed they are still frozen in their tracks. She works up the courage to ask a question through her thought projection.

CAN YOU HEAR ME?
YES, YOU HAVE TRAVELED FAR.
I CANNOT SEE YOU. SHOW YOURSELF TO ME.
THIS CAN NOT BE DONE AT THIS TIME.

WE ARE MANY.

Jaxyl's expression curls with frustration. *It's like dealing with the Matong. They are not straightforward as if they choose to keep me confused.*

EXPLAIN WHY YOU AND YOUR PEOPLE ARE HERE.

YOU DON'T KNOW?

TELL US.

Jaxyl feels as if she is floating away from her crew. She carefully reaches out to grasp Officer Cruuws who will soon be out of reach. His body is completely immobile, and he looks more like a statue than a living organism. This makes her shudder, and she feels an unwelcome flutter of panic. There is nothing he can do to save her now. *Why did I allow this to happen?* Suddenly her mind snaps open despite the awkward purple substance pervading every cell of her body both inside and out. It clings to her lungs and her breathing is labored.

WE HAVE BEEN TOLD YOU CAN STOP THE ESCOBAR GIANTS. THEY PILLAGE AND DESTROY. THEY ARE WIPING OUT PEACEFUL SPECIES ACROSS GALAXIES. CAN YOU STOP THEM?

YOU SPEAK OF THE BALA' LOODS?

THEY ARE GIANT MACHINES. THEY CONNECT TO CREATE A SHIP FOR TRAVEL. WHEN THEY REACH THEIR DESTINATION, THEY SPLIT APART AND DESTROY.

YES, WE ARE AWARE OF THESE MACHINES. THEY WERE CREATED BY AN UNFORTUNATE EVENT.

Jaxyl's body continues to wander. She has no sense of up or down except for the fact the crew remains stabilized. Her hand is still firmly gripping Joesl's sleeve, but she feels more vulnerable as time inches by.

CAN YOU HELP US?

IT WILL BE DIFFICULT.

WHAT DO YOU MEAN? WHAT CAN YOU DO?

LEAVING OUR PLANET IS EXTRAORDINARILY CHALLENGING.

WE WILL HAVE TO HAVE MORE CONVERSATIONS.

FOR NOW, YOU MUST RETURN TO YOUR SHIP. YOUR UNBORN CHILD CANNOT REMAIN HERE EXCEPT IN SHORT TIME INCREMENTS.

YOU MAY BRING ONE OTHER NEXT TIME FOR YOUR COMFORT BUT WE DO NOT WANT THE OTHERS, IT IS SUPERFLUOUS AND WASTES ENERGY.

Panic so sharp it seeps into her fingertips, causes her to momentarily let go of Joesl's sleeve. Her fingers tremble as she gropes frantically for the fabric of his uniform. *The crystal we brought with us is in Joesl's backpack. How am I supposed to get it out so we can touch it together and return if they are frozen?*

89-Making Sense of the Encounter

Jaxyl is suddenly enveloped in a dark shroud, and everything goes blank. When she awakens, she finds herself landing in a crouching position with her sword drawn. When she jumps up to look for her crew members, she realizes she is on the Ursula Weir, on the ForeSat no less. Captain Othniel and the others on deck look startled to see her.

"Jaxyl are you okay?" The captain rushes to her.

"Maybe," she says brushing herself off.

There is a general panic in the ForeSat when the others don't return with Jaxyl, but in reality, it is only a brief delay, not much longer than the time it takes for a *muldogen* on Merth to swallow a winged *catstar* whole. But at first, everyone is at a loss for why she is standing before them with her sword drawn and the others are not to be seen. Their return and hers, is punctuated by a slight dripping on the floor of condensing purple haze from the exterior of their bodies.

Fatigue swamps Jaxyl and the others, and Doctor Sandral is sent for. The entire team ends up in the Weir's medical clinic. There is lots of grateful chatter as the landing party comes to realize they are safe once again. "Man, I can't believe we missed it," one crew member is heard complaining.

"I know, I was eager for action. All our training for nothing."

"I don't really see anything out of the ordinary, but they all definitely need to rest," Dr. Sandral tells Oscara.

"That will have to wait until we debrief," she tells the first medical officer causing Dr. Sandral to rush to Jaxyl's side to scan the baby before she is ushered away.

"Officer Cruuws, please give your report."

The tall bony Talvoc, with a short boyish haircut, shrugs. "I wish I had something to tell. I defer to Officer Karda; she was the only one conscious during our brief encounter."

Jaxyl's head is still spinning from the event, and she yearns to be with Flodynhelm and take a long ride to clear her mind. "It all happened extremely fast." Instinctively her hand touches her belly, she has had to start wearing more flexible material as her red leather tunics are no longer practical.

"We were all encased in this purple haze or mist. It's what I was breathing, anyway. The Folotar did speak to me. They said next time to only bring one other. We discussed the Giants, and they called them something else. They said they were created by accident, by some catastrophic event. I asked them if they would help us, and they said it would be difficult for them to travel. I sensed no one person was speaking because I heard many voices." She was aware she was talking fast, but she wanted to get the experience out before she forgot the details.

"It was terrifying to be the only one cognizant, I did have the feeling they were sincere in their concern for us and our request, but honestly if they already knew about the Escobar giants, and they could shut them down, why haven't they already done it?"

"Perhaps…" Cruuws squirms a little in his chair. "Perhaps, that is their weakness they cannot travel, and why they haven't already taken care of the situation."

Othniel seems to be deliberating the logic of this and Jaxyl nods affirmatively.

"Yes, this makes sense and yet if it's true, it may take some creative action to make this work."

"We have reviewed your recordings and there are none," The captain shares looking toward First Officer Oscara to confirm. She nods. "We were afraid this would be the case and we are completely at your mercy Officer Karda. Do you stand by your report? Anything to add?"

90-Exhaustion

Jaxyl is beginning to stagger as she reaches her door. *I don't remember ever being this exhausted.* She tears at her clothing struggling to release herself from it and throws it on the floor. As she is about to flop onto the bed, she turns to land on her side, remembering at the last minute not to crush the baby. She is becoming more aware of her changing body, but gestation is still new to her.

There is a knock at the door. "Go away," she responds.

"Officer Karda, it is me Scorzo. Can I get you anything? I was told to escort you, but you had already left the ForeSat when I got there. Are you all right?"

"Mmmph go away,"

"I'm coming in."

Jaxyl pulls her lush comforter up over herself awkwardly, partially covering her upper body. "What?" she growls at him. "I'm exhausted. Leave me alone."

"Yes, of course, can I get you some water or some tea before I leave?"

"Water, set here." she pats the mattress.

Scorzo nods his head thinking Jaxyl is the strongest person he has ever known, and here she is like a wilted flower on her bed. He goes to the regenerator and brings her chilled water. "I can't set it there, it will spill. Sit up please and let me help you take a drink."

"Don't belittle me," she mumbles, but does as he says, pinching her bedding between her arms across her chest. "Oh, that's good," she swallows loudly, making a noise she would be unlikely to make in public.

After she has taken several lengthy swigs of the water he says, "I'll come back in a little while to check on you."

"I'm fine," she says absently as she flops back down on her pillow, nearly instantly falling asleep.

A smile slim and quiet slips across Scorzo's lips and he shakes his head slightly, recognizing he may never meet anyone again as enigmatic as his current charge.

A dream comes upon Jaxyl like a swiftly moving fog with physical sensations and music, almost as if she is attending a dress rehearsal because not everything is sequential. It starts with a loud clatter and in her mind, she jumps up from her bed, but this is not the case. Instead, she is skipping through a field of fresh grass in her mind. The pristine carpet nature has created is like a silky velvet under her feet. She is about eight revolutions again, and it is the first time she realizes the gravity of Merth has no hold on her. It's exhilarating to skip and leap and ride on the air. Suddenly she finds herself holding the hand of a small child, a girl who looks up and giggles at her. The morning starlight dances across their faces, across the field of fresh grass.

"Who are you?" she asks the child, "Should we tell Mother we can fly? Will she forbid us?" She can hear a lyrical melody in the wind and feels the warmth of the starlight on her face when her playmate trips and Jaxyl finds she is dragging the child as she leaps up into the air. "I'm sorry," she stops and cradles the child in her arms. I never meant to hurt you. Are you all right?"

In a far corner of her mind a horse whinnies and stomps his foot. It is Flodynhelm and he prances nervously rising above the ground while making a loud snorting noise as if anticipating battle. Jaxyl takes the child in her arms and places the toddler on his back. A calmness like a gentle breeze passes over them. The baby girl lifts her arms and giggles. Flodynhelm rears and paws the air with his hooves, but the child holds onto his mane and smiles. Then a voice, hard and distinct more like a soldier's than a child's voice commands Jaxyl to rise.

She lifts herself to join the child on the bare back of her horse and suddenly feels an overwhelming rush of confidence and empowerment. Without urging, Flodynhelm takes off into the borderless depth of her imagination and she is rocked into a dreamless sleep by his stride.

91-No Going Back

Jaxyl is awakened by a pounding at the door. She pulls herself up and is knocked hard by the growing being inside of her. She rubs her ribs and smiles with indignation. *Give me a break little one, or not so little one. You grow bigger every day.* "Coming," she calls to the person on the other side of the door.

Scorzo looks especially harried. "Did you not hear the signal on your console? The Folotor are hailing us and requesting your presence."

"No, I guess not," she stumbles, still soggy with sleep, but Scorzo grabs her arm to brace her. *I'm getting more awkward. Fortunately, there is no battle ahead, or let's hope so anyway.*

"We must hurry."

"Relax, Get me some tea and *tartles*, please. I'm starving, And maybe some *chantonbleau.*"

Scorzo sucks in his breath, clearly agitated by her noncompliance. "But the captain is waiting!"

Jaxyl tips up her vim finger and calls Othniel. "Yes, I'll be there shortly, sir." She quickly disconnects so there is no chance for the captain to respond.

"I even buzzed your vim, and you didn't answer."

"Relax, will you?" She gives him a condescending smirk, thinking he is the most demanding servant she has ever had.

As if he were able to read her mind, which he is not. He lets out another frustrated sigh. "You are my responsibility, yet you treat me as if I am your servant." But Scorzo's indignation doesn't even register with the Warrior Princess who begins to dress, dropping her lush robe on the floor. Scorzo looks away but not before he sees the silhouette of his charge's curvaceous and majestic body now full with child, her muscles rippling as she pulls on her newly designed uniform which allows for her growing girth.

"Here have a *tartle*, they are amazingly flaky." She takes one off the tray he has brought her and tosses it to him, which he doesn't refuse. Stuffing one down clumsily, she takes a long draft of the *chilton* juice Scorzo created to accompany her meal, and scoops up the generously sized *chantonbleau*, biting into it as they exit.

"Officer Karda, we are so pleased you chose to finally join us." Othniel's tone is kind albeit his message snide. She brushes off some crumbs that have settled on her breasts and pulls her carriage up to an authoritative stance.

"Yes sir, sorry for the delay."

"We can do little without you. They want another visit."

"Yes, sir bring it on."

"Are you prepared?"

"No, but they won't keep me for long because of the baby. The first visit was extremely exhausting, but if they call, I shall go."

Othniel nods to the security officer accompanying her and a crystal is brought forth and set on a portable pedestal. She looks straight across the stone toward her escort, a man shorter in stature than the average Talvoc, and wonders why he has been selected and not one of the previous crew members. She looks at Othniel then turns to take another studied look at her companion. His black eyes blink and she thinks perhaps he is not real, but a machine similar to the beings they encountered when the Ursula Weir first appeared at Merth. She can't tell for sure because of the mask he is wearing. As they begin the rhythmic countdown with their forearms there is no going back.

92-Time is Irrelevant

When she gains consciousness, Jaxyl feels as if the Folotar have been scanning her. It is the kind of feeling that makes the hair on the back of her neck stand up. She has no information to confirm. She feels like she is in a prone position, but there is no way to verify this as she has no feeling for what is up or down in the purple haze which appears darker this time. But she is ready with her question understanding her visit will be brief.

YOU WERE GOING TO TELL ME HOW THE ESCOBAR GIANTS WERE LET LOOSE TO DESTROY THE COSMOS.

THE BALA' LOODS WERE UNLEASHED THROUGH A CATASTROPHIC FAILURE.

EXPLAIN, she demands.

THEY WERE CREATED TO EXPLORE USING ARTIFICIAL INTELLIGENCE SO SENTIENT BEINGS WITH LIMITED LIFE SPANS COULD BE REPLACED FOR LENGTHY SPACE JOURNEYS.

BUT THERE WAS A MASSIVE FAILURE OF THE ARTIFICIAL INTELLIGENCE GIVEN TO THE BALA' LOODS BECAUSE THEY EVOLVED TO DESTROY.

THEY COULD NOT RECONCILE WITH THE IMPERFECTIONS OF BIOLOGICALS AND THEY BECAME MONSTERS, TOTALLY OUT OF CONTROL

This chilling fact momentarily stuns Jaxyl, but she needs to push forward.

HOW ARE THE FOLOTAR INVOLVED AND WHY ARE YOU THE ONLY ONES WHO CAN CORRECT THIS MISTAKE?

IT IS A GREAT SIN WE HAVE COMMITTED AND DIFFICULT TO CORRECT. WE CREATED THEM BECAUSE WE HAVE NO WAY OF LEAVING OUR SPHERE.

As she absorbs the Folotor's admissions she has a more personal angle to cover. AM I TO UNDERSTAND CORRECTLY OUR MATONG WAS BROUGHT TO MERTH BY THE FOLOTOR?

YES, WE SENT IT TO PROVIDE ORDERLY DIRECTION.

THEN PERHAPS YOU CAN SEND AN ORB WITH US ON THE URSULA WEIR TO HELP US ERADICATE THE GIANTS.

IT IS NOT SIMPLE BUT WE HAVE BEEN THINKING UPON THOSE SAME STREAMS OF THOUGHT. THIS MISSION REQUIRES THE ANHILATION OF MULTIPLE TARGETS ACROSS THE COSMOS.

Jaxyl is beginning to feel light-headed and notices her body is spinning more. CAN YOU COMMUNICATE WITH ME WITHOUT MY HAVING TO COME HERE. I FEAR FOR MY BABY'S SAFETY.

WE WOULD NEVER DO ANYTHING TO HARM THIS MOST DIVINE CHILD AND NO YOU MUST COME HERE UNTIL WE RESOLVE OUR ISSUE.

WE WILL NOT SUMMON YOU AGAIN UNTIL
WE HAVE A SOLUTION.

Jaxyl works to subdue her joy at hearing this news.
HOW LONG? CAN YOU ESTIMATE?

TIME IS IRRELEVANT.

NO, IT IS VERY RELEVANT, I'M CLOSE TO GIV-
ING BIRTH AND I WANT TO RETURN TO MY PLAN-
ET MERTH WITH MY CHILD BEFORE EVERYONE I
KNOW THERE IS DEAD. There is a strange noise in the
distance like a *moson* howling at the moons on Merth. It
sends a chill down her spine.

DON'T BE IMPATIENT THERE IS MUCH TO BE
DONE BEFORE YOU CAN RETURN.

Jaxyl's body spins and she feels a dull pain in her head.
When she comes back to consciousness, she is lying on
the floor of the ForeSat along with her travel companion,
who she now recognizes as one of the original team. Officer Cruuws comes to help her up. The pain in her head
is growing and she feels weak. She is not sure if she can
walk. "Here sit down a minute," he tells her as the crew
look curiously in her direction.

93-Your Time is Near

As the birth of her baby nears, Jaxyl becomes extremely irritable. Her massive belly blocks her from her two favorite activities, riding Flodynhelm and having sex. She is eating to excess but now is so pregnant there is not much room left in her body to overindulge in her favorite foods.

"Your time is close," Dr. Sandral warns her. I want you to come see me every morning from here on out. It's best if we handle the birth naturally, but I'm not letting you go too much longer."

"What do you mean by that?"

'We have hormones we can give you to help to flush your little girl out." Dr. Sandral gives her a rare smile, her thin lips parting in a strained fashion,

"I prefer not to."

"Of course, I understand, but there is nothing harmful about it."

"If I were at home on Merth, there would be a most public birthing. All the dignitaries would be attending as part of the extravaganza of a royal birth."

"Oh, my that sounds terrible," Dr. Sandral's smile draws up as if she has just bitten into the bitter blasomal bark.

Jaxyl shrugs, "My little planet is not very advanced."

"Look at her kick," Dr. Sandral places her hand on Jaxyl's visibly moving rounded belly.

"She's ready to get out!"

"I prefer you have the baby here in the clinic so we can address any complications that might arise.

"I don't see that happening, I'm quite robust and healthy."

"Of course, you are, but we want to be prepared for anything," the doctor tells her. "Are you drinking lots of water?"

Jaxyl rolls her eyes. "My life is abysmally boring doctor. I do what you tell me despite my propensity to ignore your expertise."

Dr. Sandral's lips again form an unusual crescent, and she realizes she is beginning to like this brazen princess, soon-to-be mother.

It happens that night after an unsettling struggle to sleep, Jaxyl finally drifts off only to be rudely awakened by the popping sound of her water breaking, drenching her bed. She sits up carefully finding she is dizzy and taps her vim finger to her mouth. "Scorzo, I think this is it. Can you get down here right away?" He is shocked by her courtesy. Then a roiling, gut-wrenching pain grasps her body and wrings her out. She groans uncontrollably. She has never been wounded in battle luckily, but this seems much worse.

When Scorzo arrives, he has a chair on wheels for her to glide to the clinic on, but she will have nothing to do with it. "Put that *flowkin* thing away. I can walk," which she does awkwardly leaning over on him as if she is going to break in half, her body laden fully with another being. Despite the late hour, they pass another crew member, a man looking to quietly return to his bed without incident, but who steps up to support her other side. In this way, she arrives at the Ursula Weir's health clinic to birth her most divine child, as the Folotar refer to her baby.

Jaxyl is determined to give birth in a dignified fashion, but it is not to be. She has severely underrated the intensity of the pain. At first, she groans so loudly they can hear her down the hall. Flodynhelm much further out of earshot knows instinctively something is wrong with Jaxyl. Rearing and thrashing his hooves, he crushes his stable corral, and the crew has to subdue him with an electronic ray, or he would have stormed down the passageway to rescue her.

Then the cursing comes like a Targa storm, sharp, brutal, and hazardous. "*Flum!* You *flowkin pistoid* Clouton. You did this to me and so did the flowkin Matong. I've been *flumed* from the moment I met you. I swear if I ever see you again, I will punch you in the groin until you scream for mercy. You *flowkin baltoff!*"

The nurse peers anxiously at Dr. Sandral with an injection at the ready but Sandral nods subtly no. "I don't want to do anything that might cause a complication. Just secure her arms so I can check and see what is going on." She nods to several beefy aides who have quietly assembled.

"Don't you touch me you *flowkin pistoids* I will kill all of you!"

"Now Jaxyl you are about to become a mother; you need to cooperate with us for the safety of your baby." Dr.

Sandral nods and they commence to secure her wrists to the table. Jaxyl makes a decisive swing at one of them and he goes flying across the floor. "Jaxyl I'm warning you! I don't want to sedate you, but I will if you don't cooperate!"

Another gut-wrenching pain comes sliding down her spine and Jaxyl nods submissively as a primal scream issues from her lips. Everyone in the room is startled by it, even those who have delivered numerous babies. "The delivery is going too fast," one nurse whispers to another.

A few more volcanic shrieks and the baby delivers. Like a defused bomb a calm settles over the room. "Let me have her," Jaxyl demands of the doctor.

Sandral turns smiling and holding the bloody little babe in a tiny blanket. "We are going to clean her up."

"No, unleash me and let me have her." Dr. Sandral, feeling the tone of Jaxyl's words, commanding but calm, releases the wrist bracelet with her vim finger. When Jaxyl sits up and stretches out her arms as any normal mother would, Sandral hesitates wondering, if after Jaxyl's previously explosive behavior, she is going to lick her baby clean like some wild animal.

"No, really it's okay, I'm safe now," she grins and beckons with her hands for Sandral to approach. It is as if a light has bled into her soul, and she is an entirely different woman than the one who had moments before threatened to kill everyone in the room.

94-Transformation

The room is still as a cold night on Merth in the middle of Asunder, when both moons temporarily disappear from the sky, as the experienced staff watches Jaxyl bond with her baby. Jaxyl stares into the tiny creature's perfect violet eyes, the same color as her aunt Galen's, and feels as if the morning star of Merth has melted away a sheet of ice that has surrounded her, her whole life. She whispers a song into the baby's tiny ear she remembers her mother singing to her as a child.

Dilta, dilta vosoon twil
Vasil, vason fone
Foltol filmon josoon longe
Twyttl, twyttl, vine

With wide eyes, Sandral looks at her nurse. She has never seen such dramatic behavioral changes in such a short span of time, and suddenly she realizes how lonely Jaxyl must be with none of her people surrounding her at this crucial moment. Instead, a handful of curious medical personnel have gathered to witness the unusually loud birth. The silence is broken by whispering on the outer fringes of the small room as reality seeps mysteriously into context and the curious onlookers file out a few at a time.

A single tear forms and runs down Jaxyl's cheek. She dabs it away and tightens her grip on the baby whose eyes focus intently on her mother, but not before the salty wetness touches the baby's face. Jaxyl kisses her lightly on her small plump cheek and words of love without syllables or sounds are transferred between them as the baby has no language yet to express, only love for the being who has brought her forth.

Dr. Sandrals's nurse brings a warm moist towel and hands it to Jaxyl to swab the baby down. The doctor and she both marvel at the gentleness with which Jaxyl performs this task, setting the baby on her back atop her thighs, she opens the blanket and begins to clean the afterbirth off. No one speaks, no one wants to break the spell. The nurse brings more towels, and they are swapped out as needed without conversation.

Finally, Jaxyl says, "She has no name. She will need a name." Dr. Sandral looks puzzled. "It is up to the Matong to name royal babies." *I can't believe I had never thought of this, she curses herself.* "She will also need a bed. She needs her own place to sleep."

"No problem. I'll have a *cholar* sent to your quarters. But for now, you must rest. Let us take the baby and check her out to see if she needs anything."

Jaxyl eyes Sandral with uncertainty. "I must hold her now. She's perfect and needs nothing."

Sandral shrugs, "I think you should listen to me. We will give her back shortly," she says firmly. Reluctantly, Jaxyl acquiesces and hands the baby to her while the nurse takes Jaxyl to relax in a steam shower.

When she is reunited with her baby the infant is crying. "What have you done to her?" Jaxyl snarls.

Dr. Sandral laughs. "Relax she's just hungry."

"Oh, give her to me."

As Jaxyl holds her child and feeds her, she is filled with a chaotic miasma of conflicting emotions. On the one hand, she is awestruck at the connection she has with her child, and on the other hopelessly confused about how to take care of her. *I was born and raised for combat and yet here I am a mother with a child.*

"It's best if you put her up on your shoulder and give her a little pat to help her burp and let her rest then let her feed on the other side." The nurse tells her and Jaxyl does as she is told. The baby feeds greedily and Jaxyl begins to relax. It is then Oscara appears in the doorway.

"Am I too late? I hear there was all kinds of excitement."

"Come in, you arrive in time for the best part. She has a full stomach and wants to meet you." Jaxyl is almost giddy upon seeing her closest friend on the ship.

"I have something for you."

"Oh, what is it?

Oscara pulls out a white leather pouch with decorative markings on it. "It is a sacramental *fosto* pouch for carrying the baby."

"It's beautiful!" Jaxyl says admiring the hand stitching and intricate beading on the soft leather baby pouch.

"There's just one caveat, it is a family heirloom and I've been saving it for when I eventually have children."

"Oh, I mustn't take it then," Jaxyl says handing it back.

"No, no, it is our tradition in our culture that mothers share things such as this, it comes from my grandmother and has been used many times. Babies grow so fast. It is good *choo chu* to share.

"Thank you, dear friend, I should use it a lot, I'm sure." But Jaxyl's face twists with angst as she holds back tears.

"What is it Jaxyl what's wrong?"

"I'm a mess, I haven't cried so much in my life, one minute I'm crying with happiness, the next minute with deep regret. I don't even have a name for my baby. It is my failing; I am already a terrible mother. The Matong on Merth always names our royal babies. There is no Matong here only the Folotor, who are the Matong's creators. They must name her. They should have told me when I went to see them last. Now we will have to wait until I am summoned, which could take a while."

95-A Surprise Visit

Oscara and Scorzo escort Jaxyl and the baby back to her quarters where they find a small reception of greeters waiting on them. "We realize you are exhausted, but we want to welcome the newest addition to the crew. We won't stay long." Oscara reassures her.

"You knew of this?" Jaxyl turns to Scorzo.

"Yes, they said to keep it a surprise." Laid out on her dining table, large enough to seat six, are dozens of wrapped gifts. And near her bedside is the *chotal* brought in for the baby to sleep in. Jaxyl sucks it up and with Scorzo there to pass out refreshments she opens the presents and lets Oscara hold the baby and show her off. To the delight of all.

Jaxyl has been given instructions on how often to feed her newborn and other incidentals like changing her, but some of the gifts, other than adorable outfits, are confusing. She doesn't admit to anyone, she doesn't understand what they are for. If she were home on Merth there would be a full-time attendant for the child.

"Scorzo will assist, he's just around the corner from your quarters," Dr. Sandral had reminded her when Jaxyl flashed her a stone-cold look of despair earlier. "Synthetic alcohol is okay to drink but you must keep your wits about you at all times with such a tiny infant," Sandral had warned her. "Always lay her down on her side when you put her to sleep and swaddle her like we have done.

They like to be bundled. She's been curled up in your womb, so it feels normal to her."

Oddly, as tired as she is the little gathering makes Jaxyl feel less alone and distant from her home with her growing circle of friends, but the minute they leave she crashes into her bed and falls into a dense sleep. She is so fatigued she doesn't wake up at first when the baby starts crying. The newborn is red-faced from wailing when Jaxyl finally sits up and picks the distraught infant up to feed her. "There sweet baby of mine don't cry. I'm here." She whispers into the infant's tiny velvety ear cuddling the newborn up to her breast. Feeling for the first time twinges of mother guilt. The strong pull of the nursing baby startles her but as she becomes more awake, she is alarmed by something else even more. There is a dull purple glow pulsing in the corner of the room.

DO NOT BE AFRAID.
WE HAVE SOLVED THE QUESTION OF HOW TO TRAVEL BEYOND OUR PROTECTIVE FIELD OF PLANETS.
THE CONCEPT IS MUCH LIKE YOUR MATONG ON MERTH
BUT WE HAD TO MAKE SOME CHANGES FOR PORTABILITY
Clutching the baby even tighter Jaxyl responds. YOU SURPRISED ME. WHAT SHALL I CALL YOU?
YOU SHALL CALL US WAYTU WHICH MEANS MENTOR OR SPIRITUAL GUIDE IN OUR LANGUAGE.

WE ARE HERE TO GUIDE YOU THROUGH THE ANNIHILATION OF THE BALA' LOODS OR AS YOU CALL THEM THE ESCOBAR GIANTS
IN THIS FORM WE CAN TRAVEL WITH YOU.

A calming sensation drifts over Jaxyl like a warm steam vapor. *Finally, I have some answers. With this kind of guidance, we can do this.* She looks at her baby's tiny face smashed against her breast with closed eyes who periodically nods off only to wake and begin anew.

YOU HAVE NOT GIVEN ME A NAME YET FOR MY BABY. YOU SAY SHE IS DIVINE AND IS TO CHANGE THE COSMOS WITH HER BENEVOLENT TEACHINGS OF LOVE.
SHE IS TO BE NAMED YEZDA ASTRAEUS.
THERE WILL BE NO ONE ABOVE HER.
NOT EVEN YOU.

Jaxyl is not sure how she likes the name. *It's a mouthful.* Still dazed from lack of sleep, Jaxyl notices the baby has stopped nursing. "Oh no you don't they warned me. You are going to have to wake up and feed on the other side." Taking the baby up onto her shoulder she pats her until she hears the tiniest of burps. "I'll have to tutor you on how to make a bolder statement," Jaxyl smiles remembering how as an adolescent she and her playmates would see who could elicit the most obnoxious noises from their diaphragms in a competition for who could be the crudest, a practice her mother had scolded her for.

"I guess we'll call you Yez," she tells the baby touching her cheek.

96-What is this About?

"What do you mean the Folotor are on board, and we are ready to depart?" Othniel questions Jaxyl when she calls him.

"I think you need to come see for yourself. There is an orb in my quarters sir, and they've already explained it is to remain here."

"This is highly unusual," the captain mutters to himself. "I'm on my way."

Jaxyl jumps into the shower and dresses hastily. Thankfully Yez is still asleep. *But I need to nurse her soon.* She calls Scorzo to put him on alert should she need him. When Othniel arrives, he has Oscara with him and several high-ranking security personnel.

"Don't touch it. I'm the only one who can touch it. I will ask it to speak aloud so you can hear the message. It… they are to be referred to as the Waytu." And of course, it is then Yez begins to awaken with gurgling sounds and Jaxyl turns nervously to Scorzo.

"Don't pick her up until she is alert, then jiggle her a little. I'll feed her in a minute." Jaxyl stands near the orb, much smaller than the Matong, and places her hand on it. Her head fills with the presence of the Folotor.

FOR PRACTICAL PURPOSES YOU MUST SPEAK ALOUD.

Of course, Captain Othniel we are the Waytu. The manifested voice is somewhat musical, rising and falling with a lyrical quality to it. **We have manifested here to assist you in defeating the Bala' Lood or as you refer to them as the Escobar Giants. We are limited in our mobility aboard the ship. In an emergency, we can move about, but it drains vital energy needed for our mission.**

"I see, but is this the best location for you? Shouldn't you be on the ForeSat where you can advise us more clearly when we are preparing for battle?" There is a soft whirring sound as the Waytu consider the captain's suggestion.

Security is of utmost importance. Noise is also a consideration. We don't want to be subjected to too many thoughts other than those pertinent to decision-making. With the Waytu engaged with the captain, Jaxyl slips away to feed Yez. As soon as the baby is satisfied, she hands her back to Scorzo and rejoins the conversation. It is apparent the Waytu are instructing the captain and others on how to construct a protective enclosure for the sphere.

Once the structure is complete, we will join you on the ForeSat.

"It's agreed, we will get right on this. We are anxious to proceed on our mission," Othniel concludes.

There is one thing more. The child.

"What about the child?"

She has been brought forth in the most difficult conditions, but unto us, a divine child is born. Othniel looks around the room at his crew feeling the pressure to say something but there are no words. Uncharacteristically he is paralyzed by the awkwardness of the moment.

Jaxyl gives him a slight nod as if to confirm what the Waytu have said. "Sir, they want you to acknowledge the child."

"But I," he gives her a confused look until his leadership skills finally float up inside of him. "We acknowledge the presence of."

"Her name is Yezda Astraeus," Jaxyl whispers.

"Yezda Astraeus and will do our best to carry out our mission, keeping her safe and all others who might be the target of the Bala' Lood."

All who stand in the tight circle wait for the Waytu to respond to the captain but there is no further correspondence. Othniel looks down at his feet as he considers this strange task before them and then looks around at the others. "We have our instructions let's get to it. Shall we?"

"I don't understand," someone whispers. "What is the importance of Officer Karda's child? What is so important about her child?"

Book V

The Bala' Lood

97-A Spark of Interest

"I am *flowkin* tired of this. All I want is to take Yez home." Jaxyl tells Oscara and Taldon who now have a little boy of their own, Tadile. He is a little younger than Yez, but they enjoy playing with each other. The cozy group also includes another couple Toosile and Flyke who also have a similar-aged boy. They get together occasionally for dinner and drinks and to let the kids play. Tonight, Oscara has invited Muir Johhson to join them ostensibly as Jaxyl's date. She has a not-so-secret agenda for Jaxyl, now she is a mother of a growing child, to settle down with a more "suitable partner." Muir is a single father with an adolescent son who has not joined them.

Oscara sips on her long-stemmed glass filled with a sparkling elixir. Her aura has become a milky white as it flutters softly around her. "Yes, the last encounter on the Flortyl outpost was a little dicey. I thought for sure we were all going to die." She looks pointedly at each friend in the circle around the synthetic fire ring. "Don't repeat me on that, I've had a little too much wine."

"Me too," Tosile giggles.

Flyke flashes his wholesome toothy smile and nods in agreement. Muir looks to Jaxyl with a neutral smile. Other than a casual interface through work they have barely spoken to each other before tonight.

"The outpost was probably our most challenging battle yet, but we have to keep pursuing until they all are crushed, or they will continue to replicate," Taldon weighs in.

"You are *flowkin* right!" Jaxyl sets her glass down a little too harshly and it teeters before she reaches to stabilize it, "But *loudon*, it feels like we are always one step behind them. What we really need is a way to seed them with a destructive virus preventing further replication. We have discussed this, but no one seems to take the idea seriously. I'm not staying out here forever chasing this *flowkin* anathema."

"Admit it, at first you took relish in the battles." Oscara chides her.

"Of course, I did, I still do really," she sits up from her relaxed position on the couch and adjusts her tunic, "but Yez is in my life now. I need to get her home in case something does happen to me. The *Waytu* keep telling me how important she is, but they do not come up with a better solution to end this war."

"Perhaps I might make a suggestion," Muir speaks up.

"Yes?" Jaxyl turns and looks directly at him. *Finally, he has something to say. This guy has been excruciatingly quiet most of the evening. He's definitely my type physically but far too quiet. Oscara should know me better by now.*

The kids come running through the room giggling and splashing their glee everywhere. Oscara smiles and Jaxyl scolds with a stern look. Taldon reaches for his son to slow him down.

Muir smiles understandingly at the children's antics then looks down at his drink. "What I was going to say is, we have a very gifted and young, very young—she's a friend of my son—scientist who has been working on a project like what you have been talking about. I don't really understand it, but she's in our quarters a lot, and I hear her talking about her work to Haldon."

Jaxyl perks up and turns to the man she has been sitting beside all night. "Let's talk to her tomorrow. Anything to give us an alternative to chasing these demons for the rest of our lives deserves consideration."

As the evening grows late Jaxyl prepares to leave and Johhson volunteers to walk her and Yez back to their quarters.

"Why? "Jaxyl spins around. "You think we might be eaten by loose *targellas* roaming the hallways of the ship?" she asks a little too snidely. Oscara frowns and her aura spikes with vivid colors and Jaxyl realizes her social error. "I'm sorry sure, why not? I can see I have angered our host."

Johhson laughs for the first time that night and shrugs. Jaxyl's voice softens. "Of course, you may walk us home. I didn't mean to be rude. No one can accuse me of being a social *bustarella*."

"Would you like Yez to stay here for the night?" Oscara asks but before Jaxyl can shake her head no, Yez begins squealing joyfully.

"Oh, mama please, please mama, please."

Jaxyl scowls at Oscara fiercely and wants to scold her, but Yez is so excited about her first sleepover, she bites her tongue, and gives in. Kissing Yez goodnight, she lets Johhson escort her back to her quarters. At first, there is a terrible awkwardness between them until he starts to ask her what it is like to bond with the Waytu, "Does it drain you?"

Turning to face him she pauses, "I don't think anyone has ever asked me that question."

"I'm no social *bustarella* either, whatever that is and truthfully, he stops and look directly at her. "You scare me a little."

"Ha, nothing new. Is it in a good way or bad way?"

"What?"

"That I scare you."

He smiles now with an expression filling his face like a fire has been lit inside of him. "Maybe you will let me show you, rather than tell you." And when he touches her, she completely zones out. They can hardly make it to her door before they start tearing each other's clothes off.

By morning Jaxyl is a little terrified of Muir, who has proven to be a great lover, and this makes her feel uneasy about how much she enjoyed their tryst.

"I sleep around a lot," she tells him.

"I've heard." He grins.

"You *pistoid!* Can't you show the Warrior Princess a little respect?"

"I think I already have. Is this some sort of marriage proposal? You warn me right off the bat you are promiscuous. Need I have a stake in this conversational trajectory?"

"Aach you are more than disrespectful!" She kicks at him playfully, and he tackles her back. "Be careful what you start again."

She grins. "I think I'm being quite careful." She says as their two mouths are joined in one thirsty drink of lust.

98-A Gifted Prodigy

"So, what we have here is what we call a sinkhole," Masalla points to a schematic diagram on the big computer screen which, is surrounded by a dense forest of mathematical equations. Muir, who holds the highest degrees in botany and plant mutations, is looking a little lost himself. He meets Jaxyl's gaze to reassure her.

"You weren't lying when you said she was young," she whispers, "but I'm almost embarrassed to bring this to Othniel. How old is she anyway?"

"The same age as my son, but she's the real thing. She's already published in the Science Academy's most prestigious journal, the *Hackenslaud*."

Jaxyl breaks in, "Forgive me Masalla, did I pronounce your name correctly?" The unusually pale girl—her translucent skin glows with the luminescence of *thisbaen* pearls—thin and petite with a tight brown bun spun on top of her head, nods affirmatively. "Have we been clear to you what our purpose is?"

"Yes, you have, you wish to plant a death virus in the Bala' Lood which will kill them and stop them from replicating. The artificial intelligence the Folotar built into them has run riot and they are now destroying biological life across the cosmos." Masalla sighs and mumbles to herself sardonically. "Who could have not seen that coming?" she continues. "Rather than be site-specific I see this application as a tool to be attached close to the proximity of the artificial brain stream infecting it and causing chaos to thwart the replication process. I wish I had a ray ready for you to use as a projection delivery, but I don't. This dissolution virus will have to be manually installed. It's been tested extensively in the laboratory, and we can count on its success."

"I'm ready to bring this to Othniel as soon as possible." Feeling jittery, Jaxyl flashes her vim to her lips and immediately decides to meet with Othniel. "Yes sir, we'll be there in ten."

Masalla looks confused. "But I'm on my way to tutor a student."

"Sorry kid that will have to wait."

As they gather in the Portal beneath the ForeSat, Othniel looks at the girl and smiles, "Yes, I am familiar with your scientific reputation and research. We have been kicking this idea around for a while now, but no one brought your research to my attention."

"Masalla gives the maneuver a 90 percent success rate," Jaxyl emphasizes to Othniel early into the presentation.

"Yes, unfortunately, our victory depends on the possibility of human error during a combat strike. There is much that can go wrong with placing the box," the young scientist says.

Othniel takes a great breath and chooses this moment to stroke Jaxyl's ego. "Yes, but we have the great Warrior

Princess, who I am assuming is more than willing to take the lead on this." He shifts his glance to her and smiles.

Jaxyl grins back at him seeing this as her chance to go home. *One last battle and we're free!*

"Okay Officer Masalla, I am giving you the rank of lead scientist on this project, and it comes with an officer's privileges. It will take some time for us to reach the closest Escobar Giant and in the meantime, I want you to gather a team of scientists to improve your current odds."

"Yes, sir," Masalla says as she squares her shoulders in salute.

"Officer Karda, you need to assemble a combat team specifically for this mission. We need to be laser-focused on the success of planting this virus effectively. This means your team will have to figure a way to board the Escobar Giant undetected, a task not easily achieved."

"Yes, sir I'm on it. Training will begin immediately."

99-Planning the Attack

Jaxyl selects two others to be on the transport team with her to board the Bala' Lood ship. "We shall be lean and mean," she tells Joesla Cruuws and Feldyn Poster frequently. Cruuws is a master warrior and Feldyn is a specialist in the viral technology they are counting on to destroy the Escobar Giants. She has been working closely with Masalla since the beginning of the project. The Waytu, the Folotor's manifestation on board, has counseled Jaxyl that Masalla's virus is sound for destroying the replicating abilities of the Bala' Lood.

The three crew members train vigorously before they get close to the Bala' Lood ship they have targeted. As they near the massive Escobar Giant the tension rises. "We must create a diversion," Cruuws warned early on. "This will help us with boarding their ship keeping the element of surprise. If we are to survive this attack, we must have stealth and confusion on our side."

While the training takes up most of Jaxyl's waking hours, she makes sure she has a stable home life for Yez who is now seven in Merth revolutions. Yez is ensconced in classes with her intellectual peers making her one of the youngest in her class, and she has many friends to keep her occupied when not in school. Jaxyl mostly sees her in the evenings when she and Yez and Muir dine together. They have moved in with Muir because he already had more spacious quarters. Haldon, Muir's son, now of legal age, has moved into his own quarters but visits often.

"Would you like to ride with me tonight?" Jaxyl asks Yez as she pulls out the *fuston* sticks and passes them out.

"Yes, Mother that would be nice, but I want to ride Flodynhelm by myself, you promised you would teach me as soon as I was big enough." Jaxyl gives her increasingly gangly daughter a second look as she inserts the serving set of *fustons* into the steaming *toslezo* and passes the handmade pottery serving bowl to Muir.

"I suppose it is time. I enjoy you sharing the saddle with me, but of course, it is time for you to learn to ride on your own." Muir, who has become an avid rider too, gives Jaxyl a quizzical look.

"Will she even be able to reach the stirrups?"

Jaxyl shrugs. "Probably not, but she can ride him bareback. He won't let her fall."

It is while she is teaching Yez to ride when Jaxyl has an inspiration. Lifting her up onto Flodynhelm's broad white back she thinks of the idea of a shield that could go around the crew members as a detection reflector or screen. Then it hits her. *Of course! Our diversion must be multi-faceted. One diversion which we have been discussing is not enough. If we transport multiple fake pods to the Bala' Lood ship and each hide in separate ones, we will create the element of surprise by manufacturing confusion. Hopefully this is enough to catch them off guard.*

When she presents her idea at the next group meeting, which includes Othniel, a wide grin spreads across his face. "The multiple pods will be like fireworks in our brains, they will absolutely lose it."

"If the scientists come up with a perfected shield design, I think I can say with confidence we have found a successful solution," Othniel concurs.

Masalla nods. "We've got this. I'll have Grilsoma in stealth technology get right on this."

100-Departure

The day comes when the predatory Bala' Lood ship looms in sight. From Jaxyl's port window, the enormous black and silver sphere gleams in the soft radiant light of a *suntana* moon the Bala' Lood are surveying for attack. The moon is occupied by a modest, peaceful community, which exists on its trade with the Tultana trade stream. Destroying it is neither politically savvy nor strategically motivated. It merely happens to be on the path of the artificially intelligent Bala' Lood species the Folotor have inadvertently created by trying to produce a foolproof method of space travel which doesn't rely on the frailty of biological beings when they must cross vast expanses of the cosmos. Their robotic answer had failed miserably. The Waytu, the Folotor entity now residing on the Ursula Weir, had conveyed to Jaxyl the Matong was delivered to Merth eons ago via the use of the Bala' Loods ships before they morphed into the Escobar Giants, so deadly to all biological beings.

As planned, the Ursula Weir hovers close enough to not be detected or attacked. The strategy is to board the menacing Escobar ship before it transforms and separates into destructive attack giants that can stomp out an entire civilization with their footprints the size of a small village on Merth.

The plan's design is to send the three warriors in a stealth ship and from there the team will transport along with numerous decoy pods. "We are hoping we will be able to get a strong microbeam image of the ship once we depart in stealth. This way we will realize where to place the virus box in the best location for success," Cruuws tells a group assembled on the ForeSat. "Unfortunately, at this point, we will not be able to communicate with the Waytu. We will be winging it a little." His voice drops. "We have rehearsed this many times, but I want you here stationed at the ForeSat during the operation to be ready for anything. If you have to leave us behind, you mustn't hesitate, but more importantly, if I give the order to abort you must do so immediately. Officer Masalla will be in close contact with us throughout, guiding us."

Jaxyl is surprisingly quiet. She had risen from her sleep cycle and taken Flodynhelm for a ride at breakneck speed until they were both dripping wet. Returning to her quarters, she had a steam cleansing and then joined her teammates for a hearty meal. Their biorhythms have been calculated and synced for the best time of departure that was approaching quickly.

Dressed in her famous attire, red leather pants and tunic with her notorious sword and shield on her back she feels ready for anything. After living on the Ursula Weir for such a long time, she rarely wears it unless she is going to battle practice.

"It's more for luck than anything," she told Muir before leaving. He had smiled fondly at her, trying his best not to allow his worry to surface, but by now she could read him far too well for him to hide anything from her. It was one of the barbs in their relationship. "You have an unfair advantage with your kinetic sight." He would often say.

Before departing to their stealth fighter launch, the group says goodbye with hugs and salutes. Jaxyl draws near to Muir and grabs him in a firm embrace with her hands grabbing his rear and plunging her tongue deep into his mouth. Her teammates smile uncomfortably and there is a hoot or two in the background. Othniel shakes his head remembering how he had to wait on her before leaving Merth so she could have one more go around with the man who caused the birth of Yez, a beloved member of their crew now. "Jaxyl it's time to go," Cruuws tugs at her arm.

Jaxyl releases her hold on Muir and gives him a stern look. "You take care of her and get her back to Merth if anything happens to me." He nods and tells her with his eyes there is nothing to worry about and yet he doesn't speak because he realizes if he does his voice will crack with doubt.

"Escort them to the fighter bay please," Captain Othniel nods to one of the security officers on deck. He wants to keep them moving before Jaxyl does something weird and wrecks their carefully crafted schedule. When Cruuws taps her elbow again she jerks away from him and gives him a scornful look. They march out and proceed to the fighter bay for launch.

101-A Crushing Blow

Jaxyl ducks, but her sword catches on the entry portal of the stealth craft causing a chill to trickle down her spine. *Is this an omen? How many times have I entered the craft in training? But not many times armed with my sword. Why do I bring it anyway? Courage Warrior Princess, the sword is your birthright. You must be a hero today for Yez's sake, for all of Merth. For all the cosmos, this is your realm now.* She takes a cleansing breath and nods to her comrades as they buckle down into their positions on the stealth craft.

The stealth fighter is one of the sexiest rides for off-lift from the Ursula Weir and it is a prestigious assignment anytime, but today there is a whole new meaning to their engagement. *This is it! Much is riding on our success today.*

"The pods look like giant eggs all lined up in here, don't they?" Feldyn laughs. Jaxyl is glad to see her be so nonchalant, of the three of them Poster is the least likely not to freeze up. *Cruuws I can depend on, but Poster is still a question mark when the blitzo hits the fozzel.*

The airy weightlessness of their liftoff is temporary as they turn to launch and propel through the launch bays like a bolt of unrestrained *lausle* energy. The force contorts their faces briefly, and in no time, they find themselves in the prescribed position to stop and get images of the Bala' Lood ship.

"There's some kind of motion going on. They may be preparing to transform into giants," Feldyn notes. Her voice comes across slightly garbled through the communication system, but she cannot camouflage her rising anxiety which both Jaxyl and Cruuws acknowledge to each other with an unspoken look.

"The scan is coming through more clearly now. Look," Cruuws points to the screen before them. "What can you determine from this?" he asks Feldyn. The question seems to calm her down.

"There you see the forward bulkhead, just inside of it is the most likely place for our sabotage. I'm going to place blobs on the screen now, where I think they will be most effective and the ones I mark with a red dot will be the ones we will beam aboard on." She quickly shuffles the images on the screen as Cruuws and Jaxyl look on.

"What was that?" Jaxyl asks as they decipher some movement on the screen.

"I don't think we have much time!" Feldyn warns. "I'm going to hit the go button on this plan and hope for the best. We need to move now!"

"But I can't tell who is who yet," Jaxyl complains.

"Don't worry," Cruuws says. "Our headsets will identify us as soon as we load."

Panic is not something Jaxyl is capable of feeling, but there is dissatisfaction with the way they have to jump ahead of schedule. She shrugs, "Oh well, here we go!"

They each leap into the pod nearest them. "Check for launch."

"Check for launch." A fear grasps Jaxyl behind the neck like a muscle cramp as she holds her breath for transport. With their helmets on they can communicate quietly without detection, and they have a full range of computer support. The stealth aircraft is set to hover in position once they transport.

"Check for launch." Jaxyl finally confirms. And in the brief moment they are transformed into whirling molecules, there is no thought.

The plan is to stay in the protection of the pod for a few moments while the invasion distracts the Bala' Lood, but timing is everything. They must accomplish their task quickly and get out. There are clanging and whirring noises so loud it is difficult to think and Jaxyl can barely hear her comrades despite the comlink in both her ears. "I think they've shut down the transformation and are focusing on us," Cruuws warns. "Eject now!" The pods transform from hard encasements to soft outerwear they pull off like clothing. Feldyn takes out the virus pack and Jaxyl gives her the nod. Carefully Feldyn heads toward the bulkhead creeping on bent knees. She is about to slap the virus pack onto the cool hard surface when she stumbles and falls flat on her face. The small package hits the floor with a metallic thud.

Flowkin faoltol! A voice inside of Jaxyl screams. Not wanting to get in Feldyn's way she unsheathes her sword and uses it to push the small cartridge back to Feldyn who grabs it and slaps it onto the short wall in front of her. All three collectively take an involuntary breath, but then there is noise coming from behind.

What the? The three of them hear the pounding of footsteps, massive footsteps and they turn to see huge robots striding toward them. There is a flash of light and Jaxyl ducks. "We have warriors on foot inside the ship. What's this about?"

"I don't know. I'm as surprised as you are." Cruuws shoots a volley of firepower back. "We don't have time for this we need to transport now!"

"You two go ahead. Stand behind me and I will defend you. Go ahead and transport." Pulling her shield, made of Targa metal, off her back, Jaxyl uses it to intervene and defend her two team members.

Not only is the shield impervious to assault, but it also reflects a blinding light. *This morning, I thought I was foolish to arm myself with sword and shield but here I am glad to have them* both.

"I'm not leaving you Jaxyl, Feldyn you transport and get back to the stealth." Cruuws orders while pelting the advancing robots with his assault weaponry. As they fire back, Jaxyl wields her shield, and the results are spectacular as the closing brutes are blinded by the piercing flashes it emits. Her adversaries recoil making a surprising squealing noise. Then there is a crashing sound as some of them fall.

"What was that?" Jaxyl asks.

"Duck and transport now!" Cruuws commands.

Jaxyl is unable to do this and instead makes a forward roll directly into the mass of stomping feet headed her way. With her shield protecting her face, she slashes at the mob of robots. Faithful to its Targa properties, the sword forcefully swings multiplying her physical strength tenfold.

She reaches for her transport crystal encased in her uniform just above her heart and disappears as a crushing blow descends upon her.

102-With Clenched Teeth

"Are you okay," Feldyn asks reaching down to assist Jaxyl to get up off the floor. Dazed, Jaxyl looks around for Cruuws but does not see him.

"I'm okay thanks to my shield. Did Cruuws make it?"

"Yes, he's over there," Feldyn points across the cockpit of the stealth craft.

"My head, it feels like it's splitting in two." Jaxyl reaches up and feels a trickle of blood on her forehead. "Cruuws where are you? Show yourself."

"Coming," the dazed warrior says. "I've been hit too." He stands and limps over to where Jaxyl is. "That was way too close."

"I'm sending the data stream to Masalla now to see if we were successful," Feldyn says.

"No, let's not do anything to give away our position. Granted they are probably in chaos right now, but I don't want to help them find us." Cruuws orders.

His warning comes too late though as shots are fired toward them. "*Sholzin fard*! Let's get the *holzo* out of here." He jumps into his seat, and buckles down, making sure Jaxyl and Feldyn have secured their seat harnesses, and heads directly away from the Ursula Weir.

"We're too far to transport and we don't want to lead them back to the ship. Go ahead and send the data and inform the crew we are headed away from the Ursula Weir for now."

With clenched teeth, Cruuws dodges the volley of firepower being launched at them. "Oh, *sholzin fard*! How can they detect us?"

Jaxyl, without skills to pilot the stealth, feels uniquely vulnerable. It is a sickly emotion that drools down her neck and nests there like a clammy *swotzel*. "You've got to get us back to the Ursula Weir, we can't defend ourselves if they can detect us." She commands Cruuws.

"Maybe not, but we should be able to outrun them. We must not lead them back to the Ursula Weir. We'll have to play a game of *clotz* and *mussle* until they implode."

"That could take much longer than you'd like," Feldyn tells them. "We are unsure how long it will take the virus to work. It must reach the universal brain and it will be a quiet ruin. There may be no explosion at all."

This whole expedition did not go as planned. I want to hold Yez in my arms and never let her go. "Maybe there is something you can do to fix the stealth mechanism so they can't see us," Jaxyl tells Cruuws.

"That's just it, the stealth should be working. They didn't detect us when we first came upon them."

"Maybe there is something on us we brought back with us like residual microorganisms we cannot see?" Jaxyl asks him.

"But that would be inside the cloak, and we shouldn't be visible. I don't understand how they can see us."

Cruuws dips the craft down steeply to avoid another volley of firepower launched from the Bala' Lood ship. "Hold on team. Here we go." The swift motion makes Jaxyl's brain curdle. "We're nearly out of range, and once we are we need to evacuate all our clothing. This ship does not have a sanitizing rig."

"You've got to be kidding, we're going to go back to the ship with no clothes on?" Feldyn looks pissed.

Jaxyl grins, "It's better than not going back at all, but what about our helmets?"

"We should evacuate them too, only it will be difficult to communicate without them." Cruuws frowns. "But perhaps our clothing can become a decoy." He looks out at the Bala' Lood ship. "It looks like we have deterred the immediate demise of the moon they were going to invade. That's a positive at least. They are still trying to track us."

"At least they've stopped firing on us."

"If it means going back to the ship buck naked. I'm all for it, the sooner the better," Jaxyl says.

Cruuws laughs, "There's got to be some blankets or something around here we can use for clothing."

"Yes," Feldyn says. "We can strip the bunks and use the bedding for clothing."

"Okay, let's get on it. Get a bag to put our helmets and clothing in and maybe it will fool them into thinking we are someplace we are not."

Jaxyl suddenly realizes she will have to part with her sword and shield from Merth. "I… can't do this. I can't let go of my sword, my shield."

Cruuws studies her, knowing how important this is to her, and hesitates. "We are not on their screens at the moment, but the decoy was the best idea to ensure our safety."

"I'm sure it is."

"Oh, *sholzin fard!* Get ready for some intense maneuvering." He jams a couple of controls all the way down and the pressure in the ship seems to evaporate causing them to feel as if they are choking. Pushing the stealth to its limits, Cruuws heads straight down from their position, and it is so abrupt it feels as if their eyeballs will exit out the back of their heads.

Jaxyl has never felt this nauseated in her life but wills her breakfast not to come up until it does, and she holds it in her mouth. With sheer willpower, she refuses to gag but forces the regurgitated wad back down. *Disgusting! I pray to the One True God for safety. Did I just do that? I haven't prayed for most of my life. What is happening?*

"Okay, team we are headed home if those maneuvers didn't spark some recognition nothing will. I think we should plot a course as close to the Ursula as we can to transport, and we will set the stealth to track away from the ship as soon as we do. This will reduce the number of stealths aboard the ship to two, but somewhere in there Othniel will have to forgive us."

"So, you think we are safe without dumping our clothes?" Jaxyl asks. Cruuws gives her a slight nod and meaningful look careful not to put anything into the official record.

"Thank you," she mouths. Grateful she will not lose her sword and shield.

103-Looking Homeward

Every fiber in her body is yearning to go home to Merth, but orders are to maintain position until Masalla can determine if the virus is working as planned. After three "days and nights" of ship time Jaxyl is more than difficult to be around.

"Go ride Flodynhelm would you?" Even Muir is getting tired of her rants, which often pour over into tantrums. "I understand you are anxious, but you are even directing your anger toward Yez."

Yez has begun to exhibit extraordinary abilities. She still laughs and carries on like a budding adolescent, but with her mother, she is prone now to only communicate telepathically. She had asked for and been granted permission to visit the Waytu chamber on the ForeSat and this seems to have advanced her divine gifts. She knows things before they happen, she can see through walls, and sometimes hear conversations on the other end of the ship if she wants to.

"Aye, you are *flowkin* right. A hard ride would do me some good," she agrees. Muir nods passively but is relieved when she stands up leaving the table with a boisterous shove and goes to ready herself for a ride.

"Yez is at the Halstead's, you needn't rush back." He is already thinking about sipping on an excellent malt whiskey while listening to some soothing *slytar* music.

It is not Masalla, but Yez who first proclaims the operation was a success. MOTHER THEY ARE DYING.

WHAT ARE YOU TALKING ABOUT YEZ?

THE BALA' LOODS ARE IMPLODING. THE OPERATION WAS A SUCCESS.

AND HOW DO YOU KNOW?

I SEE IT. THE WAYTU TOLD ME IT WOULD HAPPEN SOON.

YES, BUT THEIR SOON AND OUR SOON ARE NOT VERY SYNCHRONISTIC. ARE YOU ABSOLUTELY SURE?

IT BEGAN DURING OUR LAST SLEEP CYCLE. MASALLA IS NOT AWARE YET. YOU SHOULD CHECK WITH HER AND GET HER WORKING ON VERIFICATION. WE NEED TO GO HOME.

I HEARD THAT! EVEN THOUGH OTHNIEL RESPECTS YOU HE WILL NOT GO UNTIL MASALLA CONFIRMS WITH DATA.

Jaxyl's voice cracks slightly as she lifts her vim finger to her lips. "Masalla please check your data and confirm what Yez is telling me, the Bala' Lood are imploding."

Masalla, who has been reading a scientific journal on her screen drops it down and searches for collaborative data. "I see there is a broken stream in their tech bio. This could be a sign, let me do some more investigation."

Jaxyl's hands are visibly trembling as she calls Muir. "We've done it! The Bala' Lood are crashing. We're going home! Masalla is verifying now. It was Yez who told me."

Muir swallows and tries not to frown as he is aware Jaxyl can see him on the small communication screen that pops up in midair when a vim call is made. "Where are you now?"

"I'm in our quarters. Yez is here too."

"I'll be right there. We need to talk. If you can get Yez to find a study cubicle or a friend to hang out with…" Jaxyl doesn't like the tone of his voice, she had assumed he would return to Merth with her and Yez. *It sounds as if he is hesitant. Surely, he will come with us. I will make him my consort and rule with him at my side. He has been a good father figure for Yez.*

104-It is as it Must Be

"I don't understand why you wouldn't want to come with us. You love us!"

Muir's grim smile is unnerving. "I realize we have never discussed this. I am at as much fault as you, in that regard."

"But why aren't you coming?"

He touches her arm gently and she can tell he is mustering as much compassion as he can. "I do love you very much, and Yez is like my own, but I have Haldon to think about too."

"But he's grown and will soon have a commission of his own on the ship."

"Jaxyl listen to me." Muir fidgets but presses forward. "You are an amazing woman, but you have this huge destiny to fulfill. I have loved being your partner while you have been here, but my instincts tell me to stay here on the ship." His eyes focus with brittle conviction. "This is where I belong. But it's not where you belong." He takes a deep breath and tells her. "You must go, I must stay. I will mourn your absence, but my place is here on the ship."

Later in the evening when the three of them are together, the mood is tense and awkward, so awkward, Muir asks Jaxyl if he should leave. She rolls her eyes and looks at Yez. "Of course, not this is your place remember?"

"I understand," A bitter smile surfaces. "But your coldness makes me crazy. I don't like being around your hostility."

A jocular laugh spills out of Jaxyl. "I know I'm being a *faoltol*. It will be a very long time until we reach Merth. I don't want to spoil the rest of our trip together, and for Yez's sake, returning to Merth will be a huge deal. I want to get along until we leave."

He pulls her close and whispers into her ear something that stirs her passion, and they both realize everything will be okay.

The time comes when Merth appears in their galactic vision, the two Moons Ava and Duna orbiting the rosy-colored planet are a dead giveaway they are nearing home. Jaxyl stares wistfully at her destination wondering who will still be alive and who will be gone. According to her vim, she had been gone approximately eighty-six Merth revolutions. In contrast, Yez is now twelve revolutions old, and Flodynhelm, who had been in his prime when they arrived, was now showing gray in the muzzle which had always been a deep black in contrast to his white coat. But because he is a Matong horse, he still has half his life ahead of him. *Strange thing this relativity of time. In some ways, I have lived many lives on this journey.*

On the day of their departure, Othniel hosts a gathering similar to the one he organized for her upon her arrival, but this one is bittersweet as she knows everyone in the room by name now.

"I will miss all of you very much and if anyone would like to visit Merth, you are more than welcome." Othniel looks down at his glass with regret, he had already discussed with her they would not be able to remain near Merth for safety reasons in case there is any shred of life left to the Bala' Lood and the ship's presence might attract them.

"It wouldn't be safe, and I can't spare anyone to remain behind with you. We need all hands on deck as they say," he had told her at the time of their private conversation. The only concession he had was he was willing, and in fact, it was safer if she transported with Yez and her astride Flodynhelm, creating one transportable mass. It was the way she wanted to return, just in case they transported into a vulnerable situation.

Feeling emotional, Othniel lifts his glass and makes a declaration to Jaxyl. "Here's to the Warrior Princess, may she return to her beloved Merth and live her days in the glimmering light of Ava and Duna." Jaxyl is dressed in a flowing white gown, unusual for her, but in recognition of the gathering. She looks stunning and she knows it. Muir is across the room looking wistfully at her, and Yez stands close to him acutely aware they will be leaving him behind after the next sleep cycle.

Yez feels her mother's remorse and Muir's sadness, irreconcilable to each other as loyalty and duty burn fiercely within them both. *Mother and I shall return to my birthright, Merth. It is as it must be.*

Tales of Merth Trilogy

Thanks for reading *Jaxyl Warrior Princess*. This is the second in the *Tales of Merth Trilogy*. Don't worry, the three books don't necessarily have to be read in sequence. *Two Moons of Merth*, which caught the attention of book promoters who invited me to participate at the LA Times Festival of Books 2024, begins the saga of the royal Karda family on the planet Merth, where a lowly peasant girl, with big ambitions becomes the queen of all the land. Persistence, determination, and a sincere desire to uplift her female gender once known as breeders, are the hallmarks of her rule.

You have just finished the story of Aadya's granddaughter, Jaxyl, and the third and final installment is *Return to Merth*, which I am currently working on. I have been writing with the desire to connect with others since grade school, and never in my wildest dreams had any interest in writing a series. That changed when these characters entered my imagination and wouldn't let go.

I have been a reader longer than I have been a writer, and through my long reading career I have read a lot of science fiction, but not a lot of fantasy. Why then, I had to ask myself, was I writing fantasy? Well, it has a lot to do with the state of our world right now. We are constantly bombarded with "bad" news, and writing fantasy and reading it is a great way to escape this onslaught of chaos.

I first began *Two Moons of Merth* as a book within a book, but my critics/editors said this was too confusing, reluctantly yielding to their wisdom I pulled *Two Moons* out of *Beyond: A Tale of Discovery on the Other Side of Life*, and finished it first. But the characters pulled at me so vociferously, I almost immediately developed a plan. *Two Moons of Merth* would have female empowerment themes. The second book, which you have just read would be about female empowerment realized and the third and final book, *Return to Merth* would have parallel environmental themes and spirituality. In *Return to Merth* you will meet Yez, Jaxyl's daughter, a decidedly foil to the immaculate conception, who is born to become a spiritual star, guiding those who seek her.

I thank you for your loyal readership and kindly ask if you enjoyed the book to please review it and tell your friends. Avid readers are always on the lookout for books that meet their psychological and intellectual needs.

For more information about the author please visit: https://www.amazon.com/Ruth-Mitchell/e/B0075Y-WOGC

Author Bio

Award-winning author Ruth Mitchell has delivered another visionary tale, *Jaxyl Warrior Princess,* the second book in a fantasy trilogy beginning with the critically acclaimed *Two Moons of Merth,* which was featured at the LA Times Festival of Books 2024, with one reviewer lauding it as "a masterpiece of fantasy literature." *Jaxyl Warrior Princess* continues the epic tale of the royal Karda family and the strong women who populate it.

Mitchell has gained a reputation for gorgeous storytelling and compelling characters crafted with meticulous devotion. Prior to *Two Moons of Merth,* she wrote *Beyond: A Tale of Discovery on the Other Side of Life,* an award-winning, genre-bending sci-fi/paranormal novel. This groundbreaking story focuses on bringing the spirit world to the real world via 'seeing dogs' and cutting-edge technology.

Mitchell has also written several non-fiction books including a popular guide to co-dependency recovery, *Living Happy Joyous and Free.*

Ruth lives in the Ozarks with her husband and two entittled dachshunds.

For more information and updates it is suggested you follow her on Amazon, Bookbub, and Goodreads

Visit her author page on Amazon for more information: **https://www.amazon.com/author/ruthpmitchell**

Good Reads
https://www.goodreads.com/author/show/20017139.
Ruth_Mitchell
Bookbub
Ruth Mitchell Books – BookBub

Social Media
<u>Facebook Author Page</u>
https://www.facebook.com/Ruth-Mitchell-Author
<u>Instagram</u>
Ruth Mitchell (@ruth_mitchell_author) • Instagram photos and videos

Check out these other books by Ruth C Mitchell

Beyond: A Tale of Discovery on the Other Side of Life

Two Moons of Merth

A Request...

If you enjoyed *Jaxyl Warrior Princess* then please be so kind as to write a review. Here is a suggested review link:

https://www.amazon.com/review/create-review/asin=B-0B46V933H